What

anyway?

He'd never once mentioned how he felt about her. He'd joked about his daughter falling for Bella, *too.* He'd told her she was wonderful, beautiful, incredible, fantastic, irresistible—but he'd never once mentioned love.

Oh, he'd said he loved her body, admired every inch of it in detail. He'd told her he loved their conversations. And he'd said more than once he loved her cooking. So why didn't he say he loved her? Why didn't he create a scenario in which maybe, just maybe, they were together in some rosy future?

Sure, she'd told him in the beginning she was never getting married, never having children. She'd also told him she wasn't interested in making love with him, and look what had happened there.

He ought to realize a woman changed her mind now and then.

The least he could do was ask her.

Dear Reader,

Four more fabulous WOMEN WHO DARE are heading your way!

In May, you'll thrill to the time-travel tale Lynn Erickson spins in *Paradox.* When loan executive Emily Jacoby is catapulted back in time during a train wreck, she is thoroughly unnerved by the fate that awaits her. In 1893, Colorado is a harsh and rugged land. Women's rights have yet to be invented, and Will Dutcher, Emily's reluctant host, is making her question her desire to return to her own time.

In June, you'll be reminded that courage can strike at any age. Our heroine in Peg Sutherland's *Late Bloomer* discovers unplumbed depths at the age of forty. After a lifetime of living for others, she realizes that she wants something for herself—college, a career, a *life.* But when a mysterious stranger drifts into town, she discovers to her shock that she also wants *him!*

Sharon Brondos introduces us to spunky Allison Ford in our July WOMEN WHO DARE title, *The Marriage Ticket.* Allison stands up for what she believes in. And she believes in playing fair. Unfortunately, some of her community's leaders don't have the same scruples, and going head-to-head with them lands her in serious trouble.

You'll never forget Leah Temple, the heroine of August's *Another Woman,* by Margot Dalton. This riveting tale of a wife with her husband's murder on her mind will hold you spellbound . . . and surprised! Don't miss it!

Some of your favorite Superromance authors have also contributed to our spring and summer lineup. Look for books by Pamela Bauer, Debbi Bedford, Dawn Stewardson, Jane Silverwood, Sally Garrett, Bobby Hutchinson and Judith Arnold . . . to name just a few! Some wonderful Superromance reading awaits you!

Marsha Zinberg
Senior Editor

P.S. Don't forget that you can write to your favorite author

c/o Harlequin Reader Service,
P.O. Box 1297
Buffalo, New York
14240 U.S.A.

Bobby
Hutchinson

Harlequin Books

TORONTO • NEW YORK • LONDON
AMSTERDAM • PARIS • SYDNEY • HAMBURG
STOCKHOLM • ATHENS • TOKYO • MILAN
MADRID • WARSAW • BUDAPEST • AUCKLAND

Published July 1993

ISBN 0-373-70556-5

MAN, WOMAN AND CHILD

Printed in U.S.A.

ABOUT THE AUTHOR

In *Man, Woman and Child,* Bobby Hutchinson once again draws on personal experience. Having raised three sons more or less single-handedly, she met her own romantic hero, Alan, and extended her family to include his two small daughters. Her first story, "Pheiddipedes Was Not a Family Man," won first prize in a short-story contest, and, encouraged by Al, Bobby embarked on a writing career, which grew and thrived along with her family. Now she is one of Harlequin's most popular authors, both in North America and overseas, and *Man, Woman and Child* is destined to win her even more fans.

Bobby and Al make their home in Winfield, British Columbia.

Books by Bobby Hutchinson

HARLEQUIN SUPERROMANCE

229–MEETING PLACE
253–DRAW DOWN THE MOON
284–NORTHERN KNIGHTS
337–A PATCH OF EARTH
376–REMEMBER ME
443–JOURNEY'S END
492–VAGABOND HEARTS

CHAPTER ONE

JAKE MORENO WAS A BIG MAN, a strong man, a capable man. He'd turned thirty-seven three months ago, in January. He ran his construction business with firm and certain authority, and he couldn't remember the last time his knees had turned to jelly this way. His stained and callused hands were trembling, and sweat marked the underarms and back of the blue checked shirt he'd donned fresh not two hours before.

The nurse who'd flitted into the room a moment ago was now standing close beside him. She was young, with short, curly blond hair and blue eyes, and she was giving Jake the full benefit of a languorous smile. Her name plate said Ms. Ames, RN.

He wasn't even looking at her. He was totally oblivious to the way her pink uniform, a close-fitting jumpsuit, outlined sensational curves.

He was oblivious as well to the bustle of activity in the corridor outside the room. He didn't hear the incessant blaring of the hospital PA system and he was unaware of the amused and curious glances the other nurses on the maternity floor had been giving him as he'd hunched over Annie for the last endlessly long thirty-five minutes, cursing under his breath at his own ineptness as he tried to dress her. Tiny garments lay scattered all over the change table. The baby's toothpick arms wouldn't go through sleeves too small to fit around his own fingers, her legs snapped back up into her belly each time he tried to encase her tiny bottom in the unholy complexity of a diaper, the snaps on the white terry-cloth sleepers refused to match, and he somehow got her left leg attached to her upper chest.

Jake ran a hand through his hair in desperation. "Give me a break here, okay, Peanut?"

But Annie just stretched and yawned.

He was reasonably adept at undressing full-grown females, for cripes' sake. Why should it be next to impossible to clothe one who was eighteen inches long and weighed just under seven pounds?

At last it was done. His entire attention focused on the quiet bundle he'd finally wrapped safe and snug inside the soft pink blanket.

Goddamn. This procedure had nearly done him in. He drew a long, shuddering breath and let it out in a relieved whoosh. Finished. They could go home, he and his daughter, where his clumsy struggles would at least be private. He hadn't realized they'd expected *him* to dress Annie in the clothing he'd brought to the hospital this morning. It had taken more out of him than hand-mixing concrete for an entire parking lot.

He mopped the sweat off his forehead with the back of his hand and rubbed his palms down his long, jean-clad legs. The knot that had been in the pit of his stomach for three days had gotten bigger instead of smaller in the past half hour.

Face it, Moreno, you're scared spitless.

He had a sudden, gut-wrenching conviction that someone was making a huge mistake here, letting him walk out with this baby. Even if she *was* his baby, his own five-day-old daughter, a complex, tiny, trusting package who seemed to have arrived without an instruction booklet. Complete and fully formed, albeit minute, this human being was casually being handed over to his care from this moment on.

"Do you, Jake Moreno, take this child to be your daughter from this day forward..."

From now until...forever. His heart hammered and the painful knot moved from his stomach to his chest. He swallowed hard and anchored the blanket a little tighter around her, looking down into the scarlet face that wasn't quite as big as one of his knotted fists. The same feeling he'd had the first moment he saw her engulfed him all over again, an awesome mixture of tenderness and wonder and inadequacy and fierce protectiveness.

A tickle that was suspiciously like tears formed in the back of his throat and expanded into an overwhelming kind of love he'd never experienced before, one he wasn't at all sure he was good enough to warrant.

"All done, Tiger," he murmured, still ignoring the nurse hovering at his elbow.

She'd been patient with him, Annie had. She'd opened her blue eyes and blinked in amazement, arms flying up, starting and pouting a few times when he'd been especially clumsy. She'd managed two good wails when he got her entirely naked, and then she'd sighed, let out a loud burp and a froth of milky liquid and fallen asleep in the midst of the procedure.

Trusting him, for God's sake. Him, with his fourteen thumbs and fists like hams. His hands were so rough he was scared of leaving marks on her delicate skin. He stared down at this stranger who was part of him.

She had ridiculous eyelashes, fanned out long and curling and dark over round little cheeks. Those eyelashes were like his, but he couldn't recognize any facial features that might be similar to his, or even to Carol's, for that matter.

Annie's hair was the only other familiar item. It was as thick and dark as his own, a deep rich brown. It peeped from under the white eyelet bonnet he'd bought her yesterday afternoon in the gift shop downstairs. The ridiculous hat had seemed too small for anything human when he looked at it, yet Annie's head was almost lost inside it, and it was already slipping sideways, threatening to engulf her entire face.

Could she smother in that stuff? He tried to tug the bonnet into place, but Annie rolled her head the wrong way and screwed her mouth into a pout and he gave up. He could always take the damned thing off, if it came down to it.

"She had formula just before you came, so she should be good for another two or three hours, give you a chance to get her home and settled. You've finished with the accounts office?"

Jake nodded.

"Then I'll carry the baby down for you, hospital policy. You can take all this. It's your care package, diapers and booklets and coupons and stuff."

Nurse Ames scooped Annie up in what Jake thought was far too careless a gesture, settling her offhandedly in the crook of one arm.

Be careful, he wanted to roar at her. *Be careful with my Annie or I'll...* He swallowed and held his tongue, meekly following the nurse's rounded, gyrating backside down the corridor to the elevators.

Outside, the California sunshine made him squint and he put on the sunglasses he'd stuck in his shirt pocket. It was still early in April, but San Diego was already basking in seventy-degree temperatures.

He'd parked his battered truck right beside the entrance. He'd arranged four red cones behind it so it looked as if he was there on official business. Nurse Ames followed him over to it, chatting about the early spring heat wave, glancing curiously at the truck, giving him looks that had nothing to do with the business at hand. She was certainly in no rush to get back to the maternity floor, but it was all Jake could do not to snatch Annie from her arms.

He wanted to get him and his daughter out of here, fast. He wanted to get started on the rest of his life, the father part.

He unlocked the door on the passenger's side, tossed the stuff he was carrying on top of the toolbox on the floor and unhooked the complex arrangement of straps on the new infant car seat he'd bought. Bravely he reached out and took Annie from the nurse's arms and settled her into the tub-shaped receptacle. She was still asleep. He fumbled with the straps and finally got the hang of them.

"Well, Mr. Moreno, best of luck to you." Nurse Ames folded her arms under her breasts, making them rise like warm bread beneath her uniform. "If you run into any problems with the baby in the next couple of days that I could help with, feel free to give me a call. I'm single, but I've had plenty of experience up on maternity and in pediatrics, as well. I'm on days the rest of this week. My number's on here." She handed him a scrap of paper and he shoved it heedlessly into his shirt pocket.

"Yeah, well, thanks. I should be off." He tried for a grin and failed. His face felt frozen into anxious lines. "Thanks for everything," he repeated, feeling like a nerd. He rounded the truck, jumped into the worn driver's seat and started the engine.

Ames waved, and he watched her disappear through the wide front doors of the hospital. He folded his arms on the steering wheel and laid his head down for a long, desperate moment, trying to control the hammering of his heart and the terror in his throat.

What the hell had ever made him think he could manage this on his own? Single mothers were one thing, women were probably born with instincts about babies that he sure as hell didn't have. How many single fathers got turned loose this way with newborns?

He looked over at Annie, still sleeping peacefully, wrapped in her blanket, bonnet askew, fists curled up beside her cheeks, mouth moving in some blissful sucking dream. She was unaware of his terror.

She was so little, so new. Fragile as hell. There were untold numbers of mistakes he could make. But he was her daddy, he was all she had to rely on. He was responsible for her. He'd just have to learn how to do it as he went along. He'd read lots of books, even though right now he couldn't remember a single sentence in a single one of them.

What the hell, Moreno, there's no immediate emergency, so pull yourself together here.

The hospital had given him enough formula for another feeding, and he had all the stuff at home Annie needed. At least he hoped he had; cans of formula and disposable diapers and bottles and vitamins and clothes and baby wipes and soothers and a stack of blankets. Then there was the furniture: change table, car seat, infant carrier, high chair, stroller. It seemed one seven-pound kid required seven hundred pounds of equipment.

The wooden cradle he'd spent months making was in the room Carol had used for the past couple of months, the first room in the old house that he'd refurbished, sanding the floors, painting the walls, refinishing the ceiling, putting in new windows. For the baby, not for Carol. It was empty now of Carol's possessions, but it still smelled of her spicy perfume. He'd left all the windows open for days to get her smell out of there.

He felt a familiar twist in his gut, thinking about his wife. Ex-wife. The divorce had gone through six weeks before, and after Annie was born, Carol had wasted no time in leaving. She'd had Annie Sunday afternoon and left the hospital Monday, the country Wednesday. Yesterday.

Jake had driven her to the airport, watched her board the intercontinental jet that would take her to London, England. First class. He'd bought her ticket. Carol was a long ways out of his life already.

And Annie had just entered.

It was now Thursday, and his daughter was five days old. He'd arranged for three weeks away from the job, barring emergencies that his foreman, Charlie, couldn't handle. The application he'd made to a reputable day-care center had been accepted, but because of the irregular hours and weekend work construction demanded, he'd decided to hire someone who'd come in and care for Annie at home. Surely in three weeks he'd find someone he could trust. He figured sometimes he could maybe take her along to work, depending on the job, but he'd have to have backup. All in all, he was doing the very best he could. Annie, at least at the moment, wasn't complaining.

He pulled out onto the highway and maneuvered his way into the lane that led to the freeway, driving as if he had a load of windows in the back. A car ahead had a bumper sticker that read Today Is The First Day Of The Rest Of Your Life.

Jake grinned, and it was easier this time. "I always figured that was a dumb comment, Annie babe, but today it makes sense. It's you and me against the world from here on in, Peanut."

Parenting must do something weird to the brain. Already it felt perfectly normal to talk things over with a five-day-old baby who was sound asleep.

She was also making a noise that sounded suspiciously like a snore. Jake relaxed a bit more, and the knot in his stomach eased enough for him to remember that he was hungry. Starving, in fact. He hadn't had any breakfast and it was already lunchtime.

With Annie sleeping this way, maybe there was time to drive into a hamburger joint and use the take-out window. A couple of burgers, loaded, with a double order of fries, a large coffee, apple pie and maybe a chocolate shake....

IT WAS SUNDAY.

For the third time that afternoon, Bella Donovan was trying a variation on a recipe for tofu cannelloni with spicy tomato sauce. The last two attempts were edible but not up to the exacting standards Bella demanded for inclusion in her latest vegetarian cookbook.

The sauce was fine, full of flavor. She figured the problem was mostly the filling, a mixture of tofu, garlic, onion, parsley and mint. It was too dry. She'd tried adding spinach, which solved the dryness, but the subtle flavor of the original mixture was lost because the darned spinach took over.

Inspiration struck. "Carrots, maybe carrots." Quickly she peeled and grated a couple of cups and added them to the filling. They provided a nice touch of color, and she was almost certain they'd also supply the necessary moistness without masking the original flavor.

"Brilliant, brilliant, Madame Chef..."

Humming a Presley ballad under her breath, she mixed up another batch of dough for the cannelloni noodles and rolled it flat, cutting it into exact lengths, which she draped over several chair backs to dry while she cut the others.

She was aware of the sound of a baby crying, a crying that had been going on intermittently for the past several days. It was coming from the house next door and had awakened Bella twice in the night, mostly because her bedroom was directly opposite her neighbor's window.

The demanding wail had woven itself into her dreams, and she was sure if she hadn't awakened, the crying would have turned her sleep into a nightmare. A baby crying wasn't exactly the stuff Bella's dreams were made of.

The sinfully beautiful blond goddess who'd spent most of each day rubbing oil into and sunning her progressively pregnant, and mostly naked, body on a lounge chair in the backyard must have had her baby, and by the sounds of it the kid was colicky.

Bella shuddered. She'd dealt with enough colicky babies to last her a lifetime, and she felt sorry for the new mother next door. Carol, her name was. Carol and Jake Moreno. Bella knew their names because the guy from the cable TV company had got the wrong house and knocked on Bella's door instead of theirs when they'd moved in four months ago.

There was a plus to the baby situation, actually. A crying kid would keep Bella's exotic neighbor out of the damaging rays of the sun for a while, at least. Bella had itched to hand several articles over the fence, articles that spelled out the damage suntanning could do, except the woman next door was definitely not the friendly sort. Anything but.

She hadn't made any effort to respond to Bella's early attempts at conversation. She never returned the wicker basket—lined with a fresh linen napkin and two dozen old-fashioned oat bran and raisin cookies—that Bella had handed her over the fence the day they moved in, welcoming them to the neighborhood.

She didn't work, as far as Bella could tell, and she mustn't read much, either, because how the heck could anybody in this day and age not be aware of the danger of ultraviolet rays, for heaven's sake? Well, she had her hands full now. New babies were a ton of work.

Better her than me.

Bella wondered briefly whether or not the woman's husband, Jake Moreno, was any help. Men nowadays were supposed to be different that way, more involved in parenting.

He was certainly good-looking, as ruggedly handsome as Carol was beautiful, but he hadn't been around much since they'd moved in, coming home late and leaving again at dawn in that battered old pickup truck. He worked at some kind of construction, judging by the saws and toolboxes that littered the back of the vehicle.

Also, there'd been a couple of fights over there, real doozers, the days he was home, so maybe he had good reason for working so much.

They *looked* like the perfect couple. And they'd probably produced the perfect kid and now everything would be hunky-dory, except for this touch of colic. Pregnancy could make a woman into a crazy person, though, Bella knew that. Her mother, usually cheerful, had disintegrated into a weepy mess for most of her last three pregnancies. Mind you, if anyone had plenty to cry about, it was her mother. Having ten kids in sixteen years would give anybody a nervous breakdown.

Bella dusted off her hands and began rolling the filling into the neat oblongs of noodle dough, placing them in an oiled glass baking dish, making notes on a spattered notepad as she went along. The crying went on and on . . . and on. Nothing came close to making you crazy like a baby crying, Bella thought irritably.

At last she turned the radio to a local rock station, just to muffle the plaintive sound for a little while. But when she turned it off, hours later, the kid was still crying.

JAKE HADN'T SHAVED in three days. He hadn't done much of anything except walk the floor with Annie molded against his chest, changing her diapers when they needed changing, snatching a quick bite of something from the diminishing supply of canned food in the cupboards and collapsing into drugged sleep when she finally quieted for fifteen minutes or so.

If she quieted at all.

It had been seven hours now, and she was still wailing. Screaming. Could she rupture something this way? He jiggled her up and down and increased his pace across the bare boards of the living room floor.

Walking with her like this didn't stop the crying, but at least it made him feel as if he was doing something.

Her knees jerked up into his rib cage and her arms flailed against his chest. The urgent wails increased in volume, and Jake felt like crying himself, something he hadn't done in about thirty-odd years.

"Annie, for pity's sake, for my sake, for God's sake, could you shut up for a while?"

He knew his tone was edgy. He was exhausted, beyond exhausted, and he'd never felt as helpless in his life. He'd called the pediatrician in the middle of that first night, certain it was something he, Jake, was doing or not doing, convinced his daughter was dying. Did babies this young get appendicitis? Had he hurt her in some way? Had he fed her too much or too little?

More scared than he'd ever been, he had driven Annie in to see the doctor at the crack of dawn yesterday morning. She'd screamed every inch of the way.

The diagnosis was colic. Apparently it had nothing to do with the way Jake was taking care of her. He was immensely relieved and then appalled to learn that, in a world where medicine had made incredible discoveries over the past few years, treatment for colic was a hit-and-miss affair.

"She'll outgrow it in about three months," the casual young pediatrician assured Jake. "I'll give you a prescription that might work, but don't expect miracles. Some babies just have problems with this for a while, it's nothing to worry about."

He was a real stand-up comedian, this guy. A real first-class joker. Jake hadn't slept more than half an hour in two days, Annie either, this was going to last three months, and Dr. Smartass here was saying there was nothing to worry about?

On top of that, the prescription didn't work. Nothing worked. Not walking her, feeding her, bathing her, singing to her or reading her Louis L'Amour. Not holding her in a warm bath. Not cursing or praying or taking a couple of stiff belts of whiskey; he'd tried them all and he couldn't think of another single thing to try.

He'd called everybody he knew. The other guys on his crew were no damned help; Charlie had been divorced for ten years, and the other two were young studs who dreamed of making babies, not dealing with them after they arrived. He was seriously considering calling the crisis help line when the doorbell sounded.

BELLA WAS TAKEN ABACK when Jake Moreno yanked the door open. He looked more than a little wild, and he didn't have a shirt on. His curly dark hair was rumpled, his deep brown eyes were bloodshot, there was a dark stubble of beard on his lean cheeks and strong chin, and his worn jeans hung low on his hips.

Dangerously low. Bella swallowed hard and tried to ignore the acres of broad naked chest and flat stomach, concentrating instead on his face, which looked a bit grim and a lot desperate.

He had the kid cradled in one of his well-muscled arms, its little body pressed against him, and it was screaming and flailing around the way they did when they had a bad bellyache. It had lots of wild dark hair, the same shade as the curly mat on his chest. It had the usual screwed-up scarlet face and those unusually good lungs. Bella knew for a fact they'd been working nonstop all afternoon, which meant *she* hadn't been able to work at all for the past couple of hours. Which was why, against her better judgment, she was here.

It had a disposable diaper and a yellow undershirt on, and it looked ridiculously tiny and sort of pathetic, clamped against him that way.

She raised her voice to be heard over the racket. "Hi, I'm Bella Donovan, from next door? I hope I'm not intruding..."

"Please, come in. Please." He jogged the baby up and down in an automatic motion as he spoke, and Bella could see that he was wound up pretty tight. She hesitated, then stepped inside.

The room was a baby crash site, with bottles and diapers and tiny items of clothing spread everywhere. A bottle of whiskey about a third gone stood open on a coffee table littered with pocketbooks on baby care, a couple of westerns and an inside-out man's sweat shirt.

"Take her, would you, please?" He came close, much closer than Bella wanted, and all but dumped the baby in her arms, which was the last thing she needed. "Her name's Annie." Bella could smell baby oil and male sweat.

"Hey, I just came over to..."

He interrupted her. "I'll only be a minute, honest to God. I have to go to the bathroom, okay?"

Bella had no choice. She held the squirming, shrieking kid against her chest in a practised grasp, transferring the small paper bag she'd brought over to the other hand, wishing suddenly that she'd just minded her own business the way she'd planned on doing. The familiar smells of baby vomit and soap filled her nostrils, smells she'd done her best to avoid for a long time now. The baby writhed and jerked its legs into her ribs.

Where the heck was this kid's mother? Couldn't she hold her own daughter while he went to the bathroom, for gosh sakes?

Bella moved a bit further into the room with her volatile burden. From here she could see into the kitchen. The house had the same floor plan as her own, but it was in a deplorable mess. He must be remodeling, because the floor was bare wood, the walls had been partially stripped down to the rafters, and a ceiling fixture hung by a bare cord.

Carol wasn't anywhere she could see, and the kitchen counters looked as if a hurricane had recently struck. Bella was impressed; the general effect was far worse than any of the disasters her own cooking frenzies produced. Bags and cartons and baby bottles and a ripped-open package of diapers littered the surfaces, and somebody had spilled tomato soup and something else—vivid green—all down the cupboards.

She was aware of him behind her, and she turned and immediately held out the baby to him. It was still crying.

"Thanks." He took his daughter back with big, clumsy hands, but Bella could tell he was already used to handling her. He wasn't awkward as much as just careful, and he settled her with a sigh and a practised motion against his chest like before. He'd pulled a white T-shirt on, although his feet were still bare.

"Easy does it, Peanut." His voice was deep and rumbling. He cupped the tiny head with one hand, stroking the baby's neck with a gentle finger. The nail was broken, and his huge hands looked as though he used them for anything but holding babies. They were the hands of a man who made his living working hard at physical labor.

"She has colic," he announced, and it sounded like a death sentence the way he said it.

"I thought maybe she did." Bella wished he wasn't standing so close to her. It made her uncomfortable. He smelled of baby, mixed with a musky, male odor, not at all repulsive but definitely a signature aroma. She guessed he hadn't showered recently. Or slept, either, by the look of those eyes.

He frowned, and his voice was infinitely weary. "I suppose with all the windows open in this heat, you can hear her crying from next door, huh?"

Bella nodded. "Yeah, I can. Look, I don't want to interfere or anything, but I made up some stuff that might help her. Maybe I ought to explain to your wife exactly what's in it." She reached into the bag and took out the carefully sterilized jam jar filled with herbs. "It's a natural herbal remedy my grandmother used to use for babies with colic, nothing at all that would hurt her—"

"I don't have one," he interrupted in a harsh tone.

"Excuse me?" Bella felt as if she'd missed a portion of the conversation.

"A wife. I don't have a wife. She's gone. We're divorced. Annie and I are on our own here, aren't we, Peanut? What's in that stuff exactly? D'you know for sure if it'll work?" He jerked his chin at the jar she held.

Bella's mind was reeling. "It's a teaspoon of mixed fresh herbs, peppermint, catnip, marjoram and the crushed seeds of caraway and fennel. You boil one cup of water and then steep the herbs in it about twenty minutes. Then you strain it and let it cool. You only give the ki—the baby a couple of teaspoons at a time."

She could see him hesitate. His kid was still bawling in a kind of hiccuping fashion that signaled exhaustion.

"You've used this stuff before?" There was distrust and frantic hope in his tone.

"Dozens of times. Two of my sisters and three brothers had colic. A couple of nieces and nephews, too."

He gave her a long considering look, and his uncertainty was clear. So was his desperation.

Bella set the jar down on the littered coffee table with a thump. "Look, I'll just leave it here and you can decide on your own." She turned toward the door.

"No, hey, wait." There was a fine note of panic in his voice. "Listen, what I don't know about babies would fill an encyclopedia, and the stuff that damned doctor gave me sure didn't work. It made her groggy but she still cried." He blew out his breath in a long, hopeless whoosh, ruffling the downy hair on his daughter's head.

"I'm about at the suicide stage here. I'd try anything, honest to God. There's a package of those disposable bottles on the kitchen table. Could you fix up some of this and put a little in a bottle and we'll give it to her?"

Bella knew she should leave, but she found herself heading for the kitchen instead. The mess there was far worse than she'd realized. Her sandals stuck to the floor, and there were puddles of unidentified origin scattered around like land mines. The sink was filled with dishes that might never come clean again.

She boiled the water, steeped the herbs, strained the mixture, found the bottle and carefully measured in a minute amount. She cooled the bottle under the cold tap, secured the nipple and handed it to him.

The baby stopped crying long enough to gulp greedily at the liquid, bolting down three rapid swallows and starting to howl all over again when the bottle was empty.

"She can't be hungry. I fed her less than an hour ago."

"They act like that when they have gas. It'll take a couple of minutes for the herbs to work."

"Could you just maybe...stick around...for a little while? Please?" His request was so humble, so pathetically sincere, she couldn't refuse. "I know you must be thinking... well, probably you're wondering whether I murdered Carol and buried her in the basement, right? I mean, it must sound pretty odd, me saying she's not here."

It did sound strange. Bella's face must have revealed her feelings. "Actually, it does. Sound peculiar. Because the baby...I mean, isn't it only a few days old, right? And I saw your wife less than a week ago."

The baby's crying stopped, not immediately, but tapering off with little sobs and shudders. She belched loudly, once, and then again, long and wet, an extraordinarily rude noise to come from such a small girl. Bella met Jake's astonished gaze and had to giggle a little when gas suddenly erupted from the diaper end, as well. Then she found herself holding her breath. The room was suddenly quiet as the tiny bundle all at once collapsed into a sleeping comma in his arms.

He waited a long few moments, obviously not daring to hope, hardly breathing. He squinted down at the closed eyes and open mouth of his daughter. Then he shut his own eyes and tilted his head back, and Bella heard him expel a long, shaky sigh.

"Thank God. Thank *you.* If only she'll sleep awhile now," he whispered. He lowered himself with infinite caution to the worn brown tweed couch, carefully shoving aside a crumpled pink blanket and a pair of soiled infant sleepers without moving his body enough to disturb the sleeping baby. "Sit down... Bella. It is Bella, isn't it?"

She nodded, hesitated and finally took a seat in the armchair adjacent to the couch, her mind still going over what he'd said about his wife. It was almost as if he read her mind, because he started the story all over again, his voice weary.

"See, Carol wants to be an actress. She always did. I knew that when we got married, but I guess I underestimated how badly she wanted it." His voice was devoid of inflection, but a spark of what Bella figured was anger burned in his dark, red-rimmed eyes.

"Anyhow," he went on in the same neutral tone as before, "we've been divorced a couple of months already, even though she went on living here until after the baby came. Now she's gone to England to give it her best shot. She left . . ." He puckered his forehead, obviously trying to figure out the date. "Last week sometime, I guess, a couple of days after Annie was born. She's trying to get accepted at RADA."

Bella had never heard of RADA, and her expression must have said so, because he added, "The Royal Academy of Dramatic Art, a fancy acting school over there. Apparently you have to be good to get accepted, but Carol thinks she's got a good chance. They offered her an audition, and I guess that's pretty rare. I don't know beans about talent or any of that stuff, but she's beautiful enough to be a movie star, God knows." There was a kind of forlorn pride in his voice that hurt something inside Bella.

"But she didn't want . . ." She stopped abruptly, aware that she was prying.

"The baby? Annie?" He shook his head slowly from side to side, doing his best to keep the baby absolutely still. "Nope. She wanted an abortion. I wanted the baby. I'm thirty-seven. Time's getting on for me to raise a family. It took a lot of negotiating, but Carol finally agreed to have the baby in return for what she wanted. We . . . I guess you could say we finally came to an agreement that suited us both. She got acting lessons, a divorce and a plane ticket, and I got my baby and a hefty second mortgage on the house.'' His mouth tilted in an ironic grin that had no humor in it, then his lips gently touched his daughter's silky head in a tender caress. "Annie's worth every cent."

So his beautiful wife had fleeced him for the privilege of bearing his child. It sounded like something Bella might hear on Geraldo. She knew plenty of women were choosing to be single parents, having babies by artificial insemination and all the rest, but for a man to decide to raise a kid himself, to choose to do so when he had a choice... well, it was inconceivable to her.

It was also none of her business. She smoothed her worn denim skirt down closer to her knees, aware all of a sudden of how much thigh it bared.

"Look, I should go."

"Jake. My name's Jake." He was obviously on the verge of falling asleep himself, but he was looking at her as if he hadn't really seen her before, a bemused, grateful look that softened his dark eyes. He had the most amazing long, thick eyelashes.

It made her blush, of all things, that intent scrutiny.

"Yes, I know it's Jake. The television man told me." Aware that she was beginning to sound even more confused than he did, she lied. "There's...look, I really do have to go. I left something in the oven." She got up, and he did, as well, still as cautious with the sleeping baby as if she were a time bomb set to go off.

"You can probably lay her down now, she ought to sleep for a while. If she needs any more of that herbal mixture, she can take it as often as she needs. If you run out, let me know. Try putting her on her tummy. They usually get rid of gas easier that way." Now what the hell was prompting her to babble like that? Bella turned quickly and headed for the door.

"Bella?" His voice was heavy with fatigue and relief, and she stopped long enough to turn and glance at him.

He was smiling at her, really smiling, his bloodshot eyes crinkled at the corners, weariness plain in his rugged features. He had nice strong teeth—man's teeth. He had a crooked smile, a sweet smile, and something in her throat caught at the sight of it. He also had a cleft in his chin. She'd always been far too partial to men with clefts in their chin.

He really was a beautiful man, especially when he smiled. Carol must be a crazy person, walking out on a man like this. In spite of the baby.

"Thanks, Bella. I owe you one," he said in a husky tone.

She couldn't help but smile back at him. The trouble was, it became difficult to break eye contact.

When at last she managed, she felt embarrassed and confused and went quickly out the door.

CHAPTER TWO

IT WAS TWENTY MINUTES before seven the next morning when Bella anchored her bike to a post and walked through the open back door into the kitchen of the Artichoke Heart, the restaurant she co-owned. She could smell onions, cumin and garlic, which meant that Woody was already making his special lentil dal stew for the lunch trade.

He turned from the gas range, where a huge iron frying pan was sizzling. A long-handled spoon was in his hand and a red checked kerchief was tied over his forehead, covering most of his long black hair. He waved the spoon at her, and his wide, bearded face split into a welcoming smile. "Morning, Bell. Isn't it a great day?"

It was almost always a great day to Woody Finch. He was one of the best-natured people Bella had ever met, and she was convinced that his good nature permeated the delicious food he cooked, infecting the unsuspecting souls who ate it with blasts of good cheer they couldn't explain in any rational fashion. He was also inordinately shy of people; he loved to cook yet wanted no part of meeting the people who ate his food.

"It's just another sunny day in California, Wood. Don't you natives ever get bored with the sameness?" She liked to tease him a little. As always, he reminded her of a big, messy, unmade bed: not particularly sexy, just comfortably plump and shaggy, in baggy cotton drawstring trousers and one of the orange, outsize artichoke T-shirts some sharp-talking salesman had convinced them would be hot sellers.

They hadn't been. Woody and Bella had sold a grand total of four and had gotten left with twenty-one each, so the shirts had become work uniforms. Bella wore one now with her black tights.

Woody's spaniel brown eyes twinkled down at her. "Yup, we do get bored. So we borrow a video of Washington State, and after a solid hour of watching nothing but rain, it's funny how the boredom passes."

Woody knew that Bella had grown up in Washington State on a farm where it rained more often than not.

"Rain builds character." She washed her hands and moved close beside him to peel the gingerroot and garlic he'd need in a moment.

His huge body dwarfed hers. Part of Woody's charm was how tiny and fragile he made her feel in contrast to his tall, wide frame. And he trusted her; she'd learned that Woody didn't trust a whole lot of people.

"Who needs character, Bella *mia?* A broken arm builds character, but I can live without it."

"Many customers yesterday?"

"The usual. That new girl we hired is a dipstick. Got to watch her every minute." He was grating the fresh ginger, his wide hands with their strange, stubby fingers amazingly adept.

Bella suddenly remembered another man's long-fingered, callused hands on a baby's fragile back. It had been blessedly silent next door for the rest of the evening. She'd awakened early this morning to the hungry cries of the baby, but they only lasted a few minutes. Obviously Grandma Donovan's colic cure had worked . . . again. Thank goodness.

"So, how did your evening turn out?" she asked next. Woody had been summoned to his mother's palatial home in La Jolla for a formal late dinner last night, an event that made him nervous and edgy for the entire day before it occurred and gave him indigestion for several days after. Woody was not a social animal by any stretch of the imagination.

He groaned and rolled his eyes. "Mother outdid herself this time. There was cheese or cream or eggs in everything. There was Parmesan and a raw egg in the Caesar salad, and dessert was crème brûlée. I ate lots of bread."

They shuddered in unison. Like Bella, Woody was a vegan, a vegetarian who ate no meat and also avoided chicken, fish and all dairy products. The vegan diet consisted of fruit, whole grains, legumes and vegetables, which afforded endless variety. Woody's mother, however, labeled his eating habits both extreme and ridiculous. "Which means out of her control," Woody would interpret with a mischievous grin. "And isn't that a step in the right direction?

"She planned the menu with me in mind, obviously," he told Bella with fine irony. "And of course there was a woman there just for me. The whole thing was planned around that. The niece of somebody's great-aunt who's divorced and back on the market in a big way. The niece, not the aunt, though God knows, maybe the aunt's more interesting." He shook his large head and squinted at Bella, stirring the mixture in the frying pan. "She was a mess—done up in a designer dress that I swear she was wearing backward. It didn't seem to have any front at all, so obviously she had it on the wrong way. And all she talked about was how her ex had done her wrong and how hard it was to meet eligible men. She sounded like one of those western songs. You know, I've got tears in my ears from lying on my back, crying over you?"

Bella giggled.

"Still," Woody added thoughtfully, "it must be fairly desperate out there when my mother feels I'm a good prospect, huh?"

His words brought out all Bella's protective instincts, and she scowled at the huge, gentle man.

"You're not just a prospect, Wood. You're a catch. You're rich, you're tall, you're a superb cook. Quit putting yourself down all the time." Bella wrapped a voluminous apron around her middle and started getting out the ingredients for whole wheat pancakes. "I'd be after you myself if I thought it would do any good."

Woody shot her a knowing glance and they both laughed. They'd been through all that four years ago when they met, trying hard to fall in love and ending up in long-term like instead. Ending up partners in a restaurant instead of partners in passion, staunch friends instead of lovers.

"You get lots done on the new cookbook yesterday?" He poured the cooked lentils into the onion-garlic mixture and chose garam masala from the spice rack, adding and tasting as he mixed.

"Not as much as I wanted." She found herself telling him the story of the baby and the man next door. Jake Moreno and his Annie.

"He said his wife left when the kid was only a day or two old. They were divorced a couple months back, and he actually bargained with her so he'd get to keep the baby, can you believe it?" She was mixing whole wheat flour and soy powder, adding baking soda and oil and soy milk as she talked. "He said he's thirty-seven and time's running out for him to have a family."

There was a long silence from Woody's direction, and finally she looked over at him. "Well? Don't you think this guy's out to lunch, or what? I mean, choosing to be a single father, that's got to be a new one on me."

Woody shrugged his massive shoulders. "It's different, but I can sort of relate to where he's coming from. Women aren't the only ones with biological clocks, y'know."

Bella stopped mixing and gaped at him. "You've got to be joking."

He gave her a crooked smile and shook his head. "Nope. Just because your clock got its gears meshed years ago and kids aren't in your game plan doesn't mean the rest of us don't want any. I think about it sometimes, like on my last birthday. I know how this guy feels. I'm thirty-six already myself. If I don't get a move on, my kids'll still be in college when I'm collecting social security."

"But you don't go around bargaining with somebody to have one just so you won't get left out of the parade." She tested a bit of batter on the griddle and nodded when it swelled up and bubbled.

"I just never thought of it before. Maybe I ought to. Maybe it's the coming thing for males, raising babies on our own. The trend for the nineties. Maybe your neighbor is the front wave in a whole new tide."

Bella laughed at that.

Woody didn't.

JAKE HAD TO ADMIT to himself that he'd been watching for Bella. Why else would he be hanging around the windows at the front of the house at eight o'clock on a Monday night instead of catching the last of the baseball game on the idiot box?

Annie was sleeping. He'd checked her a few minutes before; he'd spent a lot of time checking her last night and today, uneasy with her long bouts of unaccustomed silence, amazed each time he crept into her room to find her sleeping peacefully, head to one side, tiny bottom stuck high in the air, snuggled contentedly on her belly in the cradle he'd made for her.

He'd fed her the rest of the liquid Bella had concocted when she showed signs of cramping up again, but the worst of the colic seemed to have disappeared without a trace. He just wanted to thank Bella properly and maybe get another dose of her magic medicine in case the colic came back, he reminded himself, taking another glance out the window just as his neighbor turned into her yard on her bicycle.

She braked and dismounted, balancing the bike with one hand and running the fingers of the other through her unruly mass of short, dark curls. The gesture outlined her breasts beneath the stained orange T-shirt she wore, and Jake's eyes lingered on her full-bosomed figure. He hadn't noticed what she really looked like yesterday. He hadn't really taken a good look at his neighbor before, except to note she was attractive. He'd had far too much on his mind the past few months to think much about neighbors.

She wasn't tall and bone-thin like Carol, but she wasn't exactly plump, either. She was sort of...nicely rounded, he decided. Maybe five-six or seven, and she had freckles on her nose. He knew that even though it was getting too dark to see them now.

He couldn't remember what color her eyes were, just that they were big and they gave away what she was feeling even when she tried to hide it. Like when he'd told her about the trade-off with Carol for Annie. Bella had looked at him as if he was three bricks short of a load when he told her that.

The long orange T-shirt she wore was hiked up a bit over her hips, and he decided biking did a lot for a woman's figure. The black tights didn't disguise much, and he liked the way her legs curved softly into rounded hips and bottom.

She dropped her arm and looked his way, tugging her T-shirt down almost as if she sensed his presence in the unlighted room. He moved back from the window, feeling guilty peeping at her that way. He walked swiftly to the back door and out into the yard just as Bella wheeled her bike toward the garage.

"Hi," he called, suddenly feeling bashful.

She paused, balancing the bike against her thigh and smiling over at him. She had a great smile, friendly and warm. "Oh, hi, Jake. How's the colic?"

"I wanted to thank you for that. Annie's been sleeping all day. She just wakes up every four hours for a bottle now. I can't believe the difference. I'm really grateful to you, Bella." He sensed she was about to move away and he added quickly, "You'll have to tell me how to make that stuff in case Annie starts up again."

"Sure." She nodded and began wheeling the bike toward the garage again.

"You always ride a bike? I thought everyone in California had a car."

"Oh, I do. Have a car. An old Volkswagen, it's here in the garage. There's something wrong with it. The guy at the garage said it would cost a fortune to fix it, so I've been riding my bike. It's better for the environment anyway."

He filed all that away, wondering if she'd mind if he took a look at her car someday. He liked engines. But at the moment he just wanted to talk to her some more. "You care for a beer? Maybe?"

It was all he could think of at the moment. He hoped there were three, maybe four, in the back of his fridge behind all the formula. He hadn't exactly been stocking up on beer these last few days.

She stopped again and looked at him, then shook her head no. "I don't drink."

"Maybe coffee, then?"

"I don't drink coffee, either." She paused, then added, "I'm vegetarian. Vegan, actually. I drink juice and herbal tea, mostly."

She sounded as if that explained everything. Jake knew a little—very little—about vegetarians, although he'd never had one as a friend. He knew they didn't eat meat, but that was the full extent of his knowledge. The term vegan escaped him completely. Was it a religion? Was it meant to scare him off? Did she figure he was hitting on her, God forbid?

"Oh. Yeah. Vegan, huh. Well, hey, no problem. I just thought, well, I figured we could sit out here in the yard. It's cool and I can hear Annie from here. I guess I've gone a little stir crazy, not talking to anybody but the baby." He listened to himself in amazement, hardly able to believe he was frothing off at the mouth this way. Suddenly he felt like a clumsy adolescent, overgrown and awkward. He tucked his hands into the back pocket of his jeans to get rid of them and realized for the first time that his big feet were bare.

"Babies can do that to you." She hesitated and a silence formed, thick and heavy between them.

"I could..." she began, just as he said, "Well, anyhow..."

"Sorry. What were you going to say?"

Actually, he'd been about to say good-night and bolt into the house. "Ladies first." *Now that's brilliant, Moreno. They're called women these days, you dork.*

"I could make some fresh carrot juice," she said, sounding uncertain as hell.

"Great. That'd be great. I'll bring out a couple of chairs. See you in a few minutes." By now he wished he'd stayed in the house in the first place.

"Right." She took the bike into the garage, and while he was hauling out his one lawn chair—the fancy one Carol had picked out for herself—and a straight-backed kitchen chair, Bella unlocked her door and went inside.

He scrabbled around and found a beer with an inch of frost on its side and brought it outside, popping the tab and downing almost half in one long, nervous gulp. After a moment of deliberation he pulled the straight-backed chair he sat on farther away from the recliner to reassure her about his intentions.

The deep hum of a powerful machine sounded from inside her house, and it wasn't long before she came out carrying two immense glasses of bright orange liquid, which she handed over the fence to him. Then she had to go into the alley and come into his yard via his back gate.

While she was doing that, he set one glass down long enough to shove his beer can out of sight under the steps. Then he perched on the hard chair, trying not to slop the orange stuff out of the glasses.

It was getting darker by the second. She came up his back walk and he stood abruptly, narrowly avoiding disaster with the brimming glasses. He handed her one.

"Take the lawn chair. It's more comfortable."

She did and he sat down himself, slouching back and crossing his bare ankles. "So. Hard day at work?" Had she said where she worked? He tried to remember.

She sipped at her drink before she answered. "Hectic, sort of. There weren't that many customers, at least not more than we usually get, but I had to fire the new waitress. She seemed all right when we hired her, but I swear she was high on something today. I let her go just after the noon rush, and the other one left last Friday to enroll in a spiritual growth seminar. Which means that Woody got left with most of the cooking this afternoon while I took care of the front. Woody's a fabulous cook, but he won't serve customers."

"You have a restaurant?" He took a gulp of the stuff in his glass. It wasn't any hell for taste, but he supposed he could get through it. He thought wistfully of the beer under the steps.

She nodded. He liked the way the carrot juice stained her upper lip orange. She had a great mouth, wide and full lipped, and there was a deep dimple beside it when she smiled.

"It's called the Artichoke Heart. It's totally vegan, over in Normal Heights. On Adams Avenue."

He shook his head. "Never noticed it. But I'm not much at eating out in fancy restaurants, anyhow. I mostly go to fast food joints or order something delivered."

He thought she shuddered. "Actually, the Artichoke is anything but fancy. It's part of an old bank building, nice high ceilings and thick walls, but it's not big, and it's certainly not fancy. We painted it white and blue, and Woody and I rigged up a little fountain so you get the feeling it's calm and relaxed, but there's only a dozen tables. I guess we could put in more, but we've never needed to."

We. Woody and I. Of course there'd be a man in her life, how stupid could he get? Funny, he'd never noticed a guy around next door. Well, he hadn't exactly had a lot of free time for observation since he moved here. And until the other day, he really hadn't paid any attention.

"Woody's your main man?" He downed another large swallow of carrot juice. This stuff had to be good for you. It didn't have much else to recommend it.

She shot him an odd look and shook her head. "Woody's my partner and my friend. He's not my...man at all." She sounded annoyed.

The carrot juice must be getting to his brain, because he couldn't just let the subject drop. "So who is?"

She was scowling at him now. "I don't happen to have a man in my life right at this moment. It *is* possible to exist without one, you know."

He was way off on the wrong track here. But there was a perverse satisfaction in knowing she was alone. Like him. He flashed her an apologetic grin. "Sorry. That was a long ways out of line."

Her silence told him she agreed. He gave it another try. "You lived in this neighborhood long?"

"Going on five years now. I rented the house shortly after I moved here."

"Where'd you move from?" She'd relaxed a bit on the lounge chair, resting her head against the back and crossing her ankles. She had nice ankles, slender and sort of fragile looking. It was getting darker by the minute and he couldn't see her features too clearly anymore.

"Washington State, near a town called Custer. It's a rural area a couple of hours out of Seattle. My family have a farm there."

"What kind of farm?"

She made a sound meant to be a laugh. "A kid farm, mostly, at least that's how it always seemed to me. There were ten of us. I was second oldest. I'm twenty-nine, and my youngest brother is seventeen. We had beef cattle, cows, chickens, sheep, a huge garden and a baby almost every year. Sort of subsistence farming, I guess you'd call it."

He thought about that for a couple of minutes, and envy stirred in him. "Sounds like the ideal way to grow up."

It was her turn to be silent. When she finally spoke, her voice had a tinge of bitterness. "Hardly. My father was also a minister, so a lot of the farm work fell to Mom and us kids. He expected a lot from us. There was never time to yourself. There was always too much to do, laundry, cooking, preserving, cleaning, outside chores. Taking care of the other kids. It was hard on my mother. I guess that's why I value my freedom, why I never got married and don't plan to. I enjoy coming home to my own house, knowing there's no one to care for except myself." She paused as if maybe she'd said too much, then added in a different tone, "How about you, Jake? Where'd you grow up?"

"Oh, all over the place. I was born in Florida, but we didn't stay there long. Didn't stay anywhere for any length of time. There was just my old man and me, and we traveled a lot."

"Was your dad a salesman?"

He opened his mouth to tell her about Ace Moreno, and then closed it again. After all, her father was a minister. She was bound to be pretty straight, and for some reason Jake wanted her to think well of him, not judge him by Ace.

"Something like that. Anyhow, I finally ended up here in San Diego when I was fifteen, living with two older guys, Nathan and Samuel Liposki. They were carpenters. They taught me the trade."

"You're a carpenter?" There was none of the condescension he'd heard sometimes in women's voices when he told them what he did. Instead, Bella sounded admiring. That pleased him.

"Yeah. I have my own crew now. We contract on residential mostly." It still gave him a good feeling to think about his business. It had been hard going, working his way up. There hadn't been any handouts.

"So you've got your own company." She actually sounded impressed.

"Yeah, I do. I call it Ace Construction." He hadn't really named it after his old man, he assured himself for the millionth time. It was just a handy label because it got him top billing in the yellow pages.

"That's such a great way to make a living." She sounded so enthusiastic he couldn't help but smile.

"I thought about being a carpenter myself, when I was younger," she was saying. "There weren't many women in the trade at that time, though, and one of my teachers discouraged me. To say nothing of my father. God, he almost had apoplexy when I mentioned it. It wasn't the kind of job he thought any daughter of his should have."

"I had a woman on the crew for a while, she was a good carpenter, too. Charlotte was her name. But then she married a guy with money and went to live in Hawaii. Only carpenter I ever heard of that happening to."

Bella chuckled. It was a catchy sort of sound, deep and husky and contagious. He wanted to hear it again.

"How many people do you have working for you?" She seemed genuinely interested, which surprised him. Carol was always bored and irritated when he talked about his work, so he'd gotten out of the habit.

"Two carpenters and a laborer, full time. I contract sub trades and take on extra guys now and then, but mostly it's Charlie, Manfred, Alberto and me. They're good guys, we work well together."

"You're lucky to have found them. We have an awful time getting good help at the Artichoke. We can't pay much, so that probably has a lot to do with it. We earn a living, but there's not a heck of a lot left over. Not that Woody minds. He's sort of independently wealthy. It pays most of my bills, though, so I guess that's not bad."

"If it supports you, it's a good business." He drained the last of his juice and felt relieved. There was a mouthful of some kind of pulp in the bottom, and he resolutely swallowed that as well before he set the glass down on the grass beside his chair. He managed not to shudder and felt proud of himself.

"Actually, it doesn't quite. Support me, I mean. I write cookbooks, as well, and they take up the slack. They don't make me rich, either, but between them and the Artichoke, I manage pretty well."

"You're a writer?" It was his turn to be admiring.

She laughed outright this time, a soft, happy sound in the gathering darkness. What was it about this woman's laughter that made a man go soft inside?

Her voice was pleasing, low and melodious. "I don't think cookbooks qualify me as a big-time writer, especially vegetarian ones."

"Well, they impress the hell out of me. I never got much formal education, so writing anything is a chore. Hey, I have a bad time just spelling the names on the checks at month's end." He was exaggerating to amuse her. In fact, he'd struggled through night school until he got his high school equivalency, and he was determined to tackle college eventually. Before Annie did, that's for sure. He wouldn't want his kid to be ashamed of his lack of education. He wanted the best for Annie, every way there was.

As if she knew he was thinking of her, the baby began to fuss inside the house, making the little irritated sounds that would soon lead up to exasperated wails if he didn't rescue her in time.

"She must want her bottle. Sit tight, I'll just..."

Bella got hastily to her feet. "No, I have to go. I shouldn't have stayed so long. It's getting late and I've got to be up early."

Jake felt irrationally disappointed. He'd been enjoying himself, sitting here and talking with her.

"Well, thanks for coming over, Bella." He liked saying her name, liked the soft roll of it off his tongue. He reached out and took her hand, intending to give it a friendly little shake. Instead, he ended up holding on to it for much longer than he ought to have.

She finally withdrew it gently. "I enjoyed talking with you, Jake. Thanks for asking me over."

He could hear Annie really winding up now, and he couldn't seem to find the right words to say to Bella. Finally he blurted, "Let's do it again soon."

"Great. Good night now."

He walked her to the alley and along it to her own back gate. She slipped through, and he could see her blurred shadow crossing the small yard, hear her key in the door lock.

"Good night," she called softly.

Then the light came on in her kitchen, and he could see her outline against the filmy curtain. He watched for a second and then hurried to his own yard, trotting inside to recover his insulted daughter, scooping her up with a practised gesture and balancing her against him.

"Calm down, Peanut. Your old man's on the job, just a little slow tonight."

Her round little head bumped against his collarbone and he felt the deep sense of delight and tenderness that holding her stirred inside of him. Cradling her with one arm, he warmed her formula with the other.

"We've got a foxy lady living next door, y'know that, Annie?"

Annie's screwed-up face and wide-open mouth telegraphed that she didn't give a hoot.

Jake settled into an armchair, propping the baby in the crook of an elbow. She gave one last wail, broke it off and snuffled at the nipple, then clamped on with greedy fervor, her eyes crossing with the effort of gulping down the bottle's contents.

"Sexy, too."

What was he doing, thinking sexy here? He'd decided when Annie came that his libido and its demands were going to have to go on hold for a good long while. Fatherhood was a serious proposition, and his spare time was spoken for.

But what the hell, he wasn't dead, either. He'd actually gotten six hours of uninterrupted sleep last night, and today he felt like a new man. New enough to notice that Bella did have luscious breasts—in spite of being vegetarian.

Because of, maybe?

"Tell me, how d'you personally feel about carrot juice, Miss Annie Moreno? And be honest, you're among friends."

BELLA CLOSED THE DOOR behind her and switched on the light in the kitchen, kicking her sandals off. As she set her empty glass on the counter, she remembered that she'd left the other one behind at Jake's.

Well, he'd probably return it, which wasn't a bad prospect at all. It felt good having a neighbor to talk to. The weariness that she'd felt when she first came home was gone entirely, replaced with a giddy sense of elation and well-being.

She liked Jake Moreno. He was interesting to be with. She'd enjoyed the past hour, probably because it had been spontaneous. He was a down-to-earth sort of guy, totally unenlightened when it came to diet, but what the heck. She could gradually introduce him to the dangers of cholesterol and triglycerides.

If their friendship continued.

Meat eater or not, he was a sexy man, but she was determined to ignore that side of him. The presence of Annie, the choices he'd made by becoming a single father, spelled out a set of values and life-style that Bella had weeded out long ago from her garden of possibilities.

Still, he had a great body. Nice muscular arms from all that hammering. A physique that looked virile and lean. Strong. Just think what he'd be like if he ate right.

She wandered through the kitchen into the small living room, gathering up her mail from the mat by the door. There was a letter from her mother, Marion, and Bella slumped on the couch and opened it, scanning it quickly for major news and then more slowly for detail.

A sister-in-law and a sister—Penny, sixth in the Donovan lineup—were both pregnant again. Her father was on different medication for his arthritis. Aunt Lottie's daughter's husband was on sick leave. They thought he'd had a heart attack and he was only forty-four.

Then, the crux of the letter. Marion was worried sick about Leah, Bella's eighteen-year-old sister, not that that was unusual. She'd been worried sick about Leah since the wayward child started to walk.

Two years before, Leah had dropped out of school and run away with her boyfriend, Mervin, a long-haired rebel with a motorcycle. She'd come back alone via bus two months later, unrepentant and fortunately not pregnant, but oblivious to her mother's tears and her father's pious lectures. All she ever said about the trip was that it hadn't worked out and Mervin was a real jerk.

Bella had to admit she was in awe of the kid. How had Leah ended up with so much spunk so young? It had taken Bella until her mid-twenties to get up enough gumption to break away from her family.

Marion wrote that Leah had now quit her job at the convenience store and signed up with a company that supplied nannies to families abroad, and she was leaving for France in two weeks. Leah didn't speak a word of French and she wasn't good with children. She even refused to baby-sit for her nieces and nephews, Marion wrote. Father—Marion always called her husband Father, as if he were the pope or something, Bella thought with disgust. Father had tried to talk her out of it, but Leah was determined, and she brazenly reminded Father that she didn't need even his signature now that she'd turned eighteen. Father had resorted to prayer and Marion wasn't sleeping right. What did Bella think they should do about Leah?

Off the top of her head, Bella thought they ought to give her little sister a French-English dictionary, a copy of *Baby and Child Care,* a gross of condoms and their blessings. But she knew it would never work that way. Her mother and father wanted their children close to them. They wanted them to marry, preferably someone they'd grown up with and whom the elder Donovans knew, settle in the area, assume a mortgage and start a family. They wanted control, even after the kids were grown up. Maybe not Marion so much, but her father certainly did. Peter Donovan was heavy into control. Most of all, Bella figured, they wanted their children to follow the pattern they'd set for them.

So far most of them had, amazingly enough. The only two real renegades out of the Donovan tribe seemed to be Bella and Leah, eleven years apart, second oldest and second youngest.

It was ironic that her mother had started asking Bella for advice after all the commotion her own move to California had caused. Peter Donovan considered California a modern-day Sodom and Gomorrah. One of the few letters she'd ever had from him had come after she told them she'd become vegetarian. Peter had written her warning against extremes and asking her where she was getting her protein from. He warned that protein deficiency resulted in mental illness, and she wouldn't be aware of its onset until it was too late. Bella considered the letter a meat eater's classic misconception and had found it extremely funny. She planned to have it published one day in the Carrot and Stick column of *Vegetarian Times.*

Marion ended the letter with her usual one-liner. "I'm fine, hope you are well and happy."

God almighty. Three tightly written pages and not an inkling about how her mother *really* was, what she thought about or dreamed of or wanted or hated. And not a single authentic question about Bella's life, either. Marion had lost her selfhood somewhere along the way, and it made Bella sad. Mad, too. Furious, in fact. Furious at her father for taking that away from her mother.

Bella remembered Jake's comment about her big family and the farm. "That sounds like an ideal way to grow up."

What a laugh that was. She leaned her head against the back of the sofa and closed her eyes, her earlier feelings of elation fading into tiredness and depression. Growing up the way she had was an ideal way to put a woman off marriage and children. For life.

CHAPTER THREE

THE PHONE CALL CAME the next day just before noon.

Jake had Annie fed, bathed and in a clean set of terry pajamas, a morning production that took him a good three hours, all told. He kept forgetting to get all the stuff he needed collected in one place, which meant he had to rush around the house locating lotion and powder with Annie over his shoulder, often wet and stuffed inside a towel.

Right now she was propped in her infant seat, staring around with a bemused expression. He was just as bemused, gazing at the chaos the bathing procedure created and thinking that he ought to make a stab at cleaning up, when the phone rang.

"Ace Construction? Mr. Jake Moreno?" The caller was male, polite and, by his accent, Oriental.

"Uh, yeah, hello. Jake Moreno speaking."

"This is Tho Van Chung, Mr. Moreno. I am pleased to make your acquaintance. You see, I am interested in having your company build a house for me, a special house. Your bid was very competitive, and I would like you to meet with my architect as soon as possible. Would that be convenient, Mr. Moreno?"

Half an hour later, Jake slowly replaced the receiver and stood staring at the phone.

"We just might have landed the biggest contract of our lives, kid," he told his daughter in a strangled tone. He'd bid on the job a full year before and entirely forgotten about it because he figured from the beginning he didn't have a snowball's chance in hell of getting it; every small contractor in San Diego was after the same job.

Tho Van Chung was the owner of a string of local restaurants. He was a wealthy man who'd bought a breathtaking piece of property with a wraparound view of San Diego Bay, and he wanted a half-million-dollar house built on it. If Jake could complete the project in four months, he'd make a sizable profit—enough to pay off the second mortgage he'd taken out on his own house to raise the money he'd needed for Carol. The fly in the ointment was the fact that, after taking a year to make up his mind, Tho Van Chung now wanted to begin instantly.

"Which is going to cause us a few problems, Annie, m'girl. I can take you to the preliminary meetings all right, but after that, once work starts, we're gonna have to find somebody to stay here with you or else drop you off every day at that day-care place."

That part bothered him a whole lot. He'd wanted at least three weeks with her before he had to leave her with someone else, and although the day-care center seemed efficient enough, it was also impersonal.

Still, it was a windfall, a major happening. His first stunned reaction began to give way to elation, and Jake suddenly wanted to tell someone besides Annie, share the good news, maybe celebrate a little. He glanced at the clock. His crew were finishing up a house out in Escondido and wouldn't be back till late evening, so they were out of the question.

Everybody else he knew was at work right now. Well, he couldn't exactly take Annie out for a beer, but why not treat himself to lunch somewhere? Apart from hurried trips to the supermarket and drugstore, he'd hardly left the place since Annie came home. They both deserved some R and R.

He glanced out the side window toward Bella's house. He'd watched her leave on her bike this morning, just about the time he was giving Annie her six o'clock bottle. She'd had a blue dress on, he remembered.

Bella was good to look at in the morning. She was freshly showered, dark hair gleaming, and she seemed filled with energy as she pedaled vigorously away, shapely legs pumping up and down in a way that filled Jake's sleepy brain with X-rated fantasies. He wished she was home today. He'd invite her along to celebrate. But she'd be at her restaurant, that artichoke place.

Well, it's open to the public, right?

He didn't give himself time to get cold feet and change his mind. He flipped through the phone book and found the address, scooped up a couple of diapers and a spare bottle and stuffed them into Annie's traveling bag, wrestled the eyelet bonnet onto his daughter's reluctant skull, then gathered her up and loped out the door.

What the hell, there must be more on a vegetarian menu than carrot juice. And he could tell Bella his good news. Sort of offhand, casual like. Without making a real big deal out of it, but letting her know it was important to him. After all, what were friends for except to share good news?

THE NOON RUSH at the Artichoke hadn't amounted to a heck of a lot, and Bella was in the kitchen rolling out pastry for a couple of apple pies when the bell dinged, signaling that someone had just come in.

Woody was deep in the intricacies of making spring rolls, delicately stuffing chopped fresh vegetables into their rice pastry wrappers.

"Your turn," she said to him. He gave Bella such a pleading look that she muttered under her breath, washed the pastry off her hands and ducked out of her apron, dusting flour off the bodice of her blue cotton dress.

"I'll go, but we've got to find another waitress, that's all there is to it. This business of running the front and cooking at the same time is totally nuts," she grumbled.

Woody grinned at her affectionately. "I absolutely agree. I'm working on it, trust me. You've got flour on your nose."

Jake was already seated at a table by the window. Annie was sound asleep in her infant seat, propped on two chairs shoved together.

"Hi there, neighbor. Thought I'd come and check out this place of yours. How ya doin'?"

He was wearing a clean gray T-shirt with the sleeves cut out and the usual faded blue denims. His muscles bulged, his curly hair was rumpled, his dark eyes twinkled up at her as if he was high on life. He grinned, white teeth flashing against the deep tan of his skin.

God, he was one good-looking man. Bella felt ridiculously pleased to see him. She didn't even try to curb the answering smile that spread across her face. "Hi, Jake. I'm really glad you came by. How're things going?" She studied the baby. "Looks like everything's well under control with her."

Actually, the baby looked adorable... and funny. She had on a huge white eyelet bonnet that engulfed her head and half her face and a one-piece terry sleeper in a particularly bilious shade of green that made her complexion appear slightly jaundiced. Jake had attached her soother to the front of her sleeper with an immense safety pin, and he had her wrapped in a neon pink blanket that fought vigorously with the green terry.

"Annie's behaving like an angel. She just eats and sleeps—and messes her pants. She does that quite a lot, in fact." He sounded so smug and proud and slightly disgusted that Bella had to laugh.

"That's what babies are supposed to do."

"Yeah, well, if she hadn't had colic, I probably wouldn't appreciate her being this way. But it still seems like a miracle, having her sleep like this. You're a magician, Bella."

He met and held her eyes for too long. Finally he looked away, studying the sunny high-ceilinged room, smiling at the tiny fountain tinkling water into a miniature basin.

"This is real nice. Sort of homey." The tablecloths were blue checked, the tables and chairs an odd assortment of mismatched finds from the local junk stores, and the floor was plain scrubbed wood. Wide windows with crisp blue curtains framed the street, and outside pedestrians ambled along exploring the antique emporiums, junk shops and used bookstores that lined both sides of this section of Adams Avenue. Inside, several relaxed-looking people were finishing plates of food, but the place was almost empty.

"What can I get you, Jake? Do you want some lunch, or did you just drop by to case the joint?"

"Lunch, I think. I'm starving." He cast a curious and rather apprehensive glance at what the others were eating. "Normally I'd order a burger and double fries, but I guess that's not quite what you guys serve, right?"

"Right." Bella handed him a menu. "The lunch special is steamed vegetables over rice with homemade chapatis. You get a salad with it."

Jake handed the menu back unread and nodded. "Sounds fine." He'd never heard of chapatis, but what the hell.

"What would you like to drink? We have all kinds of juices, herbal teas and perked caf-lib." He raised an eyebrow and gave her a questioning look.

"Caf-lib's a caffeine-free coffee alternative. It's grain based, it tastes great and doesn't wreck your nervous system."

He didn't appear convinced. "I guess I'll have that. And, Bella? Any chance you could sit down and have a cof—ah, a caf-lib with me?"

She thought of the unfinished pies, but the decision wasn't tough at all. "Sure. See you in a few minutes."

Back in the kitchen, she deftly heaped grated carrot, sliced beets, sprouts and shredded cabbage on a bed of chopped lettuce, drizzling their special mustard-honey dressing over the top and finishing the salad off with a generous sprinkling of sunflower seeds. Woody was still fussing with the spring rolls.

"That's my neighbor out there, Jake Moreno. I'm going to sit and visit with him for a while."

"Sure. I'll be done with this in a minute and then I'll finish up those pies. Did he bring the baby along? Maybe I'll come have a look at her when I'm finished here. I haven't seen many babies that fresh out of the oven."

Bella was amazed. Woody never volunteered to meet people. The baby must be a big drawing card.

"This one looks slightly underdone at the moment, Wood. Anyhow, she's sleeping right now. Let's hope it lasts."

She served Jake's salad and got herself a bottle of apple juice out of the cooler, taking the chair across the table from him so that Annie was between them. The baby's face was now almost totally obscured by the bonnet.

"D'you think she needs that hat on?" Jake frowned uncertainly at the baby, and Bella carefully untied the bonnet and took it off, sticking it in the bottom of the infant seat and smoothing Annie's dark hair back with a finger. Her skull felt soft and vulnerable to the touch, her hair as fine as silk thread. Bella jerked her hand away when she realized what she was doing.

"I never know how many clothes to put on her or whether she needs a hat or not," Jake said in an apologetic tone. "How the heck do you tell?"

"Just use your common sense," Bella said. "Babies react faster to hot and cold than we do, because they're lots smaller, but basically just go by how you feel."

"Guess you learned all about babies from having so many brothers and sisters."

Bella grimaced. "Yeah, I sure did. By the time I was five, I could diaper and burp a baby like a pro." She meant the remark sarcastically, but he looked at her with admiration.

"I wish I'd been around kids more. I'm scared half the time that I'll do Annie serious damage. She's so damned little, and I'm clumsy."

Bella had to smile at his earnestness. "She's a lot tougher than you think."

He didn't look convinced, but he didn't say anything more. Instead he took a tentative mouthful of salad and chewed thoughtfully, lifting an eyebrow at her. "Y'know, this isn't bad at all."

"So what did you expect, castor oil and weeds?" There was just a trace of acerbity in her tone. "There's not much a person can do to wreck a salad."

He munched another mouthful before he answered. "I wouldn't know. I've never made one."

She was utterly aghast. "Never made a salad? You're kidding me."

"Nope, I'm not. I don't cook much at all. I was never around anybody who did. The old carpenters I lived with used to make beans once in a while, but mostly we ate stuff out of tins or got take-out."

"But surely your wife—" She stopped abruptly, aware that maybe it wasn't a subject he wanted to get into.

But Jake didn't seem to mind. "Oh, Carol never cooked, either. She used a lot of frozen dinners and stuff like that. Cooking wasn't her thing."

As she sipped her juice, Bella thought about that. Carol hadn't wanted a baby, cooking wasn't her thing, and it seemed Jake hadn't been her thing, either. So why had she gotten married in the first place?

Bella looked at the man across from her and figured it probably had a lot to do with plain old sexual attraction. Jake exuded a kind of raw male magnetism that would likely convince a lot of women they wanted him on a long-term basis, even though they'd never thought about marriage much before.

Not her, of course. She knew exactly what she did and didn't want. She knew herself far too well to ever imagine things could work out over the long haul with a man like Jake. Friendship was fine, but anything more was out of the question.

Jake was almost finished his salad. Bella brought him a heaping plate of brown rice topped with steamed vegetables and a generous basket of chapatis.

The other patrons were leaving, so she took their money and chatted a moment with them before she again sat down with Jake. He'd made impressive inroads on the food.

"Did you make all this, Bella? It tastes really good."

"Yeah, Woody and I trade off. If I make the lunch stuff he does dinner. We share making the bread and desserts. We also have a woman who comes in two days a week and spells one or the other of us off with cooking. She's kind of cranky but she's reliable. Her name's Mrs. Montgomery. Every now and then we hire a couple of kids who do cleanup in the afternoons, but they seldom last long. We really need someone reliable for the front. When we first started, we were here all the time and it got to be too much."

"I know what you mean. That's what construction's like. If you've got a job going, you pretty much have to work steady at it till it's done. It's feast or famine." He paused for a moment and then added almost shyly, "In fact, that's what I came over to tell you. I landed a big job this morning." He told her about Tho Van Chung and the house he wanted built, his voice betraying his pride and excitement. "The grapevine has it that he's also investing in other residential property around the city, so if he's happy with the work we do for him, there'll probably be other projects."

Bella's wide smile reflected her pleasure at his news. "Jake, how terrific for you. Hey, I'm really pleased. Congratulations."

She held up her apple juice in a toast and realized she hadn't brought him anything to drink. She sprang up and got him a bottle of juice and also his caf-lib, and they toasted his good fortune.

Jake's dark, gentle eyes met hers as they raised their glasses. An intriguing sparkle, an aura of excitement that had nothing to do with his job caught them both in its wave, and she was suddenly aware just how attracted she was to him.

Dangerous, Bella. Out of bounds.

She slid her eyes away from his and deliberately focused on Annie, sound asleep but stretching tiny arms and legs as she wriggled more comfortably into her nest.

Jake was a package deal, Bella reminded herself. And the package was a time bomb, because babies grew and became even more time-consuming and energy draining. Annie was a lifetime project, one Bella wasn't about to take on. Even if she had a chance.

What made her think Jake was interested, anyway, she chided herself—apart from the way his eyes caught fire when he looked at her now and then. Like now. Her heart betrayed her head and hammered away in her chest as awareness kindled between them.

Fortunately, Woody chose that moment to amble out from the back like some bear coming out of hibernation, his portly figure swathed in a striped apron. Bella introduced the men and they shook hands. She could sense them sizing one another up like a pair of awkward, wary animals.

"So this is the baby," Woody finally said, turning his attention to Annie. He spent several unhurried moments studying her, crouching down and leaning over until his large nose almost rubbed hers, cautiously touching one of her miniature hands with one of his fingers.

He started asking questions. How much did she sleep? Had she grown a lot since she was born? How did Jake know how much to feed her? Were her legs always curled up into her stomach like that? Would her hair come out and new stuff grow? When would she get teeth?

Jake took each question seriously, answering in detail, asking Bella's opinion when he wasn't sure of the answer. Bella had to smother a giggle. All of a sudden the two macho men sounded like a pair of doting nannies.

Woody finally straightened. "You're doing a good job on her," he complimented Jake earnestly, as if he'd been admiring a rebuilt engine.

"Thanks. You have kids yourself?"

Woody shook his head, and Bella was astonished when he dragged a chair over from another table and lowered his bulk into it. Woody was being downright sociable, for gosh sakes.

"No kids. Never had the pleasure, unfortunately. I understand from Bella you're going solo with this parenting thing. Wish I had your guts."

"Yeah, well, fools rush in and all that. You want kids?"

Woody nodded. "Always have. Problem is finding a lady who wants me and kids, as well. Never seem to connect with the right person, you know what I mean? And I ain't getting any younger."

Jake nodded. "Exactly how I felt. Don't get me wrong. I don't think raising Annie on my own is ideal by any means. But it's better than not having kids at all, and I'm getting up there, too. I'm thirty-seven. I figured it was now or never."

Bella listened to this conversation in disbelief. She'd heard female variations of it countless times, but hearing two men seriously discussing their biological clocks seemed nothing short of bizarre. If she had a tape recorder, she could probably sell it to Oprah for a bundle.

A buzzer sounded in the kitchen, signaling something was ready in the oven. Woody hurried off after one last look at Annie.

"So, when does your new job start?" she asked Jake.

"I have to see Mr. Chung and his architects tomorrow morning. We'll get the permits and everything in order, and we'll start right away. My crew's just finishing a job, and we've got one more small one I promised to do. We'll have to juggle the two of them for a little while."

"Sounds like you'll be busy. You have a baby-sitter for Annie, I take it?"

He frowned and shook his head. "Not yet. There's a day-care center that'll take her, but with my hours it's not gonna be practical. It's a big worry. I'm going to have to find someone reliable in the next few days who'll come in and baby-sit. See, I'd arranged my schedule so I'd have three weeks off, more or less, and I was going to interview baby-sitters during that time." He shot her a hopeful look. "You don't know anybody really trustworthy who loves kids, do you?"

Bella shook her head. "Afraid not. But I'll put the word out to some of our customers who have kids of their own. Maybe they'll know somebody."

"I'd appreciate that."

She'd be home Friday and Saturday. She could offer...

What was getting into her? Offering to baby-sit was the last thing she ought to do. She got quickly to her feet. "You want some dessert? We've got tofu cheesecake or fruit pudding with pear cream."

"I'll try the pudding."

Bella got the dessert for him and filled his cup, getting herself some herbal tea while she was at it. When she sat down again, Annie was starting to fuss, letting out little anxious cries and wriggling around. Her eyes were open and she gazed around with the myopic intensity little babies always had.

Jake scooped her out of her chair and propped her over his shoulder. His dessert was only half-eaten, and to her own amazement, Bella reached across and took the baby from him. "You finish eating, I'll hold her. Does she need a bottle?"

"It'll have to be warmed." He dug one out of the diaper bag. Bella took it and the baby into the kitchen, where Woody actually asked to hold Annie while Bella heated the bottle. She had to show him how to support the baby's head, but he caught on fast.

"Hey, she smells good, sorta like fresh bread," Woody commented, resting one hip on the counter and cradling the baby cautiously with both arms. He was snuffling at Annie's hair.

"They don't always smell like that, Woody. I hate to tell you this, but there's times when they positively stink." She was becoming a little irritated with him and his fascination with the baby. She suspected she was also irritated with herself and her reactions to the baby's father. "Didn't you have cousins or friends' kids you had to baby-sit?"

"Nah. My mother and dad were divorced before I was three. After that I shuttled back and forth from one to the other. They both married and divorced a couple more times each, but there weren't any more kids."

Bella knew there hadn't been any shortage of money, either. Each parent had vied with the other to give Woody the best of everything.

"You poor kid, you really led a deprived life." She meant it sarcastically; to Bella, heaven on earth would have been growing up as an only child with plenty of money.

But Woody nodded, totally serious. "Yeah, I sure did. I'd have given anything for a couple of sisters and brothers."

"Too bad I didn't know you then. I'd have happily donated a couple of mine to the cause. God knows we had plenty to spare."

She tested the bottle on her wrist and offered it to Annie, who attacked the nipple with undisguised greed.

"You better take her. I don't know how to do this. I might drown her or something." There was a note of outright panic in Woody's voice, and Bella had to laugh.

"You'd better take a few courses if you're serious about getting pregnant," she teased. She took the baby from him and walked out to Jake.

He was finished eating, so she deposited Annie in his arms. In the process, Bella's skin brushed against his, her breast touched his muscular shoulder for an instant. She could smell the freshly washed pine odor of his thick hair and the dusky male aroma of his skin. Warmth spread through her belly.

He settled Annie in the crook of an arm and looked up with a curved grin. "Thanks, Bella. I guess I oughta be going. She's gonna mess her pants right after she eats. She always does. And I need to put some ads in the papers, try to find a baby-sitter fast."

Later, Bella would curse herself for what she said next. But the words slid out as if she had no control over them.

"I'm off on Friday and Saturday this week. If you need someone those days I'll take care of her for you."

The look on his face, the slow-breaking smile and the gratitude in his deep dark eyes were wonderful payment. "That's really great of you, Bella. The thing is, I don't know anybody else I'd trust with her right now."

"Yeah. Well." Bella became brusque, clearing the table as if her job depended on it. "Let me know."

"I will. I'll tell you tonight how I make out finding somebody." He collected Annie's paraphernalia, paid the bill and left.

Bella spent a good four minutes crashing dishes around and swearing under her breath, using all the pithy words she'd learned as a kid in order to shock and horrify her father.

She needed a good swift kick right where her legs started to grow. She'd moved thousands of miles away from her family just to get out of things like baby-sitting. And here she was, after all this time, actually offering. What the hell had gotten into her?

"I figure that neighbor of yours has the hots for you, Bell," Woody greeted her when she slammed the armload of dishes down in the kitchen. "There's a definite energy field every time he looks at you."

She shot him a bad-tempered, evil look, and mischief danced in his spaniel brown eyes.

"Y'know, I read this study about celibacy. It said that prolonged periods can have the same detrimental effect on the system as eating meat and dairy. Isn't that interesting?"

Bella said something so crude Woody roared with laughter and grinned at her knowingly for the rest of the afternoon.

CHAPTER FOUR

"HEAR THE TRUCK, ANNIE? That's your daddy home from work. Let's hurry and get you cleaned up for him." Bella whisked the soiled diaper from the baby's narrow bottom and washed her off. In seconds, the tiny girl was diapered and snapped into a fresh outfit.

It was like riding a bike, Bella thought with a satisfied grin. Once you learned to take care of a baby, you never forgot.

"You have junk all over your jaw, kid, and your hair's a mess." Bella wiped traces of dried formula off the minuscule face and used her fingers to curl Annie's topknot into a single loop on the crown of her head. "There you go. Now you're ravishing."

Annie squirmed and gave her what looked like a smile. Even though she knew it was probably gas, Bella grinned. It was late Friday afternoon and the baby had been with her since six that morning, when Jake had brought her over. Despite Bella's misgivings, she and Annie had become friends.

Not bosom buddies or anything like that, Bella assured herself, tipping the sweet-smelling bundle over her shoulder just as the back door opened and Jake came in. His eyes were all for the baby. His face lit up and he gave Annie a kiss on the forehead when Bella plopped her into his arms.

"Hey, Peanut, how'd you make out? Were you a good girl?"

"She's a model houseguest. Well, apart from a few minor problems with sloppy burps and bowel movements. She just ate, so don't jounce her too much. You want to sit down?"

He shook his head. "I need a shower, we'll head on home. I can't thank you enough for taking care of Annie for me, Bella." His warm brown eyes were filled with gratitude. "It makes a long day for you. I felt bad getting you up so early this morning, but construction's like that. You either work from dawn till dusk or you don't work at all."

"No problem." Bella turned toward the oven as the timer signaled that her casserole was done. She pulled on oven mitts and slid it deftly out and onto the counter. "I had a nap with Annie this afternoon, and then we took a walk to the store. I'm not at all tired, but she's probably going to conk out any minute now. Fresh air's harder on you when you only weigh ten pounds or so."

She realized that he wasn't paying much attention to what she was saying. He was gazing instead at the casserole and the fresh loaf of bread on the counter, and if ever she'd seen a hungry man, it was him.

Well, what the hell, she thought. In for a penny, in for a pound.

"Why don't you leave Annie here, go over and shower and then come back and have some of this dinner with me? I always make enough to feed the military. It's a habit from cooking at the restaurant. It's not fancy, but it's filling. Vegetable mushroom casserole, fresh bread, apple pie."

"That doesn't seem fair, you baby-sit all day and then ask me for supper. It should be me taking you out for a meal." But there was no conviction in his voice. He couldn't seem to take his eyes off the golden loaf of fresh bread.

She grinned. "I'll take a rain check. In fact, you can sign an IOU."

"Consider it done." He handed her the baby. "I'll be back fast, before you change your mind."

It took him exactly seventeen minutes. Bella hardly had time to lay the baby in her carry cot and set the table before he knocked once then came through the back door. His curly dark hair was wet and his face shone from a recent scrubbing. He had on fresh jeans and a short-sleeved checkered shirt, wrinkled but very clean. He left his worn runners at the door and handed Bella a bottle of wine.

"I know you said you don't drink, but here in California wine doesn't count as drinking, right?" He gave her a teasing grin.

"I'm not that much of a fanatic. I do enjoy a glass of wine every now and then. We'll have some with dinner. Come and sit down. It's all ready and your daughter's fast asleep over there." She gestured to the quiet corner where she'd parked Annie.

For the next half hour, they ate with honest hunger. Jake was full of praise for the bread and the casserole. He had a second helping and then, looking a little shamefaced, agreed to a third.

"Y'know, Bella, you're the best cook I've ever met."

Bella couldn't help laughing. "You've forgotten that you confessed to me you've never really met anybody in your life that could cook at all. So I figure I'm the only cook you've ever met."

"True. But I'll bet if I had met others, you'd still be the best."

"For that, gallant sir, I'll give you a piece of apple pie."

They finished the meal and Jake insisted on washing the dishes while the kettle boiled for tea.

"Living alone teaches a guy how much skud work there is to keeping a place halfway clean and tidy," he remarked, up to his elbows in dishwater. "And I still can't believe how much extra mess a baby makes."

"That surprises lots of people. I couldn't believe how easy it was to be responsible only for myself, after I left home."

"You still want a family of your own someday, though, don't you, Bella?" It wasn't as much a question as a statement.

She took a deep breath and concentrated on the glass she was drying. "No, matter of fact, I don't. I got enough of mothering when I was growing up. I decided by the time I was fourteen that I'd be a career woman, and I've pretty much stuck to that."

He stopped washing dishes and turned to stare at her. "But you're so good with babies. You're such a good cook." He gestured around with one hand, dripping water. "This place—you're wonderful at making a house look and feel like home."

She shot him a challenging look. "So?"

He flushed and turned back to the dishwater. "Don't get me wrong here. I'm not violating any woman's liberation stuff by saying those are the only things women *should* do, or be good at. I just mean you have a special talent along those lines . . . family lines. It shows. And it seems a real waste—"

"Not in my books it doesn't." She knew she sounded snippy and she didn't care. She attacked a pot with the tea towel. "All this garbage about women and their biological clocks gives me a pain behind my ears. Just because I can cook and keep a house from being condemned by the city doesn't necessarily mean I should marry and have twelve kids. Nobody goes around telling men they're perfectly suited to domesticity and fatherhood."

"You're right. I'm sorry. I was way off base. All I was doing was trying to pay you a compliment and it came out the wrong way. Cool down, okay? You're gonna wear the pattern off that plate, rubbing on it like that."

Bella knew she'd overreacted. She felt the angry tension in her neck and shoulders. She put the plate in the cupboard and tipped her head back, drawing in a deep breath, then glanced at Jake with a shamefaced smile.

"I'm sorry, too. You just managed to push one of the buttons that sets me off. My father used to lecture me endlessly about how suited I was to be a wife and mother, and it made me insane. You're just getting the backlash."

"Did you fight with your father a lot?" He was scrubbing a pot, and as he looked up at her, the apprehension was plain on his face. "Just say the word if you figure I'm being too nosy." His gaze shifted to the sleeping baby in the carry cot. "It's just that I kind of think of Annie and me, in a few years time. It would help to know what girls fight with their fathers about, so I'm kind of prepared, y'know?"

She nodded. "Sure, I understand. And talking about my father doesn't bother me at all." She gave a wry grin. "Probably because I've done so much of it over the years to anybody who'd listen." She sighed. "Yeah, we fought, all right. It started when I was still really young and got worse the older I got. As the years passed, I started trying harder and harder to get him to listen to my point of view for a change instead of just laying his beliefs on me, but it was like banging my head on concrete. I was a slow learner, I guess, because it took years for it to gradually dawn on me that he'd made up his mind at some point that he knew everything there was to know and he wasn't open to discussion on anything. I used to imagine a tape in his head that clicked on and played out the same message over and over whenever I opened my mouth."

"You said he was a minister. I thought ministers were supposed to be good at counseling people."

Bella was pouring boiling water into the teapot. She laughed, but there wasn't much humor in it. "Believe me, I told him that more than once. And maybe he was better with his congregation than he was with his family. I don't really know."

"Do you go home to visit very often?"

Bella shook her head. "Maybe once a year, at Christmas. I didn't go last year, though. The Artichoke was really busy and we couldn't get extra help. I'm pretty close to my mom, but it's such a zoo back there. Somebody's always in labor, there's one crisis after the other with my nieces or nephews or sisters or brothers, and it seems there's never time to just talk with anybody about things. Especially not Mom. She's always up to her eyeballs cooking or helping somebody out with baby-sitting." She took two mugs down from their hooks and poured tea, thinking about her relationship with her family.

"I guess what I really mean is that none of them are all that interested in my life or what I'm doing. Not that I particularly want to be the center of attention." She thought about that for a moment and amended her words. "Well, let's be bone honest here. It might be nice to be the center of attention for ten minutes or so, at least once in my life. With nine brothers and sisters you never get the chance to be a star."

Jake grinned at her. She smiled at him and tried to explain. "I love my family. It's just that they don't understand why I'd choose to live in California, far away from the rest of them. They don't know my friends, they think being vegetarian is totally nutty, and quite naturally they're involved in their own lives, but they're also incredibly self-centered about it. We don't have much in common, I'm afraid."

He rinsed out the sink, dried his hands and accepted the mug of tea. "That seems kind of a shame. I always had the idea that a family was like having built-in best friends, people who knew and supported whatever you decided to do."

She shook her head. "I guess it can work like that, but not in my family. Let's go sit down." She led the way into the living room and perched in her favorite spot, curling her legs under her on the old, comfortable sofa she'd recovered in soft shades of peach and green.

She remembered the sketchy details he'd given her about his own background. "How about you, Jake? Do you visit your father often? Where does he live, anyhow? I don't think you ever said."

He chose to sit beside her, setting his mug on the low table in front of them. "That's because I don't really know," he said in a matter-of-fact tone. "Ace is a bit of a drifter. The last I heard of him he was in Ohio, but that was almost a year ago."

"You haven't heard from him in a whole year?" Bella couldn't keep the astonishment out of her voice. Her family were often a pain in the neck, especially her father, but she always knew exactly where they all were. It was a whole new concept to think of someone having a parent and not even knowing where he was living. "Heavens. Then he doesn't even know yet that he's a grandfather."

"Nope." Jake took a long gulp of his tea.

"Ace, you said. You named your business after him." She watched him and was surprised when his ears turned red and then the rest of his face grew ruddy underneath his tan.

Jake Moreno was blushing. And she had no idea why. It was kind of sweet of him, naming his business for his father, but it was nothing to be embarrassed about.

"I didn't really plan on it being named after him." He sounded defensive. "It was the only name I could think of that would give me top billing in the yellow pages. I'm not too imaginative at naming things."

She didn't believe that for one instant. She'd read a few books on Freud. Not that she thought the old chauvinist was very bright in all areas of the human psyche, but he did have some insights into parent-child relationships. She'd bet her best recipe for carob brownies that there was a lot more to the name Ace than the yellow pages.

"Aren't you ever afraid...." She reconsidered what she'd been about to say and hastily revised it. "I suppose if he had an accident or something, somebody would call you."

"Yeah, for sure." He didn't sound all that certain, however. "Ace is pretty healthy, and he's sure as hell street smart. I don't worry about him much."

Jake seemed uncomfortable talking about his father, so Bella let him off the hook.

"How's the job going?"

For the next half hour, Jake made her laugh with anecdotes about the men in his crew and the sometimes ridiculous problems that could come up on a contracting job.

"Tho Van Chung is over at the site before I am in the morning. I swear he's going to get an ulcer if he keeps worrying over this house the way he's doing now. Or maybe I'll get the ulcer, having him around all the time."

It was after ten when Annie started to fuss and Jake glanced at his watch.

"Past time to get on home and let you get some sleep, Bella." He got to his feet and reached out a hand to her, catching her fingers in a strong grip and pulling her up beside him. "Thanks for everything. Tonight's been really special." His voice was filled with feeling.

Before Bella realized what he was going to do, he'd leaned over and planted a kiss on her lips. The contact was warm and brief, just long enough to convince her that she liked it. Lots.

He gave her hand a final squeeze and released it. "I only have to go down to the site for a couple of hours tomorrow, and I could take Annie with me..."

"Nonsense." She was glad her voice was steady. "A construction site's no place for a baby. I'll be here all day anyhow. She might as well stay with me."

Warmth emanated from his dark eyes. "I'm grateful as hell, Bella. I've got interviews lined up all day Sunday for housekeepers who'll come in and care for her, but these two days caught me sort of unprepared. I arranged the business so I'd have time off with her, but I can see now I should've lined up somebody long before Annie was even born. I guess I didn't because I never really thought Carol would carry through her end of the bargain. I always figured she'd take one look at the baby and change her mind."

He walked over to Annie and lifted her and her little cot into his arms, pressing a kiss on his daughter's downy head. "I figured when she saw the baby, she'd go back on her word and want to keep her herself. I couldn't believe it when she walked out of that hospital and left me Annie."

He gazed down at his daughter, and the adoration and wonder on his face made Bella's heart contract.

For a long moment she wondered if Jake Moreno would lavish that same wholehearted adoration on a woman, and with wistful longing she thought about how it would feel to have him look at her that same way... Well, not in a fatherly fashion, she corrected.

Anything but.

"See you about eight in the morning, Bella, if that's all right. And thanks again, more than I can say."

Bella closed the door after him and turned off the kitchen lights. She sank down again in her spot on the sofa and poured herself another cup of tea, thinking about Jake Moreno.

He was fun to be with. He had a wry sense of humor, and they talked easily together. She loved his open grin and his occasional teasing, and she felt comfortable with him. Most of the time. Except when sex reared its ugly head.

They were friends, and she'd better make damn good and sure they'd stay that way, because she valued having him as a neighbor. And the way to stay friends was to ignore how warm and...receptive his casual kisses made her feel.

She'd learned in the past that the best way to lose a friend and gain a whole lot of hostility was by making a friend into a lover. So she'd have to stop looking at Jake's body and fantasizing about it. Friends didn't daydream about erotic encounters with each other. She never imagined Woody taking her forcefully in his arms and dragging her down to the rug and kissing her all over. Lord, what was it with her, anyhow?

Get a grip on yourself, Bella, old girl. If your hormones don't stop working overtime, you'll be headed for trouble.

SATURDAY BEGAN as Friday had, with Jake knocking on the door to deliver Annie, already bathed and fed. She squirmed in her chair, gazing around with unfocused eyes at the strange surroundings in Bella's kitchen.

"You got a short memory, kid," Bella told her. "You were here all day yesterday, remember?"

Jake hurried off and Bella set the baby's chair on the counter and sang to her as she made herself a bowl of oatmeal. Bella knew perfectly well she couldn't carry a tune to save her life, but she enjoyed singing all the same. And Annie didn't seem to mind.

"Poor kid, you're a captive audience. But I have to say you're not very discriminating. Don't be too good-natured and eager to please, young lady. Those are the traits that land lots of good women in serious trouble. We're taught not to rock the boat and to smooth everything over for everybody else from the time we're your age. We never learn to stand up for ourselves. Develop a mind of your own, Annie. You paying attention here? I'm giving you the benefit of my twenty-nine years of experience as a woman, so listen up. Feel free to take notes if you have to. There's a pencil in that cup by the phone."

Annie yawned and went to sleep, and Bella was irrationally disappointed. She liked talking to the kid, although she'd never admit it to another living soul. Woody had already had far too much to say just because she'd offered to baby-sit.

Jake was home early in the afternoon, just as he'd promised. When he drove into his driveway, he spotted Bella sitting outside with Annie beside her, both of them shaded from the sun by the huge tree that grew in the center of her backyard.

It was an exceptionally warm day, and Bella had put a short romper and a big sun hat on Annie. She was wearing white shorts and a light blue blouse, and a pair of sunglasses shaded her eyes. Bella was reading a book and Annie was staring into the leaves overhead as if mesmerized by the patterns the branches made against the sky. There was something cozy about the scene, and it made Jake nostalgic for things he'd never had.

He jumped out of the truck and slammed the door. "Hello, ladies. Nice day, huh?" He grinned at them over the fence, wishing he had his camera handy. They made a delectable picture, both of them looking dainty and feminine. Waiting for him.

Bella smiled at him, closing her book. "Go have a shower if you like. Annie's fine over here. She ate just a while ago."

Jake hurried through a shower and shave and pulled on a pair of khaki shorts and a green sweatshirt. He took an extra few moments to throw a load of baby clothes into the washer. Over the past week he'd figured out a system for keeping the household from complete disorder and he was quite proud of himself.

Outside, he vaulted the fence into Bella's yard then made a low, sweeping bow to the two ladies.

"Showoff," Bella teased. "Those pickets are lethal. You could do yourself serious harm."

"An athlete like me? Never."

She tipped up her sunglasses to look at him, and he was startled at how blue her eyes were. How come he'd never noticed she had blue eyes before?

"You've got beautiful eyes," he blurted out. "How'd you get eyes the color of the sky with that dark hair?" He was unduly pleased when she blushed a little.

"They're a legacy from my long-ago Irish ancestors. Irish on my father's side, English on my mother's. What nationality were your relatives, Jake?"

He shrugged. "Got me. Ace never talked about things like that, and I never thought to ask him." There were usually far more urgent things to ask Ace, like whether or not the cops were likely to pick him up again for passing bad checks.

"When you see him again, you ought to. Annie's going to want to know all about her background. Kids always do. I used to spend whatever little spare time I had as a kid poring over my mother's old family photo albums."

Jake hadn't thought of Annie wanting to know things like that. He didn't have a single picture of his relatives, apart from a few old blurred ones of Ace. He didn't know exactly where they were, either. He'd heard Carol talk about parents and grandparents in Minnesota, but he'd never paid much attention. Carol hadn't been close to any of them that he knew of, and he sure as hell didn't have any pictures. There'd been a lot of pictures of Carol around the house, but he'd packed them up and given most of them to her when she left.

He guessed maybe he should have kept a few more. If Bella was right, it stood to reason Annie would want to know all about her mother someday, as well as her other relatives. It gave him an uneasy feeling, wondering how many things he was totally unprepared for with his daughter. Now that Bella mentioned it, he remembered wondering himself when he was a kid why he didn't have grandparents and uncles the way other boys his age did.

Well, he'd have to do the best he could, just be honest with Annie and try to put down roots here in San Diego so they had friends to take the place of an extended family. Bella was a great beginning.

"I'm taking you ladies out to dinner. The place isn't fancy, so neither of you need to change." He glanced at Annie. "Well, maybe a diaper change for Ms. Moreno here, but you're perfect the way you are, Bella." The blue shirt she wore had a V neckline that showed the beginning of some cleavage. He approved a whole lot.

Bella looked a bit apprehensive. "Maybe we should eat here, Jake. Most restaurants don't have a heck of a lot of stuff that I can eat."

"The place we're going does. I did some research on this whole vegan eating thing."

She was sitting up straight on the lawn chair now, squinting at him. "How'd you do that?"

"I checked it out in the phone book, actually. The yellow pages have a whole list of places under vegetarian, so I just called them and found out which ones are vegan."

The smile she gave him was well worth the effort. "That was brilliant of you. Where are we going? I hardly ever get to eat anywhere else but the Artichoke." She sounded excited.

"It's a surprise. You hungry right now?"

Bella nodded. "What with feeding Annie, I forgot to have any lunch."

"I skipped it, too, so I could get back sooner. I'm famished, but I also have to get back here by seven in order to interview some baby sitters. I'll take Annie over and change her bottom, and we'll go right away, all right?"

THE SPOT HE'D CHOSEN was called Soup Plantation. It was on West Point Loma Boulevard in a small shopping center. In typical California style, the airy restaurant had a forest of hanging plants, wooden beams, glass walls and colorful posters.

It was cheerful, bright and not too crowded, and Annie was one of many children. The menu consisted of the largest salad bar Jake had ever encountered, along with a bread bar with freshly baked muffins, another area that offered homemade soups and chili and a fruit and yogurt bar, as well.

Bella was enthralled. "This is absolutely perfect, Jake. I've heard of this place, but what with working and my car not running, I've never gotten over here. It's too far to bike."

They'd taken turns loading their trays, one of them staying in the comfortable booth by the window with Annie while the other chose dinner. They were beginning to eat when an elderly couple passed by and the woman stopped and cooed over Annie.

"Baby girl?" she inquired, and Bella nodded because the woman was looking at her.

"What's her name?"

"Annie," Jake supplied. He loved it when people admired his daughter.

"Annie, honey, you look just like your mummy, don't you? Especially around the eyes." With a doting smile at Bella, she moved away with her husband.

Jake looked at Bella, hoping the comment hadn't bothered her. But she was grinning at the baby.

"Stop misleading people, kid," Bella warned Annie in a teasing voice. "I'm innocent here. You look just like your daddy, you know you do."

To their amazement, Annie pouted and then began sobbing. Bella dug out the soother and popped it into the little girl's mouth, but for several moments Annie wouldn't respond. Finally Jake picked her up and held her in one arm while he forked up his dinner with the other.

"Guess you hurt her feelings," he joked.

Bella stared at the baby. She was sucking hard on her soother, but every now and then she'd give a heartrending sob.

"Okay, Annie, I apologize," Bella said. "If you insist on looking like me, it's your bad luck, kiddo."

Jake frowned at her. "Any kid that looked like you would be lucky, Bella. You're an attractive woman."

He studied her short cap of willful curls, her pert nose, her wonderful eyes.

Bella frowned at him. "Of course I'm attractive. But I'm well aware I'm not any raving beauty. Your ex-wife, now, she was what I'd label gorgeous."

Jake chewed a mouthful of salad and swallowed. "Outside, maybe. Inside, she's one messed-up lady." His voice had the same wistfully sad note it always had when he talked about Carol.

They ate and drank in silence for a while, and Jake thought about his ex-wife and how much easier his life was without her moodiness, her dissatisfaction with everything he could afford to provide for her. She'd never have been satisfied to come to a place like this with him, he mused. Carol wanted what she labeled "class," which always translated as expensive. Invariably he'd ended up feeling like Scrooge when he had to say they couldn't afford this or that.

"D'you figure she'll be involved at all in Annie's life? Carol, I mean." Bella was dunking her herbal tea bag in a pot of hot water and she glanced up and caught Jake's eye. She flushed and looked down again.

"Hey, I'm sorry. Your private life isn't any of my business."

Jake reached across and touched her fingers with his own. She looked up, her blue eyes suddenly shy and uncertain.

"We're friends, Bella. You can ask me anything you like. About Carol, it's hard to say for sure, but my guess is by now she barely remembers she has a daughter. Her acting career is everything to her. She's never written or phoned or anything to ask how Annie's doing, that's for sure."

"Does that bother you?"

"Damn right it does." He didn't even try to disguise the pain he felt. "It's hard to get it through your head that somebody you loved and married and had a child with can walk away and never think of either of you again. She's Annie's mother, after all."

He thought over their earlier conversation about children needing their families, and for the millionth time since Annie's birth, he wondered if he was insane to think he could raise a little girl on his own. Maybe little girls couldn't develop the right way without a mother. How the hell was he to know? He'd been a boy and he'd had a screwed-up childhood, at that. An uncertain lump seemed to block his throat, and he had trouble swallowing.

Bella took a bite of the crunchy whole wheat bread on her plate and chewed it as she stared across at Annie, now falling asleep on Jake's broad shoulder.

"Well, Annie's sure lucky to have a father like you. You're one of the best fathers I've ever come across, and I saw my brothers and lots of my cousins with their kids. None of them were the way you are with Annie. She's going to grow up secure and happy, I know it."

Jake felt as if a light had just gone on in some dark and frightened place in his soul. He wished with all his heart he was somewhere he could have grabbed Bella in his arms and kissed her. Her words were a vote of confidence right when he most needed it.

"Thanks, Bella," was all he could manage to say, but he looked across at her and suddenly he knew she wasn't just attractive.

She was absolutely beautiful.

CHAPTER FIVE

THEY GOT HOME just after six, and Jake barely had time to feed and settle Annie in her cradle before the first applicant arrived for the baby-sitting job he'd advertised. He'd had a dozen responses and had set up five interviews tonight and the rest on Sunday. He felt optimistic—surely out of the whole crowd one of them would be perfect for Annie.

Within fifteen minutes, he knew the first young woman wasn't going to be the one. She had a toddler of her own, which would have been fine with him, but he wasn't impressed by the way she treated the little boy. She had a high, whiny voice and she nagged. The child seemed to be used to ignoring her. The first question she asked was whether or not he had cable television.

The second woman wiped her nose and sniffed all during the interview. She claimed it was her sinus, but to Jake she looked more like an addict. He got rid of her fast. The third was fifteen years old with no fixed address, and the fourth, a young male student, admitted he'd never laid eyes on a live baby before.

"But hey, man, how tough can it be to take care of a kid? They sleep most of the time, right? Heck, women do it all the time. I figure I can handle her and finish my thesis at the same time."

By the time the fifth applicant was due to arrive, Jake knew it was hopeless. He'd have to resort to the day-care center he'd applied to before Annie was born.

Number five was Mr. Geary, an elderly man who admitted to being seventy. Jake suspected he was probably at least five years older. He was gentle and sweet-natured and claimed he'd taken care of several grandchildren. At first Jake thought he might be great for Annie, but within a half hour he realized that Mr. Geary repeated himself and couldn't seem to remember what he'd told Jake even moments before. He asked the same questions over and over, and Jake felt profoundly sorry for the old man, but there was no question of having him baby-sit. There was a problem getting him to leave; Mr. Geary seemed to have settled in for the night.

Jake felt hopelessly depressed when he finally got the old man out the door. Bella's lights were still on, and he was tempted to pick up the phone and call her to tell her about the weird collection of people he'd met that night. But it was after eleven, and she might be in the bathtub or busy doing the mysterious things to her hair and face that women did before they were ready to go to bed.

Thinking about Bella in the bathtub took his mind off baby-sitters and cheered him up a little, and he watched the late news and the sports results and then went to bed himself. Bella's lights were out by that time, and Jake imagined her sleeping, curled up on her side with the blanket slipping off her shoulder. He went to sleep wondering what she wore to bed.

SUNDAY MORNING AT ELEVEN he started interviewing more baby-sitters, and by two o'clock he was nearly suicidal. Weren't there any normal, trustworthy people left in San Diego capable of caring for a tiny baby? He'd never come across such a collection of crazies in his entire life.

The next to last applicant rang his doorbell at two-thirty. Jake was giving Annie her bottle, and he didn't answer right away. He considered letting the doorbell ring until the woman went away. He glanced at the list he'd made. This one's name was Turner and there wasn't any reason to think she'd be any better than the last ten had been.

With no enthusiasm and little hope, he finally let her in, holding Annie over his shoulder and patting her back to burp her.

"How do you do. You're Mr. Moreno, I presume. And this is the dear little baby. Annie, you said her name was on the phone. I'm Miss Florence Turner."

She was tall, thin and ruler straight from top to bottom. Her hair was a peculiar shade of blue-gray, cut and permed tight to her rather large skull. She wore round glasses that magnified her gray eyes, and her mouth was knitted into a tight knot when she wasn't using it, as if she'd taken a bite of something particularly nasty. The blue suit and crisp white blouse she wore looked as if they had had military beginnings, and she seemed to have more teeth than she needed. Jake remembered a grade three teacher he'd had for a few months who'd looked and talked like Florence Turner. That woman had put the fear of God into her students, Jake included.

Miss Turner gave one quick perusal of the living room and sniffed her disapproval before she sat down gingerly on the sofa.

"I'm fixing the place up. It takes time." Jake also realized how much the house needed dusting. More than dusting; it needed a heavy-duty mop squad. He'd never even noticed the extent of the mess until he saw it through the eyes of Florence Turner.

"If you don't mind me saying so, don't bang that poor wee girl's back so hard, Mr. Moreno. A gentle rubbing motion is just as effective and less stressful on her nervous system. Here, give her to me and I'll demonstrate."

Before he knew what was happening, Annie was in Florence Turner's arms. The woman changed entirely when she held the baby, cooing and talking away to her in a soft voice hardly recognizable as the one she used with Jake. It was obvious she knew what she was doing as far as babies were concerned. Annie belched twice and then curled up in her arms and went straight to sleep, while Miss Turner somehow managed, one-handed, to dig out an impressive bundle of references from her suitcase-size handbag.

"As you can see, I'm retired now, but I was a dietitian and a practical nurse for many years. There's a list of respectable, upstanding local citizens there for you to call, so I won't waste time telling you my strong points. They'll tell you whatever you need to know, and of course I expect you to call every one. A person can't be too careful about whom they leave their children with these days. However, there *are* questions I must have answered if I choose to take this job. Where, if you don't mind my asking, is this dear little girl's mother?"

Jake did mind, but he told her briefly that he and Carol were divorced and that Carol wasn't going to be around.

For the next half hour, Florence Turner interviewed Jake, questioning him closely on Annie's diet, her regular routine, her bowel movements, her formula, her vitamins, her sleep patterns. She asked to see Annie's room, laying the sleeping baby with infinite care into her cradle and making certain the window was open and the blinds shut so the afternoon sunshine wouldn't disturb her.

"I will, of course, do some light housekeeping—I can't abide having nothing to do, and goodness knows, this place could use a good going over. But my first and foremost concern would be the baby, you understand that, Mr. Moreno?"

Jake understood that Florence Turner was probably going to be a major pain in the butt, and that she was also far and away the best applicant he'd had for the job. She made him feel as if he hadn't washed behind his ears, but he couldn't deny the gentleness and affection she showed for Annie. If her references checked out—and he intended to check them very carefully—he'd hire her.

He phoned Bella later that evening. She'd been working; the Artichoke served brunch and an early dinner on Sundays, but she was home by nine. He watched her lights go on and waited what he considered a decent interval, in case she had to use the bathroom or something.

"So how'd the interviewing go? Was it hard to decide who to hire?"

Her warm, throaty voice made Jake smile into the receiver. There was something about Bella that always made him feel good. He filled her in on the strange assortment of people who'd answered his ad.

"The thing is, I even screened them on the phone before I gave them my address. If those were the ones I thought were reasonable, what the hell were the others like?"

Bella laughed, and the rich sound of her laughter relaxed him even further.

"So none of them were even possible?"

"One." He described Florence Turner. "I phoned seven of the references she gave, and five of them were home. They all gave her glowing reports, said she's as responsible as they come, honest, hardworking. One guy added that she might have a little too much of a mind of her own and didn't hesitate to express an opinion."

"Hmm." Bella was quiet for a moment. "That probably means she's a dreadful know-it-all, but it sounds like you already guessed as much on your own. So are you going to hire her? She sounds kind of intimidating to me."

"You got that right. She scares the daylights out of me. But she *was* good with Annie, and it sounds as if I can trust her."

"That's what's really important, isn't it?"

He realized he'd been holding off making a final decision until he talked with Bella. She had a way of making everything come together for him.

"You're right, it is. She also said she'd come early, which I need sometimes. I think I'll hire her. I'll give her a call right now. I was going to take Annie over to the day-care center tomorrow, but if Florence Turner can start right away, I might as well bite the bullet and get used to her."

Five minutes later, Annie had a baby-sitter. It was an immense relief. Jake felt as though a heavy timber had been lifted from his chest. He called Bella right back and told her the news, then suggested she come over and celebrate with him. To his delight, she agreed right away. From here on in, the evening was going to be great.

He'd rented a video and it turned out to be funny. They made popcorn and shared the sofa. Jake put his arm around Bella's shoulders in a friendly fashion, and they laughed their way through the next several hours.

"Well, I guess I ought to be going home." The movie had ended, they'd rehashed the best parts, and the popcorn was gone. Bella made a move to get up, and Jake playfully tugged her down again.

"Not so fast, pretty lady." He took her face in his hands and put his mouth on hers. "Mmm, you taste just like popcorn," he mumbled.

She did, but there was also an undertone of something sweet, like honey. He slid his tongue between her soft lips, tasting, exploring, and his body reacted with a bolt of white-hot desire when her tongue met his.

His hands slid to her shoulders, then slowly trailed down to cup her heavy breasts. The nipples were already wondrously hard through the flimsy cotton of her shirt, and he made an involuntary sound in his throat, a groan of desire and need. He could feel her heart hammering beneath his fingers.

His own heart was pounding like a bass drum and his erection strained against the denim of his jeans.

"Bella?" It was both question and appeal. His voice felt as if he had a throatful of gravel. "God, Bella, I sure do want you..."

She pulled back, placing her palms on his chest and holding him away from her. Her deep blue eyes were clouded with passion, and her breath came in short gasps, but she was shaking her head.

"It's...it's too soon for this, Jake." She moved back, taking his hands in hers and holding them, keeping him from touching her. "I...I want us to go on being friends, and if we...if we make love now, everything will be different."

She drew in a deep, shuddering breath. "Besides, you just came out of a difficult relationship. I'd feel...I'd feel as if this was only a rebound thing."

He didn't want to listen. He considered dragging her into his arms, using his mouth and his hands to smother her objections. But gradually, as control returned, his brain reluctantly accepted what she was saying. It almost killed him to admit it, but she was right.

In his experience, friendship and sex were like oil and water. He'd started out being friends with women before, and as soon as they became lovers everything changed. He liked having Bella as a friend; he didn't want to spoil what they had.

And she was right, he *was* pretty screwed up still. If he was honest, he'd have to admit he had a lot of bitter feelings about Carol and their so-called marriage. He had no idea whether those feelings would affect his relationship with another woman, but he guessed they probably might.

"Ah, hell." He rested his head on the back of the sofa and closed his eyes.

"You sound like a kid who's just been told he can't have a candy bar."

He opened his eyes and looked at her to see if she was annoyed or just teasing him. There was hesitancy and a kind of shyness in her blue gaze, and he realized that she probably figured he was the one who was mad.

She seemed so vulnerable. He reached out and grazed a knuckle down her satiny cheek, gently bumping her rounded chin with his fist. "I sort of thought we could share it... that candy bar."

His words brought a semblance of a smile, and he grinned at her. "How the hell can a bad idea feel so good?"

She gave a little half shrug and shook her head, wordless, but he knew that the regret on her face was the same as on his own.

WITHIN THE NEXT SIX WEEKS, Florence Turner had Jake, Annie and the entire house organized to her taste, which was way too organized for his taste, Jake mused as he struggled to remove a stubborn bolt on the underside of Bella's Volkswagen Rabbit early one Sunday morning in June. He was flat on his back beneath the car in a makeshift pit he'd dug, and he cursed under his breath and strained at the wrench. The bolt finally gave, and flecks of dried mud along with globs of grease landed on his face and in his eyes. He wriggled out from under the vehicle and swiped at his face with a rag he kept in his toolbox.

Annie, two months old now and full of smiles, gave him a huge, toothless grin and an excited wave of her arms and legs from her recliner chair. He'd perched her under a big sun umbrella a few feet away from where he was working, and he'd tied some of her toys to the fringe with lengths of fishing line so she'd have something besides the bottom of his feet to look at. Her hair had all fallen out and she was almost bald, so he'd put a sunbonnet on her. She looked like a round-faced cherub, and she smiled at him again.

"I look that funny, huh, Peanut?" He grinned at her and rubbed his nose, realizing too late he had grease all over his hand. "I better not get anywhere near you. Florence will have me drawn and quartered if I get grease on your clothes."

Florence. He cringed every time he thought of her. The only thing that kept him from firing the old fusspot was the meticulous and loving care she took of Annie. She was a good baby-sitter, no question about it. His daughter was healthy and happy and extremely well taken care of, and that was the name of the game, wasn't it?

But being told he wasn't allowed to set foot in his own house in his work clothes rubbed him the wrong way, to say nothing of having every single thing he laid down for two seconds put away in some impossible place where he couldn't locate it.

Granted, the house looked clean. Clean, hell. It looked like a sanitation unit, for God's sake. He'd managed to finish the floors and the electrical wiring and the drywall. The painting was coming along. But the place smelled of bleach all the time, compliments of Florence. He'd never realized how much he detested the smell of bleach.

"Your baby-sitter's a clean freak, Annikins."

She thought that comment was hilarious, and he couldn't help laughing at her, pumping her miniature arms and legs like pistons.

That reminded him of the oil pan he was trying to dislodge. He got back under the car and resumed working, whistling through his teeth.

Through the open window, Bella heard his cheerful whistle as she stepped out of the shower. She'd come home the day before and found him up to his elbows in grease, happily taking the engine of her car apart.

"Thought I'd see if I could get this old girl up and running for you," he'd explained.

"But the guy at the garage told me it wasn't worth fixing."

"Maybe she isn't, but I thought I'd have a look anyhow. One of the guys on my crew has a lot of old parts around. He used to have a Rabbit about the same vintage as this. It's sort of a challenge. You don't mind, do you?"

Of course, she didn't mind. She'd be an absolute fool to mind all the things Jake did for her. She toweled her hair and thought about what he had repaired, built or improved for her in the past six weeks.

There was the bookshelf he'd built in her living room, the taps he'd repaired in the kitchen, the bedroom light that had never worked properly till he took it apart and replaced something or other. He'd put decent locks on both her doors and fixed the front steps. A woman could get awfully used to having Jake next door.

A woman could get awfully used to having Jake.

Not that she had him, she reminded herself. Not that she ever would. She'd called the shots in the beginning, and they were friends. Period.

She pulled on her tights and artichoke T-shirt and brushed her curly hair into some semblance of a style, trying to make sense of the turmoil of emotions he stirred in her. He'd been scrupulously careful about avoiding physical contact since the night he'd kissed her, but more and more often she wished she'd kept her big mouth shut that night and just let things get out of hand. The fact was, the more time she spent with Jake, the more she wanted to be with him. In the biblical sense, as her father would put it.

She couldn't be around Jake without noticing the beauty of his strong body, the appeal of his rough-hewn, handsome features. The memory of his kiss disturbed her dreams and intruded into her waking moments, and she kept looking at his muscular arms and imagining them around her.

It wasn't just physical, either. She'd found they could discuss almost anything together. They hated the same movies and more or less liked the same music, and she loved his humor. Humor, hell. Maybe—and the idea scared her spitless—just maybe it was the *man* she loved.

Mind you, he was still heavy into meat, and that could be a problem. She was working on it, though. She stuck her head out the back door.

"Morning, you two. Want some breakfast? I'm gonna make tofu scramble and toast."

She wasn't going to do anything of the kind. She never fixed breakfast for herself on Sunday if she had to go to the Artichoke and make brunch. She and Woody usually ate there.

Well, it was Woody's turn to start early this Sunday, so she had plenty of time to make something here if she felt like it. It was barely seven o'clock.

Long legs in dirty jeans and what at one time must have been a red T-shirt slowly wormed their way out from under her car. Jake rolled to a sitting position, brushed dirt out of his hair and grinned at her. He had grease on his nose and one cheek, and he hadn't shaved yet. He looked...delectable. Her traitorous heart did a flip-flop.

"Sounds great, Bella. I finally got this infernal thing loose, too. We'll be right in."

"I better come get Annie or you'll have Florence hollering at you about grease on her clothes." Bella hurried over and picked up the baby's chair. Annie smiled at her, and something inside Bella went all soft and mushy.

"Y'know, Jake, this is one gorgeous kid you've got here. Smart as can be, too. I'm sure she knows me already."

"GREAT DAY, HUH, BELLA?" Woody waved a spoon in greeting and opened the oven a crack to check on his muffins. "Jake drove you to work again, huh?"

"How'd you know?" Bella washed her hands and wrapped her huge apron around her.

"Your hair's not egg beaten the way it is when you ride your bike. And you've got that smile on again, the giddy one you always get when Jake's around."

Bella glowered at him, but his back was turned. He was pulling muffin tins out of the oven.

"Don't be a smart ass, Finch. It doesn't suit your sunny personality."

"Okay, I'll be direct instead. How's the romance progressing?" He poured bancha twig tea into a mug and handed it to her. "Or are you still pretending you're just friends?"

She set the cup down with a thump on the worktable and started cutting up potatoes for hash browns. "That's exactly what we are. Friends."

"Uh-uh. I think not. You and I are friends, Bella *mia*. You and Jake are... let's see... what would the in expression be?" He plucked fat bran muffins out of the tin and lined them up in precise rows. "Preinvolved? Nearly amorous? Almost enamored?"

Despite her annoyance, Bella had to laugh at his nonsense. "You're a hopeless romantic, Woody, and I hate to disillusion you, but I'm going to anyway. Read my lips here. Jake's looking for a wife, some nice lady who wants a white picket fence and thirteen more babies. And I've got exactly what I want, a house of my own with its own picket fence, an income of sorts, a batty partner who forgets to mix up the sourdough pancakes..."

"Crap. I knew I'd forgotten something. I was just going to start on them when that new waitress, Justine, phoned and said she can't come in today. Or tomorrow, either. Her mother's just had twins, or was it her grandmother? I forget. Anyhow, we're going to have to work the front ourselves this morning."

Bella groaned. "I don't believe it. That's the third time she's let us down this week. We're going to have to let her go, and she's the second one we've had to fire this month. We must be doing something wrong, Woody. We just can't seem to hire good help. Or maybe kids these days have no sense of responsibility. God, I'm starting to sound like my father. Next thing I'll be blaming it on lack of animal protein in the diet."

"Maybe you're on to something, though." At her shocked look, he added, "Don't have a heart attack, I don't mean lack of animal protein, but maybe it's because they've all been too young, too unsettled. In our next ad, why don't we say no one under forty need apply?"

"Because we'd get sued for reverse discrimination, idiot. Maybe we could just say Mature Vegan Preferred."

"Makes it sound like we're partial to extraterrestrials, but hey, I'm easy."

The bell sounded.

"There's our first round of customers, Wood." She teased him a little. "You serving out front, or am I?"

"You, I fervently hope. I'll flip you for it." He picked up a hot muffin and tossed it in the air. "Tops or bottoms? Aha, tops. Thank God, I win." He gave her an appealing look. "Please, Bella? I promise not to say another word about your non love affair with Jake."

"I want it in writing." Bella untied her apron and tried to neaten her hair with her fingers. "You ever think maybe you have a problem with meeting the public, Wood, old boy?"

"The public's fine. It's just individual people that make me nervous."

Bella rolled her eyes and headed out to wait on customers.

JAKE HAD GIVEN ANNIE her noon feeding, changed her and put her down for a long sleep in her cradle. With the windows open, he could hear every whimper, so he went back to the intriguing puzzle of Bella's car, letting himself dwell on how pretty she'd looked that morning.

Voluptuous, that was the right word for Bella. Those breasts and wonderful swelling hips... He wondered if she had any idea how aroused he got watching her run around in tights and that crazy orange shirt. Here she was maybe the best friend he'd ever had, and damned if sex didn't keep interfering. Well, he hadn't a clue what to do about that state of affairs, so he'd better just concentrate on her car.

He had the motor pretty well dismantled, parts strewn over most of Bella's lawn, when he heard his front doorbell ring. He swore under his breath, swiped at his hands with a rag, vaulted over the back fence and jogged around the corner of his house, hoping to get there before whoever it was rang the damned bell again and woke up Annie.

He rounded the corner and came to an abrupt stop. His gut felt as if somebody had landed him a good one right in the old bread basket.

"Hello there, Jake. How ya been, son?"

He swallowed hard and at last his voice worked after a fashion. "Not bad. Not bad at all. How about you?"

"I'd feel a hell of a lot better if I got out of this confounded sun. I ain't used to it. You maybe gotta a beer or somethin' to drink?"

Jake recognized prison pallor when he saw it. He'd seen it often enough in the past. The pale man standing at his door sweating in the noon heat was his father, Ace Moreno.

And Ace was the last person in the world Jake expected—or wanted—to see.

CHAPTER SIX

"SO HOW LONG WERE YOU in the slammer this time, Ace?" Jake handed his father a cold bottle of beer and sat down on the sofa. While he was in the bathroom trying to scrub grease off his hands, Ace had taken the scruffy old recliner that was Jake's favorite chair, settling himself in as if he owned it.

"Six months. They set me up on some phony charge, passing bad checks or something. The sentence was a year but they let me go early for good behavior. Damn well ought to have, too, charging an innocent man for something he didn't do." He looked self-righteous and took a long draw on his beer.

Ace always insisted he was innocent of any wrongdoing; Jake remembered the injured tone of voice his father had used each time he was arrested and phoned Jake to get him to arrange for bail. Jake knew how to arrange bail by the time he was ten.

Jake looked at his father, really looked. He hadn't seen the old man in years. He sat the same way, talked the same, but there was something different about him. He'd changed in subtle ways, gotten older looking.

He must be...how old now? Jake calculated quickly and came up with sixty-three. His father had always been tall and rangy, but now he had the beginnings of a potbelly and his shoulders didn't seem as wide as they once were, or as straight. His thick curly hair, several shades darker than Jake's, was turning white at the temples and thinning on top. Jake could actually see the old man's skull, although he'd combed his hair to hide his balding crown.

His pin-striped suit had once been expensive and in fashion but was now dated and showing signs of wear. His flashy pink shirt was frayed around the neck and cuffs, and his shoes, shining like patent, had several holes in the soles. Ace had tipped the recliner back and crossed his ankles, which wasn't a cool move when it came to worn soles on your shoes. Jake would bet Ace had probably spent his last couple of bucks on a shoeshine. Ace always said you could tell a gentleman by the shine on his shoes and the trim on his hair.

Jake smiled a bit at the memory, but he sobered fast. Ace was obviously down on his luck. He had to be, Jake concluded bitterly, or he wouldn't be here. His father didn't exactly pay him regular visits out of loneliness or paternal devotion. Ace was broke, he'd bet on it.

Right now he was looking around the room, openly assessing the place, which made Jake decidedly nervous. In another minute he'd be asking to see the guest room or trying to float a hefty loan.

"This is not a bad place you got here, Jake. Needs a lot of work, but I guess you being a carpenter, you can fix it up, right? Landlord paying for the renovations? I guess rents are pretty high in this area."

"I wouldn't know about rents, I'm buying the house. Scraped together a down payment and took out a whopping mortgage, but it's all mine." Deliberately, Jake decided to put the old man on the spot. "Did you ever get the letter I sent you when I got married?"

Ace looked almost flustered for a moment. "Well, yes, now that you mention it, I did get that letter." His eyes flickered around the room, darting toward the kitchen. "Guess it's kinda late for congratulations. Should have asked you right off where your wife was. Went right out of my head there for a minute. What was her name again?"

"Carol. She's not here. We're divorced."

Ace clucked his tongue. "Sorry to hear that, son." He didn't sound at all sorry. "But you know what I always said, a man's better off on his own. Nobody tellin' you what to do or how to do it."

"A rolling stone gathers no moss. I remember you saying that all the time." Jake had wondered when he was a little boy if he was the moss Ace meant when he said it. It used to make him feel bad. He never figured moss was such a good thing to be.

Ace chuckled and drained his beer. "Ain't that the truth. You got another of these nice cool ones around, son?"

From the other room, Annie started the quiet fussing sounds she made when she first awakened, and Jake watched the expression on Ace's face turn from bland to horrified as the cry became more distinctive.

"Is that... That can't be a baby I hear?"

Jake was almost enjoying this. "Yeah. I guess you didn't know you were a grandfather, huh?"

Ace set the empty beer bottle down on the polished coffee table with a thump—Florence was going to have a fit at the white rings—and sat forward so that his feet clumped to the floor. His face had turned florid with the beer, but it went pale again.

"Grandfather? Me?"

Jake nodded and got to his feet. "Yup. I have a daughter, that makes you a grandfather. I named her Annie. You used to tell me that was my mother's name, remember? Anyhow, she's two weeks old now. I'll get her."

He headed into the bedroom and scooped her out of the cradle. She stopped fussing when he picked her up. She smiled at him as he laid her on the change table to do a diaper job.

"Go get him, Tiger," he murmured into her ear, planting a kiss on her downy cheek. Expertly he snapped her pink rompers into place then used his fingers to curl the sparse silky hair growing in on the top of her head into a semblance of a curl. She smelled fresh and sweet. Propping her in the crook of his arm, he walked into the living room.

Ace was still sitting bolt upright, and he stared at Annie as if she were going to leap out of Jake's arms and bite him.

"You just got her for the day, right? Your wife—your ex-wife, she just dropped her off for the day?" He couldn't seem to take his eyes off the baby. "She's sure a small one. Looks almost new."

Jake shook his head. "Nope on all counts. Carol's in England. Hasn't laid eyes on Annie since the day she was born. Annie's mine. I have a baby-sitter for her while I work, but the rest of the time I take care of her by myself."

"Geez." Ace looked thunderstruck. "That's a rough one. Woman just walked out and left you with the kid, did she?" He shook his head. "You 'n' me, we sure as hell know how to pick 'em, huh, Jake? Walking out on you, leaving you with a little nipper like that... At least your mother waited till you was older before she took a powder."

Jake had to suppress the sudden rage Ace's words filled him with. His mother might have deserted him, but damn it all, Ace sure as hell had, too. He took two deep breaths and had to force himself to loosen his hold on Annie. He was clutching her far too tightly.

"It wasn't that way at all," he finally managed to say. "I bargained with Carol to have my baby. See, I wanted Annie more than anything."

Ace looked as if he figured Jake had taken total leave of his senses. "Now why in hell would you do a harebrained thing like that?"

Jake didn't answer. Instead, he just gave Ace a long, scathing look, and for the first time, the older man seemed to realize that Jake wasn't exactly amused by what he was saying.

"What I mean is," he stammered, "a baby, a girl at that, it's just not natural... It's not something a man knows how to do, raisin' up a baby. How d'ya know what to feed it or anything? You was eatin' ordinary food by the time... I mean, that's women's territory, all that baby stuff."

"Why should it be? Lots of women don't have any idea how to raise a kid before they have one of their own. They get forced into it and have to learn on the job. Why should it be different for a man?" Honest pride filled Jake's voice. "I've learned how to care for Annie, it wasn't all that tough. I made a few mistakes along the way, but she's doing fine, aren't you, Peanut?" He jogged his daughter and she obliged him with a smile.

"But it's gonna tie you down somethin' awful, you ever think of that?"

"Yeah, well, I never fancied being any rolling stone, Ace." There was a hardness in Jake's voice. "See, I'm not like you. I'm no drifter. I want a home where Annie can grow up knowing the neighbors, going to school with the same kids. A place and people she can count on to stay the same, year in, year out."

Ace's gaze shifted from Jake and the baby to a picture on the wall behind Jake's head. His expression seemed frozen. "Everybody's different, I reckon."

"Yeah, everybody sure is." Annie wriggled and Jake grinned down at her. He couldn't stay mad at the old man with his daughter giving him that big new smile she'd perfected in the last week.

"You hungry, Ace? I'll put her in her chair and make us a sandwich."

Ace was hungry, all right. He devoured four sandwiches and half a bag of oatmeal cookies along with most of a pot of coffee, eyeing the baby warily the whole time.

"She don't cry much, I'll say that for her," he remarked after lunch when Annie was fed and asleep again.

Jake thought of those first few days of Annie's life when she'd cried nonstop. "She had colic there for a while, but the woman next door gave me some stuff that really helped. I had to use it half a dozen times or so, but Annie's all over it now."

"What the hell's colic?"

Jake did his best to explain, remembering that first meeting with Bella. It all seemed a long time ago, and he wondered for a moment what life would be like, not knowing her.

Pretty damned empty, he decided. Bella was his best friend.

Ace was showing no signs of leaving, so Jake finally led the way outside and over to Bella's yard, where the car waited to be reassembled. No point wasting the whole afternoon entertaining the old man.

"What's the problem with her?" Ace had always liked engines.

"One of the main bearings is worn. I'm replacing it."

"Might go again right away, ya never know."

"Might," Jake agreed. "But it might also go for sixty thousand miles trouble free. It's worth taking a chance."

"I'm a gambling man myself," Ace said blandly, as if Jake hadn't known. "I'd give ya a hand if I had my old clothes with me," he added conversationally, staying a careful distance away as Jake bent over the greasy engine again. "I'm pretty good around motors, if I do say so myself."

When Jake didn't respond, Ace added in a far too casual tone, "Suitcases are down in a locker at the bus station."

Jake straightened and looked his father in the eye. The time had come for some straight talk here, and his heart sank as he realized what was coming.

"You got anyplace to stay, Ace?"

Ace shrugged and tried to look nonchalant. "I can always get a hotel room."

"You got money?"

Ace tried to look insulted but it didn't work. "A little." He shifted and stared at the engine. "Not much. Matter of fact, I'm sort of flat right now, between jobs as it were."

Jake sighed and made up his mind. Reprobate or not, he couldn't put his father out on the street. "When Annie wakes up, we'll go get your things. There's a spare room here you can use, but there's conditions."

"What's that?" Ace was frowning.

"You keep right out of trouble. I don't want any cops at the door. I've got neighbors I care about, and there's Annie to think of. No passing bad checks, no gambling, no crooked stuff at all."

Ace appeared offended. "Hell, I'm no criminal. I told you I got a bum deal..."

"Just like all the others, huh?" Jake gave his father a scathing look. "Don't forget, I know you pretty well. And I want your word on this before you move in, Ace. You're welcome here only as long as you keep out of trouble."

The older man stared at Jake for a long moment and then seemed to deflate like a balloon. "All that's behind me now, son," he whined. "I'm gettin' a little older. I been kinda thinking of settling down, gettin' a job of some kind. You got my word, no wheelin' or dealin'."

"I'll hold you to that." Jake felt as if a heavy weight had settled on his shoulders. Having his father as housemate was the last thing he'd expected or wanted, but there seemed no way out of it. No way that would let him sleep at night, anyhow.

Well, it probably wouldn't last long. Ace was incapable of staying out of trouble, and the moment that happened, Jake would have no qualms about asking him to leave. It was only a matter of time, he told himself.

BELLA PEDALED HER BIKE into the yard just after eight that evening, astonished to find Jake still working on her car. Another man was there, as well, older, tall and well-built, Even in faded green work pants and shirt, he looked strangely elegant. Annie was in her buggy a few feet away from the men, sound asleep.

"Hi, everybody. I can't believe you're still working on this car. Jake, are you sure it's even worth it?"

Jake was crouched on the ground doing something intricate with a greasy-looking clump of steel and a pail of gas, and it took several moments before he acknowledged her. When he did, Bella thought he seemed weary, although the smile he gave her was as wide and welcoming as ever. The older man smiled, too, and when he did there was something eerily familiar about the lines of his face and the deep cleft in his chin.

"Another couple of hours, we'll have this thing running like clockwork. Bella Donovan, this is my father, Ace Moreno."

No wonder the guy looked familiar. Jake hadn't said a thing about his father coming to visit. It must have been spur of the moment, she concluded, smiling at the older man and extending her hand.

"What a lovely surprise. I'm really pleased to meet you, Mr. Moreno."

Now that she realized who he was, she could certainly see the resemblance between him and Jake. Both of them had strong, rugged features, and Mr. Moreno was well over six feet, just like his son.

Handsome, too, for an old guy. There was a trace of Jake's sweet, crooked grin in his father's courtly smile. It gave Bella a funny feeling in her stomach, seeing what Jake was going to look like when he got older.

"Name's Ace. Really pleased to make your acquaintance, ma'am. Jake mentioned you earlier, but he didn't say how pretty you were. All right if I call you Bella?"

"Please do." He was smooth and charming. The admiring way he eyed her made her blush. She bent over the carriage and tucked the light blanket closer around Annie's tiny form. "It must be wonderful for you to come here and meet your granddaughter."

When she straightened, she thought Jake had a strange expression on his face, but he didn't say anything. Neither did Ace, and the silence began to be uncomfortable.

"Well, why don't you both come in and have some tea and poppy seed cake? It's getting too dark to work out here anyway. We'll just roll Annie's buggy right through the back door and into the kitchen."

Soon they were seated around Bella's kitchen table, drinking chamomile tea and devouring the cake she'd made the day before. The men had scrubbed their hands in her bathroom, but the faint smell of grease and gas still lingered about them. Bella decided she rather liked the odor; it gave her feminine kitchen a homey, slightly masculine atmosphere.

"It's awfully nice of you to help Jake with my car, Ace." Bella smiled at the older man.

"My pleasure. Man's gotta have something to do. Had enough of just sittin' around doing nothin'. Inactivity's enough to make you crazy."

"What sort of work do you do?" Bella realized after she'd asked that maybe Ace was laid off or retired. Or perhaps he'd been ill. He looked pale and drawn.

"Between jobs at the moment, but I guess I've tried my hand at almost everything over the years. People, now. I like doing anything that involves people. Guess you might say I'm sort of an amateur...what-you-call-it? Sociologist, that's the word."

Jake choked on his cake and had a coughing fit. Bella banged on his back but Ace was unconcerned.

"How about you, Bella? How do you spend your days?" Ace seemed genuinely interested, so Bella went into detail about the Artichoke Heart and her vegetarian cookbooks.

He nodded his head thoughtfully. "Been doin' a fair bit of reading these past few months, and there's plenty of articles nowadays about vegetarians. Seems like it's a real healthy way to eat."

Bella beamed at him. So few people had even a minimal understanding of true vegetarianism, but Ace seemed more enlightened than most.

"C'mon, Ace, let's go home. I've got to get Annie to bed. It's getting late and I have to be up early in the morning." Jake stood up and gathered the teacups, taking them over to the sink.

Surprised at his abruptness, Bella glanced at her watch. It was only nine-thirty. Usually Jake stayed till well past ten or even eleven. He seemed a little out of sorts tonight, Bella thought.

"Well, it's nice to meet you, Ace. Maybe before you leave Jake can bring you over to the Artichoke for a meal. Are you going to be in San Diego long?"

"An indefinite period, my dear. Indefinite. Certainly I'd enjoy visiting your restaurant. If Jake's unable to come with me, well, I'll just come on over by myself one day. Thank you for the delicious cake, much appreciated."

What a nice man to have for a father, Bella mused after they'd left. Easy to talk to, not at all like her own father. Ace was sort of quaint, like an old-fashioned gentleman. Jake was lucky. Still, it must be a strain on him, having his parent around. He'd hardly said a word all evening.

She washed out the cups and set them to dry, thinking about Jake. She spent a lot of time thinking about Jake. It was probably a good thing his father had turned up, because she and Jake were spending far too much time in one another's company these days.

It was enjoyable, no question about it. She was getting attached to Annie. For all their drawbacks, and Bella knew every last disadvantage intimately, babies were still hard to resist. Especially babies like Annie. She was unusually bright and beautiful and responsive, Bella mused.

She wandered into the bathroom, stripping off her clothes as she went, dropping T-shirt, tights and underwear in puddles along the way. Being comfortably messy was one of the best things about living alone, she reminded herself.

She filled the tub with cool water and poured in a handful of sweet-smelling hyacinth herbal bath salts. As she eased into the fragrant water, she found herself thinking of Jake once again. Even though she and Jake got along amazingly well, there were still chasms between them that could never be bridged, like his fantasy about a wife and family of little Morenos.

Little Morenos brought to mind the subject of sex. Well, the lack of sex, to be precise. She felt irritated with herself over sex these days. If she'd allowed matters to take their natural course weeks ago, the whole troubling problem would probably be gone by now. She and Jake would have fallen into bed, found out that it wasn't as great as they'd expected and either stayed friends or drifted apart.

The way it was now, she couldn't be near him without constantly wondering what it would be like to be loved by him, damn it all. She imagined his big, callused hands on her, his mouth doing things...

She stopped the erotic direction her thoughts were taking. There was no real basis for a significant relationship between them, she reminded herself. Not the slightest, faintest excuse—unless you counted the fact that they truly liked one another, got along wonderfully well, laughed more than two people had any right to laugh. Why, he even seemed to be enjoying the vegan dishes she cooked for him.

And damn it all to hell, she really wanted to go to bed with him.

Well, having Ace around—and it sounded as if he planned on being around for a long while—would certainly curtail any fantasies she might have in weaker moments of tumbling Jake down on his living room rug and taking advantage of him.

Now why should the thought of having Ace around for an extended period of time depress her? There was always her own living room rug, come to think of it.

FLORENCE TURNER ARRIVED at Jake's back door at seven on the dot every weekday morning.

Jake paid her extra for coming early; most of the time he had Annie bathed and fed by seven, but this morning he hadn't. He'd overslept, and so had Annie. When Florence marched into the kitchen, he was still trying to give the baby a bottle and eat his toast at the same time.

"Give that child to me." She settled Annie in her arms and took the bottle from Jake. "A baby should have all your attention when you're feeding her, otherwise she'll get gas." Florence sat and clucked to Annie as Jake bolted the last of his breakfast, glancing at the clock and mentally reviewing the day's work.

Tho Van Chung was meeting him on the job site at quarter to eight, and there were some papers he had to remember to take along, estimates of various materials. The job was going pretty well, but Tho Van Chung was driving him nuts. The guy insisted on knowing every last detail of the job, and then he'd weigh and consider every decision endlessly, discussing it over and over with Jake, asking his opinion, arguing with whatever that opinion was, changing his mind and then finally taking Jake's advice as often as not.

"I see there's grease on the back doorknob. I certainly hope it's not all over the bathroom. I cleaned thoroughly in there on Friday. The mess was quite disgusting," Florence was saying in her disapproving voice.

He'd cleaned the bathroom himself last week, so it couldn't have been that bad. He tried to remember how much grease had come off on the towels yesterday. Well, he'd probably hear about that in detail when he got home this afternoon. Between Tho Van Chung, Florence Turner and the arrival of his father, he could easily go over the deep end here.

Patience, Jake counseled himself, downing the last of his lukewarm coffee. He'd used tap water to mix up some instant, and if the taste practically turned his stomach, at least the caffeine would give him the kick start he needed.

"I've told you I don't expect you to do housecleaning, Florence. Taking good care of Annie is all I expect."

Florence snorted. "And how can I take good care of her in the midst of total chaos? Besides, she still sleeps a great deal and I never was one to sit and do nothing."

Jake was reminded of Ace, relaxing in Bella's kitchen last night and telling one whopper after another about how industrious he was and how he couldn't abide sitting around. Afterward, Jake had spent half the night lying awake and wondering whether or not he ought to clue Bella in about his father before the old man went any further with this disgusting English gentleman act of his. He didn't want to prejudice Bella against the old man, but neither did he enjoy having his father charm the pants off his best girl. Figuratively, of course.

That had given him pause for thought and kept him awake another hour and a half. Was Bella his best girl? Did normal sex-crazed people really go on year after year like this in platonic relationships? Had the world changed that much while he was waiting to be a father? Could a man die from relentless amicability without hope of carnal knowledge?

Why couldn't his father have stayed on the missing persons list? Which reminded him, he'd better tell Florence that Ace was staying here.

He drew in a deep breath and let it out slowly as he made his announcement. "By the way, my father's here for a visit. He's sleeping in the back bedroom, probably won't be up until noon.'' Ace had never been a morning person, although prison might have changed all that. Jake didn't think so, though.

Florence's nostrils flared. ''How old a man is he, may I ask?''

Jake could see she was thinking of senility and bedpans and soiled sheets and stuff. He was tempted to tease her, but he had a suspicion teasing Florence would be like baiting a rhinoceros.

''He's about sixty-three, he's perfectly healthy and able to take care of himself.''

''And how long will he be here?''

Jake sighed. If only he knew the answer to that question. He fell back on Ace's own response when Bella had asked. ''An indefinite period, Florence. He's here on an extended visit.''

Florence sniffed. ''Well, I won't tolerate him interrupting the baby's daily routine, you understand that, Mr. Moreno. I'm quite firm about Annie's routine. I must insist you tell her grandfather so. And I won't appreciate him messing up this kitchen at all hours of the day and night, either.''

Jake thought about Ace's negative reaction to Annie.

''Believe me, there won't be any problem with the baby.'' He tactfully avoided the subject of the kitchen. The last time Jake had lived with him, Ace hadn't exactly been housebroken, and he doubted things had changed much. Florence and the old man could battle it out on their own.

Looking at the clock again, he hurriedly got to his feet. "I've gotta go." He reached out and took Annie from Florence and kissed her, ignoring Florence's obvious displeasure. "Bye, Peanut. Be a good girl. Daddy will see you later."

He gave her to Florence. "You have the number of my mobile phone if you need me." Grabbing his work papers from the top of the fridge, he headed out the door.

"I'm quite capable of handling any emergency should it arise, Mr. Moreno," Florence called after him. "And I must ask you again not to phone here every afternoon. There's never any problem and it wakes the baby from her nap."

Jake stifled the urge to take the woman's scrawny neck in his hands and squeeze it a little. "All right. See you about four."

Bella was coming out her back door. Over the past weeks, Jake had managed to perfect his timing so that he met her this way most of the mornings she worked. She was wearing white shorts today, and he noticed all over again that she had great legs—shapely, probably from riding her bike all over the city. He wished the shorts were shorter, but hey, a guy couldn't have everything. Some of the sour aura Florence had given off began to dissipate as he gazed at Bella.

"Morning, neighbor. Nice day, huh? Can I give you a ride to work?" He usually put her bike in the back of his truck and drove her over to the Artichoke on his way to work. It sort of made his morning.

"That would be super, Jake. Thanks." She smiled at him, and he thought that her wonderful smile was the best thing that had happened to him this morning. One of the two best, actually. Annie had also given him a big smile when he lifted her out of her cradle.

He settled the bike in the back. These few moments with Bella were a great beginning to the rest of the day. He pulled out of the driveway and headed down the street, whistling under his breath. Maybe he shouldn't be so swift about fixing her car.

"I really like your father, Jake. He's so interesting to talk to. I can't get over how open-minded he is about things. It must be wonderful to have a father you can actually discuss things with."

Jake's whistle caught in his throat and his morning began to go downhill all over again.

CHAPTER SEVEN

FLORENCE TURNER and Ace Moreno despised one another on sight.

Jake heard all about it in extensive detail from Florence when he arrived home that afternoon, then heard about it all over again when Ace turned up at six, just in time to eat more than his share of the pizza Jake had ordered in for supper. Ace said he'd gone to a triple feature movie just to get away from Florence.

"Wouldn't have that miserable women around for longer than ten seconds," Ace declared, taking a huge bite out of his fourth piece. "Bad news, that's her. Some women are just too mean to live, and she's one. Frustrated old bitch."

"I didn't exactly hire her to keep you company." Jake had had a bad day and it wasn't getting any better as it went along. Tho Van Chung had changed his mind twice about the location and size of a door, which caused a blowup with the carpenters, who'd already framed it in. They'd threatened to walk off the job unless Jake got his act together.

"You sure she knows what she's doin' with this nipper?" Ace jerked his chin at Annie, who was occupying half the table in her infant carrier. Annie wriggled and smiled at him. Ace stared at her and then gave her a surprised grin.

"Cheerful little thing," he remarked, reaching for another slice of pizza. "You sure that woman knows what she's doin'? Sure as hell she's never been married or had a kid of her own, I'd bet my bottom dollar on that. No man on earth would take on a sourpuss like her."

"She had good references," Jake snapped. "You think I'd leave Annie with someone I wasn't altogether convinced would take the best care of her?"

As he said it, he couldn't help remembering how Ace had dumped him on Nathan and Samuel Liposki years before. Granted, he wasn't any baby—he was fifteen at the time, already half-grown and streetwise. But still, now that he had a kid of his own, he couldn't imagine doing something like that, no matter how old Annie was.

And how much checking had Ace done before he left Jake with the two men? Not a hell of a lot, he'd bet. He'd been dumped more than once before that, with people Jake wouldn't exactly classify as reliable. The memories didn't make him feel any more loving toward the old man, that's for sure.

Suddenly Annie upchucked a good portion of her last bottle along with a sampling of rice cereal, all down the front of her yellow pajamas. Jake casually used a piece of paper toweling and cleaned her off, but Ace gulped and swallowed hard, then set down his unfinished piece of pizza and fled from the table.

Jake grinned at Annie. "Way to go, Peanut." He reached for the last piece of pizza and slowly munched his way through it, enjoying every bite.

TO JAKE'S UTTER AMAZEMENT, Ace began to make supper for the two of them shortly after that, and his cooking wasn't at all bad.

"Worked in the kitchen this last trip to the big house," he explained, serving up pork chops, mashed potatoes and turnips.

Bella dropped over while they were eating with some soy buns she'd baked, and Jake made her a cup of tea—he'd bought a selection of herbal teas especially for her. She wrinkled her nose at the pork chops and gave them a short lecture on the dangers of fat and the need for greens in their diet, and she and Ace were soon deep in a discussion about cooking that left Jake feeling ignored.

"I'd like to learn more about this vegetarian way of cooking food," Ace declared. "Trouble is, at my age I guess it's hard to teach an old dog new tricks, eh, Bella?"

Jake could have sworn there was a tremor in Ace's voice that hadn't been there before.

"Why, you're not at all old, Ace," she insisted with such warmth in her voice Jake wanted to punch something, preferably Ace. "Why don't you come over to the Artichoke tomorrow afternoon and meet my partner, Woody? He's one of the best cooks I've ever met, and he'd never so much as boiled water until he was an adult."

Ace beamed. "Thank ya kindly, I'll do that. Get me out of here while that woman's around. Can't abide her." He shuddered dramatically.

Bella laughed. She'd met Florence, and although she admired the way the older woman cared for Annie, she shared Ace's opinion of Florence's personality.

Jake felt his stomach tighten at the thought of Ace becoming even friendlier with Bella. He ought to have told her the truth about his father, he thought, as he watched the two of them laughing like old friends. He'd wait until he and Bella were alone and then somehow he'd break the bad news about Ace's background. The problem was, would he ever get to see her alone? He doubted it, not with Ace hanging around her like a bad smell.

Bella finally got up to leave. She hesitated a moment at the door then blurted out, "Jake, I hate to bother you, but water's leaking out from under my bathroom sink. I've got towels down to soak it up so there's no real hurry, but I wondered if maybe you could come over and have a look at it sometime?"

At least she was still asking *him* to come over and fix things, Jake consoled himself.

"Tonight's a good time. I'll be there as soon as I get Annie settled. You won't mind listening for her, will you, Ace?" He knew damned well the old man didn't relish the idea of baby-sitting, but Annie never fussed once she was fed and settled in her cradle. Even if she did, he could hear her from Bella's place with the windows open. He had to talk to Bella alone. "Bella's number is right by the phone, so if Annie cries at all you can just give me a call.''

Ace didn't seem very pleased with the arrangement, but Jake could not care less. Within an hour he was tapping at Bella's back door.

''Hi, Jake, c'mon in. I didn't expect you quite so soon.''

She'd obviously just gotten out of the bathtub. Her skin was flushed and shiny and she was wearing a long red wraparound cotton robe, a thin one. Her hair was a mass of damp curls, and she smelled like apple shampoo and perfumed soap. She looked so delectable that Jake had to shove his hands into the pockets of his jeans to stop himself from reaching out and taking her into his arms.

She led the way into the bathroom. It was small, and he was uncomfortably conscious of her brushing against him as they both leaned down to look under the sink. The robe gaped a little at the neckline, and of course he peeked. Bella rested a hand on his arm as she crouched down beside him to point out the exact location of the leak, and he was treated to the sight of one silken thigh. All he could think about was what she might not have on under the red robe.

''I tried to tighten this pipe myself with a wrench, but it just made it worse. I probably should call a plumber instead of bothering you about it—''

''Don't talk nonsense. I can fix this in no time at all.'' Even to his own ears, his voice sounded strangled.

She was pressed close to his side. He wasn't paying any attention at all now to the pipe, because the damned robe had slithered open again right up to her thigh. And from what he could see out of the corner of his eye, there wasn't any sign of underwear, top or bottom.

Jake gulped and tried to concentrate on the plumbing, but parts of his anatomy were reacting with urgent insistence to Bella. He could smell her delicious fragrance, and the warmth from her body seemed to reach out and envelop him. His jeans were way too tight and his breath wouldn't reach his lungs. He struggled valiantly, pitting his finer sensibilities against his baser instincts, but all of a sudden he knew it was useless. He just gave up the fight and let his gonads win.

With a groan, he turned and pulled her into his arms, forgetting they were both crouching in awkward positions. Thrown offbalance, she half fell against him and the top of the robe came open, revealing those lush, naked breasts.

He was lost. The next thing he knew, they were on the floor, squashed somehow between the sink and the tub. Bella was underneath him and he was kissing her with all the pent-up passion he'd subdued with such ruthless determination during the past few weeks.

And the miraculous, unbelievable, spectacular part of it all was that Bella was kissing him back, making little hungry sounds in her throat even when he lost all control and held her head between his hands, ravaging her lips, her cheeks, her eyes. He recaptured her mouth, meeting the challenge her tongue provided, then let his lips wander down her chin and throat until at last, with an impatient, stifled exclamation, he shoved the red fabric of her robe aside and tasted the sweetness of her breasts.

She was luscious, she was intoxicating. Her large nipples were hard as pebbles, her breasts full and soft. Now it was her turn to cradle his head between her hands and encourage him as he suckled first one breast and then the other.

"Jake..." He heard her saying his name, and he knew by her tone she was going to make him stop. He slid his palms across her breasts and down the silkiness of her torso, desperate to remember how she felt, how she tasted. She was breathing in short gasps, her ribs heaving.

"Jake, my back's breaking. This floor is tile over cement."

He slowly realized that his own legs were folded into pretzels against the bathtub, and if either of them moved, they were in danger of getting their heads stuck in the small space between the sink cabinet and the toilet. There wasn't any human way possible to finish what he'd started here and now, but he knew the moment they stopped and Bella came to her senses again, she'd call a halt to the whole operation.

He felt absolutely suicidal. Why in God's name couldn't he have chosen a better spot for this than her damned bathroom floor? Had he lost any finesse he might once have possessed in the art of seduction? Abstinence had affected his brain, no doubt about it. With great reluctance, he began to untangle them. Trembling, he staggered to his feet and pulled Bella up, snuggling her into his arms one last time before the inevitable protest came. God, she fitted so well.

It took a long five seconds for him to realize that she wasn't objecting at all. To the contrary, she was pressing delicious parts of her body against urgent areas of his and responding to his kisses. God help him, he still had his clothes on and he couldn't take very much of this fully clothed.

Her lips were pressed close to his ear. "Why don't we move into my bedroom, Jake? It's lots more comfortable in there."

He'd been afraid to hope. Jubilant, he swept her up into his arms...and then realized there was no way on earth he could fit them both through the bathroom doorway. He made several abortive efforts with no success. Bella started to giggle.

The damned room had been designed for elves. With a muttered curse, he put her down again and quick-stepped them both through the narrow passageway. At the door to her bedroom, he scooped her up again.

She was laughing now and couldn't seem to stop. As she twined her arms around his neck, he could feel her body shaking. He didn't care. Laughter was fine. Anything was fine, just as long as she didn't make him stop. He breathed a silent prayer that the condoms he'd carried around in his shirt pocket for weeks wouldn't have rotted with age.

"Bella, God, Bella, I have to make love to you, I'm going out of my mind wanting you..."

The giggles subsided in a long sigh, and he heard her whisper, "Me, too. Oh, Jake, me too. It took me over two hours to loosen that damned pipe enough to make it leak, and I think I've wrecked my wrist."

HER BODY ACHED in delicate places. She felt feather light and totally at peace. Her head was pillowed on Jake's shoulder, and she could feel the rhythmic pattern of his breathing. He'd fallen asleep a few minutes ago, and she needed time to assimilate what had just happened.

Who'd have imagined it would be like that? Who'd ever have dreamed it *could* be like that?

Not her. Oh, she'd wanted him, all right, and finally stooped to a little intrigue to satisfy that wanting. But what had happened between them after that had gone way beyond anything in her experience—or her imagination, for that matter. Granted, her experience was limited. But if the lovemaking she'd just enjoyed with Jake was the norm, she'd been living in a state of serious deprivation.

She tried to reconstruct the scene, so she could figure out how and what he'd done to make her body and soul explode the way they had, but after the preliminary kisses and cramped caresses in the bathroom, she began to get muddled. Well, maybe the scientific approach was best. Maybe she ought to reconstruct the entire experiment.

Turning her head to the side, she trailed a line of kisses down his shoulder, using her tongue to explore the texture of skin, tasting the slightly salty essence of him as her lips ventured further, to his chest. She propped herself up on one elbow and took his nipple gently in her teeth.

She knew he was awake. His body went from relaxed to alert in the space of a millisecond. She peered at him from under her lashes. He was staring at her, not moving a muscle as she teased and suckled him, but his dark brown eyes were riveted on her face. The passionate look in them made her breath come fast, and a thrill of anticipation wove its way through her abdomen.

She moved slightly, raising herself higher so she had better access to his body. As she worked her way down his torso, licking and tasting and teasing, she could feel him tense. His breathing was audible, a loud sighing in the stillness of the room, but still he didn't move.

The muscles in his stomach were like bands of steel beneath pliant skin. Bella touched him with both her hands and mouth now, hungry to savor all of him. When at last she took him fully into her mouth, he made an agonized sound deep in his throat.

For long moments she tantalized, feeling her own body respond. Need rose in her in direct proportion to his desire, and her breath sobbed from her lungs when at last he grasped her, lifted her, flipped her over and settled her beneath him in one deft and easy gesture.

"Enough, Bella. Now it's my turn." His voice was gruff and guttural, and it seemed to reverberate through every pore. She shivered as his clever, callused hands touched her everywhere she needed to be touched, while his lips sought and found her breasts, her ears, her mouth.

He was tender and rough by turns, never hurting but adept in knowing exactly what she wanted and when. Her desire grew beyond the level where control was possible, and still he waited, watching her eyes, murmuring words of encouragement .

At last she could wait no longer. She gripped his shoulders and pulled him down to her, into her, frantic with craving. And at that moment his control fled. He cried out and drove himself deep inside her, blossoming in the same inferno consuming her.

"YOU OKAY, BELLA?" His voice was thick with satisfaction, sleepy and slow.

"What do you mean, okay?" She was locked against him, her bottom to his belly.

There was a moment of silence.

"I guess what I mean is, was that as great for you as it was for me?"

She was amazed to detect a slight note of insecurity in his voice. It was touching, but this whole thing was scary, too. She had to be careful here. She had to be sure she didn't reveal how magnificent it really had been, being loved by him. If she was bone honest, he might get nervous and embarrassed about the whole thing, and she didn't want that. She wanted things to go on just as they were—just as they were as of tonight, that is.

"It was very nice, Jake." Talk about the understatement of the year. It's a wonder her nose wasn't growing by leaps and bounds.

"Yeah, it was, wasn't it." There was a flat sound to his voice, as if he might be a little disappointed by her less than effusive reaction. A long silence followed, and then he said, "Bella, did you really fake that leak in the bathroom, just to..."

She could kick herself now for ever admitting that.

"Yeah, I did." At least it was dark in the room, so he couldn't see the blush she could feel stealing up her chest and over her neck.

She felt him press his lips against the back of her neck. "You didn't have to, you know. I've been crazy with wanting you for weeks now. If you'd just said something..."

Honestly, sometimes men were impossibly dense. "What exactly do you think a woman's going to say, for heaven's sake? Call you over here and say, Jake, I've changed my mind, I want to go to bed with you now?"

"Yeah. Something like that. Hell, you could have totally screwed up the whole drain in that bathroom, fooling around with a wrench. As it is, it's going to take me a couple hours to fix it."

The hint of laughter in his voice told her he was joking, and she was relieved the conversation had become less intense.

"But right now, sweetheart, I've got to go home. It's a wonder Ace hasn't phoned or come banging on the door already. If Annie had cried, we'd probably have heard her, though, the way these windows are situated."

"I think it's wonderful that Ace is here, getting to know Annie. My grandfathers were both dead by the time I was born, so I never had the chance to know them. A kid needs grandparents."

He seemed about to say something, but didn't. Instead, he gave her a satisfying hug and rolled off the bed, searching for the clothing he'd abandoned.

"You want a ride to work in the morning?"

"Thanks, not tomorrow. I'm not going in till noon. I'm working on the cookbook in the morning. The publisher wants me to have it done by September. Then I thought I'd ask your dad if he wanted to walk over to the Artichoke. It would take about an hour and a half, but it's a nice walk. Think he's fit enough for that distance?"

"If that's what you want to do, I'm quite sure Ace can go the distance."

There was a decided coolness to his voice. Could Jake be jealous of his own father? The idea was preposterous.

Before she could ask him what *was* wrong, he bent over and kissed her, long and hard. "Tonight was a great beginning, Bella."

Her heart skipped a beat and she tried to sound flippant. "You don't mean you want to do this again?"

In reply, he trailed kisses from her mouth to her ear, and she caught her breath. "Again and again and again, until we get it right. Night, lovely lady. I'll lock the back door on my way out. Sleep well."

She heard him walking through her house, stopping at the back door to pull on the runners he'd left there. As he slipped out and the lock on the door snapped into place, Bella suddenly felt very alone.

EVEN THOUGH IT WAS AFTER one in the morning, Ace was slouched on the living room couch, sipping a beer and watching a bowling tournament on TV. Beside him, wedged between two rolled-up blankets, Annie slept peacefully on her stomach.

"Sorry I was so long. Did she cry much? You should have given me a call." Jake felt guilty. He and Bella must have been too involved to even hear the baby. Hell, the truth was they probably wouldn't have been aware of a major earthquake.

"Didn't cry at all." Ace kept his eyes on the television screen. "This is the damnedest sport. I never woulda believed it could get on television."

"If she didn't cry, what's she doing sleeping out here?"

Ace still wouldn't look at him. "Figured if I was gonna watch her, I should watch her right. So I brought her out. She never even woke up."

Jake stood and stared at the two of them for several moments, digesting what Ace had said. Finally, he walked over and picked Annie up. "I appreciate you keeping an eye on her, Ace. I'll put her back in her cradle now."

When he came out of Annie's bedroom, Ace had turned off the television. He gave Jake a long, accusing glare.

"Little thing like that shouldn't oughta be in a room all by herself, I don't think. Oughta have her in with you."

Jake was flabbergasted. "All the books say a baby needs a room of her own. Besides, I always leave the door open so I can hear her if she cries."

Ace snorted. "Books. In my opinion, you can't learn how to raise a baby out of books."

"Exactly what would you recommend instead? There aren't exactly any videos on the market." The last thing Jake had expected was that Ace would start telling him how to raise Annie.

"Like I said before, a girl baby needs her mother. Where exactly did you say her mother was again?"

"England. And I told you she was out of the picture for good." He sank down in the recliner, aware of how exhausted he was. "All Carol wanted was a plane ticket out of here and enough money to pay for acting lessons at some fancy studio in London. She wasn't even curious about the baby. You can bet she's forgotten she ever even had a daughter."

Ace clucked his tongue in disgust. "Nice little baby like that. Hard to figure. What'd you say her name was again, this ex-wife of yours?"

Jake sighed. Why did Ace have to choose the middle of the night to catch up on family history? "She goes by her professional name, Carol Proctor, unless using Moreno is to her advantage."

Ace pursed his lips. "One of these liberated females, huh. Bet the day comes when she's sorry she ever took a powder."

"Why'd you think that?"

"They all are, sooner or later. Hell, even your mother was."

Jake sat forward in his chair and stared at Ace. "What do you mean? I thought my mother walked out when I was about three and you never heard from her again. That's what you always told me."

Ace looked as if he'd said more than he intended. "Ah, hell. Fact is, I happened to run into her once, when we were living in Spokane that time. You were about fourteen. She cried and carried on, wanted to see you. But I figured it was way too late by then.''

Jake's heart was hammering. ''You never told me. You never let me meet her.''

Ace shrugged. ''No point. She was hooked up with some high roller, living it up footloose and fancy-free. Couldn't see how she'd find room in her life for a kid, once the novelty wore off. Ann was always like that, all steamed up over something in the beginning and then she'd lose interest. I figured there was no point in makin' things worse than they were for you. Just confuse you, her comin' and goin' again.''

A million questions flooded Jake's brain. He wanted to know about his mother, what she looked like, how she talked, where she might be now. He felt a new, intense anger toward Ace for not letting him meet her.

''That must have been just before we moved here to San Diego. Just before you left me with Samuel and Nathan.'' He tried to keep the resentment out of his voice, but he couldn't manage it.

Ace got to his feet and yawned. ''Wanted you to have a trade, son. Meetin' her made me do some thinking about things. I figured you needed more than I was doin' for you. Figured gettin' to be a carpenter would stand you in good stead, and it has. You got your own company and all, this Ace Construction. Good name for a business, too. Night, Jake. I'm off to bed.''

Jake wanted to grab the old man and hold him down until he'd revealed every last thing he knew, until he confessed it was his fault and his fault alone that

Ann had left them, until he apologized for abandoning Jake.

He clenched his fists and listened to the old man's steps go down the hall, telling himself that one thing living taught you was that there were no easy answers. Maybe it hadn't been all Ace's fault that his wife left.

Had it been his—Jake's—fault that Carol left? He thought about it for a long while, and had to conclude that the marriage hadn't had much chance of success, even though he'd believed he was in love with her in the beginning.

He and Carol had expected different things from marriage. She wanted a husband who would worship her beauty and give her the freedom to pursue her career without the pressure of earning her own living. Jake had sort of thought their life together *was* a career, a secure foundation for the family he craved.

There'd been fault on both sides, no question. Even sexual desire, which had drawn them together in the first place, had withered and died once he realized Carol didn't enjoy their lovemaking as much as she enjoyed the power it gave her over him.

That brought his thoughts full circle to Bella and what had occurred between them tonight. Lovemaking with Bella had taken on a whole new dimension, one that he wasn't ready to examine just yet. The memory was enough right now.

It would have to be, until he had the chance to love her again. He turned out the lights, locked the doors, checked Annie and went to bed, plotting ways and means of being alone with Bella.

IT WAS TEN O'CLOCK in London. It was early July, and it was raining. As usual.

Carol Proctor pulled aside the dusty curtain that covered the single window in the dingy bed-sitter she shared with two other women. She peered out, wondering if there was any point in getting dressed and going through the time-consuming process of doing makeup, just to answer some cattle call for a bit part she wouldn't get anyway. Damn. It was pouring buckets out there, yet the calendar showed it was the middle of summer. Or was there any summer on this godforsaken island?

One of her roommates, Betty, came storming through the door, towel and makeup case in a plastic shopping bag, flaming red hair bunched together into a clip on top of her head, housecoat not quite covering acres of bosom and yards of leg.

"Linda's still in the bath, the stupid cow. She's been there for over an hour. I must have banged thirty times already. I'm going to be late for work, and if I'm late once more, old man Evans will give me the boot. You going to that audition?"

"Haven't decided." Carol put water in a battered saucepan and set it on the hot plate.

"I'm going to have to wash my face in a bowl again, so don't use up all that water. And we're out of instant, if that's what you're planning."

"Damn." Carol hated tea. She hated having one bathroom for god knew how many people, she hated the constant rain, she hated this miserable city, she hated sharing a room too small for one person with two deadbeats. Most of all, she hated feeling a failure.

The Royal Academy of Dramatic Art had sent an encouraging reply to her application and an invitation to audition. Naturally she'd believed there'd be no problem enrolling. She had stretched the truth a bit and told everyone she knew in California that she was already accepted. Of course they were green with envy. RADA, the London stage. It had real panache.

Then when she got here and acted her guts out for them, an ugly woman with thin hair and a horsey face told her she'd failed the audition. A person enrolled in an acting school to *learn* how to act, right? So how the hell could they fail you before you even got in? Well, that was England for you.

She poured hot water into a mug and dunked a tea bag in it.

"We're out of milk, too," Betty added in a waspish tone. "It was your turn to bring some home yesterday."

Carol muttered an obscenity under her breath and put two spoonfuls of sugar in her cup, trying to forget about the extra inches she still had around her waist and hips. Having a kid didn't do a damn thing for your figure.

England didn't do a damn thing for your disposition, either. As she sipped her tea, she thought longingly of San Diego's sunshine. It hadn't taken her two weeks over here to realize she'd been hasty about leaving California. God, when she thought now about the house she and Jake had lived in, her coffee maker in the kitchen, the bathroom she'd had almost to herself, the roomy closets. The money he gave her every week, regular as clockwork.

Not that she wanted to be married again. Marriage was the last thing she wanted, especially to a go-nowhere dude like Jake Moreno.

He was a hunk, though, no denying that. Jake had sex appeal oozing out of his pores. She used to get a charge out of the way other women eyed him with greedy hunger and her with envy. But marriage? She rolled her eyes. Forget marriage. Unless, of course, the next man who proposed happened to be filthy rich—and didn't want kids. One pregnancy was enough as far as she was concerned.

She knew now that she'd been too quick to accept the settlement Jake had offered in return for having a baby. Now that she thought about it, having a kid just because he wanted one should have been worth a hell of a lot more than he'd given her. All those months spent getting fatter and fatter, heartburn and indigestion starting once the morning sickness stopped. And nobody had warned her about the pain involved in childbirth, either. She'd had to scream the damn labor room down before they gave her something to deaden the pain. She'd been a fool to agree to Jake's proposition.

Granted, she still had a fair amount of her settlement in the bank, which meant she didn't have to wait tables or type boring business letters in order to pay the rent, the way Betty and Linda did. But then, they weren't as smart as she was, either.

But she did get nervous and edgy when week after week went by without one single bit part. Why, she had more talent in her toenails than most of these London bitches had in their entire bodies. She knew that, despite RADA and their snobby attitude. Look at the way she managed to keep Linda and Betty thinking she actually liked them. Now that took real talent.

And there was the dinner date tomorrow night with that chinless producer she'd met at a party. Harvey something or other. She'd convinced him she was hot for him; maybe that would result in something besides an invitation to bed. She'd wear the tight red mini dress, it showed off her legs well. And she'd have to touch up the roots of her hair.

If Chinless didn't come through and worse came to worst, she still had enough money for a plane ticket back to California. She could tell her friends that RADA had nothing left to teach a California actress.

There was always Jake, of course. Good old Jake. She was pretty certain she could fall on her back and get anything she wanted out of Jake now that she had her figure back again. You couldn't blame him for not getting turned on when she looked like a blimp. Oh, he'd been attentive enough, waited on her hand and foot while she was pregnant, but she knew that was because he was concerned about the baby.

Funny about Jake, how that kid had turned into an obsession with him. For a moment she remembered the wrinkled, red, squalling baby and Jake's expression when he first saw his daughter.

Carol set the cup down with a bang and her full mouth thinned with annoyance. Even in his most passionate, vulnerable moments Jake had never once looked at her the way he had at that naked scrap of a kid. No doubt about it, she'd put too small a price tag on that whole operation.

CHAPTER EIGHT

IT WAS WOODY'S IDEA to hire Ace as part-time waiter at the Artichoke Heart, but it was an idea Bella wholeheartedly seconded. She figured it was nothing short of brilliant.

That first afternoon Ace visited the restaurant, he volunteered to help carry orders from the kitchen to the customers when the place became unexpectedly busy, and it turned out people responded to him.

"There ya go, eat up. Good for your gizzard," he'd say with a quirky grin, and the customer would laugh. He was quick and efficient at setting up and clearing tables, and he learned the menu and prices faster than Bella thought possible.

"You're either a natural or you've worked in the food business before," she remarked at the end of his first official day as Artichoke's front man.

"Jack of all trades, master of none," he responded. But Bella could tell he was pleased by the praise she and Woody heaped on him.

To Bella's surprise and disappointment, Jake wasn't pleased at all.

He and Annie arrived that first evening to give Bella a ride home. Having Jake pick her up after work had become a pleasant routine.

"Hi, sweetie." She bent over to give Annie a kiss on the cheek. The baby was three months old now and getting more appealing every day, cooing and smiling whenever anyone paid attention to her.

"Guess what?" she said to Jake. "Your father's turning out to be the best waiter we've ever had. He's actually getting tips from people who've never tipped anybody in the Artichoke before. He's fast on his feet and he learns really quick."

Jake clenched his jaw the way he always seemed to do when Bella brought up the subject of Ace. "Let's just hope it lasts," he said, his tone openly skeptical. "Ace isn't exactly reliable."

Bella glared at him. "I don't get it," she said after a minute. "Sometimes I get the impression that you don't like your father at all."

Jake shrugged and paid much more attention to the traffic than Bella thought necessary. "I just know the old man a lot better than you do."

Bella felt irritated with him. "I'm sure you do. After all, he's your father. But surely once in a while you could be more positive about him."

Jake stared out the windshield a minute then turned and gave her his lopsided grin. "You're right. I'm sorry. I'm being an ass. Now, you want to drive out and see the moon set over the ocean, or would you rather go somewhere and eat food you didn't have to cook? I'm easy, and Annie's clean, full and raring to go."

It was impossible to stay mad at Jake. She chose the ocean.

THEIR LOVEMAKING was like an addiction. Bella had naively thought that once they were lovers, the novelty would wear off and they'd become bored with each other in short order. Exactly the opposite was happening. The instant they were alone together—and Jake made certain they were alone together almost every night as the hot San Diego summer slipped from July to August—they fell into one another's arms with a hunger and intensity that Bella found almost frightening.

"It must have something to do with our particular chemical balance," she told Jake one night. "Don't you figure that's it?"

They were in her bedroom, sprawled naked on top of the sheets. The window was open, but the air was totally still.

"What's that?" He sounded groggy. Bella knew he'd been leaving for work earlier in the morning and letting his crew go home before the late afternoon heat became unbearable. But Jake himself invariably stayed on until five or six; it seemed Tho Van Chung demanded daily bulletins on the building's progress, and filling him in was a slow, laborious process. Ace was being called on to watch Annie for an hour or so late afternoon, because Florence had a thing about leaving on the dot of five.

"There must be something about our combined body chemistry that makes it this good between us," Bella explained. A new, disquieting thought struck her. "Unless it's always this way for you."

It was meant to be a tactful question, but Jake didn't respond.

"So is it?" She needed an answer. "Always like this?"

His hand splayed across her stomach, his fingers moving in a gentle caress. "Never."

"What do you mean, never?" Sometimes getting information out of him was like walking in molasses.

"I mean never. It never worked this way with anybody before."

Making it sound like a well-oiled machine was just Jake's way.

"For me, either."

He glanced at her bedside clock. "Speaking of work, I'd better get home. I'm beat and I've got to be up at five. There's a delivery coming and I want to be there when it arrives."

"Does Ace ever say anything about you being over here so late and so often?"

"Nope, not a word." Jake hadn't moved. "He's too busy complaining about Florence to think of much else. Besides that, he's taken a sort of shine to Annie. I think he actually enjoys keeping an eye on her in the evenings."

Bella snorted. "There's nothing unusual about that. He's her grandpa, after all."

"Yeah. Well. I wish he'd find a way to get along with Florence. The two of them fight like a pair of mad dogs. I get back from dealing with Tho Van Chung, and one or the other of them is waiting to fill me in on the latest battle on the home front. Tonight it was Florence. She's in a snit because Ace wears his shoes in the house and picks up Annie without washing his hands."

"So what? I do that, too. Don't you?"

Jake sighed. "I hate to admit it, but she's got me washing my hands and taking off my shoes all over the place."

Bella had to giggle at the embarrassment in his voice. "She's a scary lady. More power to Ace for standing up to her."

Jake snorted. "He doesn't just stand up to her, he instigates full-scale riots. I'm not exactly in love with her, either, but I can't fault her as far as taking care of Annie goes. I trust her opinions about child care a heck of a lot more than I trust Ace's. Annie's probably the first baby he's held in his entire life." The familiar bitterness was in his tone.

"C'mon. Surely he held you."

"Don't bet on it." His hand wandered from her stomach downward, and Bella's breath caught.

"I thought you said you had to go home." Her voice was uneven.

He rolled over and kissed her, intensifying the hunger his fingers were creating. She did her best to be sensible. "Five's awfully early, Jake."

"Lots of time. The night's young."

"MORNING, MR. MORENO. What in heaven's name are you feeding that child?" Florence gazed in horror at the soft white substance in the bowl Jake was holding.

"Steamed tofu. Bella gave me this book on feeding babies, and it said if a kid's not breast fed, the best thing you can start them on is soft, steamed tofu. Annie likes it."

"I've never heard of such a thing. She's one of those vegetarians, isn't she? That woman next door."

Jake leveled a look at Florence that made her lips compress, but she held back whatever else she might have said.

"Bella knows a lot about food. She helps run a restaurant and she writes cookbooks, as well."

Jake's voice was even, but there was a decided warning in his tone that Florence thought it wise to heed. She held her tongue, but she knew what kind of person the woman next door was by the state of her unwashed windows and the shocking condition of the tea towels she hung out on the clothesline. A bit of bleach would go a long way over there, she'd bet on that. And then there was the way she dressed, those skin-tight black pants and brazen orange shirts. She was a hussy, that Bella was. And there was something going on between her and Mr. Moreno, Florence was sure of it.

She wasn't going to hold back on the subject of nutrition, though. After all, she'd been both a nutritionist and a practical nurse, and that made her an expert on feeding babies.

"Pablum, that's the only thing Annie should be eating, isn't it, lovey?"

The moment Jake laid the spoon down, Florence took the bowl to the sink and rinsed it repeatedly under hot water, as if the tofu might contaminate something.

"Well, she gets plenty of that, too." Jake wiped Annie's chin and kissed her goodbye. As soon as he was gone, Florence scrubbed the table off and set up the plastic tub and all the necessary paraphernalia for Annie's morning bath.

"Cleanliness is next to godliness, isn't it, sweetheart?" She undressed the baby, thinking that even a modicum of hygiene was a hard thing to maintain in this household, what with that dreadful old man around. At least the younger Mr. Moreno was gone a great deal of the time. But the old one—Florence sniffed, carefully using her elbow to test the water so it would be just right for Annie. The old one made her hackles stand on end. Why, her blood pressure rose just thinking of him. She'd caught him singing Annie a risqué song two days before. He played with her before naptime and made her overexcited. He was trying to teach her to spit. He made insulting comments to the baby about Florence, which was blatant undermining of her position and authority, even if Annie was too young to understand him. He was despicable, that was all there was to it.

"Here we go, angel. There now, isn't that nice for the baby?"

She lowered Annie into the water, and the dear little thing waved her arms and legs and smiled at her. Florence soaped her head with baby shampoo then rinsed it off. The child's hair was growing in, and Florence was certain it was going to be thick and blond and curly to boot. Annie's eyes had lost their newborn blueness and were now a deep, rich brown. Her eyelashes had stayed ridiculously long and dark. She was a picture-book child, good-natured and beautiful, and Florence was becoming more and more convinced that this household was no proper place for her to grow up.

There was no question that Mr. Moreno loved his daughter, she thought as she swept the little girl out of the water and into a thick, snowy bath towel—the result of the quantities of bleach she'd used on the towels in this house. But Mr. Moreno was a man, after all. What did he know about raising a beautiful little girl?

Annie was diapered and in a fresh pink romper when the doorbell rang. Florence popped her into her infant carrier and went to answer it, leaving the chain on the door and peering out. A young man in a blue suit and tie stood on the front steps.

"Good morning, ma'am." He held out a business card, which Florence took but didn't immediately read. "I'm Carl Skellings. And you are...?" He smiled at her.

"I'm Florence Turner, the nanny of the household." Florence detested the term *baby-sitter.* She felt it demeaning, considering her abilities. "What can I do for you?"

"I'm here to confirm that Mr. Ace Moreno resides at this address."

Florence held the man's card up and slid her glasses down her nose so she could read the small printing. Carl F. Skellings, Parole Officer, the card said. Her heart rate increased as she realized the possible ramifications of this, and she unhooked the chain and opened the door wider.

"Is Mr. Ace Moreno in some kind of trouble?" She waited breathlessly for the answer, but Carl F. Skellings just smiled and shook his head.

"No trouble. I'm just here to verify residence."

"But he *was* in trouble, wasn't he? Why else would a parole officer be here asking about him? Was...was he in jail?"

Skellings smiled again, but all he said was, "Does Mr. Ace Moreno reside at this address?"

Florence was annoyed with the imperturbable young man.

"Surely you could give me a straight yes or no?" she snapped. "Is he or is he not a jailbird? What did he do?" It would confirm her most dire suspicions to learn that the despicable man was a rapist or a murderer. She'd put nothing past the likes of him.

"As I said, ma'am, I'm simply here to verify residence. Now, does Mr. Moreno live at this address or not?"

"Yes, of course he does, more's the pity. You must have known that in the beginning or you wouldn't be here." She glared at Skellings. "Coming here and then not giving me a straight answer, you ought to be ashamed of yourself."

"Is this the correct telephone number?" He reeled off the numerals.

"That's Mr. Moreno's number," she confirmed. "*Young* Mr. Moreno, that is. The other one, the old one, I'll lay odds he doesn't even pay for what he eats, never mind the phone or anything like that. Cheap as dirt. I can tell his kind a mile away. A sponger, that's what."

"Is Mr. Ace Moreno in at the moment?"

"No, he's not, thank goodness. He's gone to that woman's café or whatever it is she runs. That woman next door, Bella something or other. He works for her, I gather." She snorted. "To think the health department lets places like that stay in business. Why, I wouldn't eat there if I were starving. And a dirty man like that, touching the food." She shuddered. "Someone should report it to the authorities."

Skellings was single-minded. "When would Mr. Ace Moreno likely be home?"

Florence was losing what little patience she'd ever had. "How should I know? I wish he'd stay away permanently, if you want the truth. Nasty, foul-mouthed individual. People like that shouldn't be around little babies, I'll tell you that much."

"Is he home in the evenings?"

Florence had had enough. "I'm just the nanny, as I already told you. I'm not here in the evenings so I don't know. I go home promptly at five every afternoon. It's part of my contract. Start the way you plan to go on, I always say."

Bingo started at six, and it gave her time to have a bite and freshen up a little.

"But if you want my honest opinion, my bet is he spends his evenings in the nearest bar getting himself drunk. He's that kind of man. I can spot a drunkard a mile away."

"Thank you, Ms. Turner." Skellings turned to go.

"You mean you're not even going to tell me why he was in jail?" Florence's outraged voice squeaked toward the upper registers. "An innocent person doesn't even have the right to know when she's in danger these days? What's this country of ours coming to?"

The parole officer turned and looked at her, smile firmly in place. "I can assure you you're in no physical danger from Mr. Ace Moreno, ma'am." He strolled to the curb, where he'd parked his dark blue sedan, and Florence slammed the door after him.

She gave Annie her bottle and settled her in her freshly made cradle. The whole time her brain was buzzing with what she'd learned. It was exciting, and a little frightening as well. She wished there was someone she could talk to.

She put a load of clothes in the washer, added soap and bleach, then poured herself a cup of coffee. *General Hospital* was about to come on, so she settled herself into the recliner. But she couldn't get her mind on the story. She kept wondering what Ace Moreno had been in prison for.

Just two weeks ago, there had been a story on TV about child abuse. Florence shuddered when she thought about it. Imagine, precious little Annie in this house with a common criminal. Alone with him, at that. When Florence's quitting time came these days, that man was often the only one here to take care of the baby. Young Mr. Moreno was working long hours, and he'd told her that his father would look after Annie until he got home and she was to explain in detail before she left what the baby needed until then.

Why, who knew what that foulmouthed convict got up to when he was here alone with that little girl? Her mind leaped from one disgusting scenario to the next. Finally, Florence got the phone book, and sure enough, there was a number for a child abuse hot line.

She filled her coffee cup, turned the sound off on the television and dialed the number.

It wasn't as easy as she'd expected to explain what was going on in the Moreno household. The woman on the line kept asking questions about whether Annie had bruises or evidence of sexual assault or obvious signs of neglect, and Florence had to admit—reluctantly—that there were no visible signs of such atrocities. But she emphasized that in her opinion, it was merely a matter of time.

In the end, the woman referred her to the Children's Home Society. She assured Florence that a social worker would be assigned to the case and she thanked her for calling.

"We need more concerned citizens like you," she added before she hung up.

Florence felt elated and not a little proud of herself for taking charge. She dialed the number the woman had given her, and within a few moments she was on the line with the nicest man, a social worker named Manuel Arbuckle.

MANUEL ARBUCKLE HAD worked for the Children's Home Society for two weeks and three days. He was a small, fastidious man, inclined to be a little shy, and he was seriously beginning to wonder if he hadn't made a disastrous career choice.

His supervisor was a man-eating dragon lady who'd told him the very first hour of his first day on the job that she seriously doubted his ability to stand up under the pressure her department endured during the course of every single working day, and that if at any time he was giving less than two hundred percent to the job, she'd be the first to know because she was *watching* him.

It didn't exactly make for a relaxed work environment. Not that anyone human could ever be relaxed with the caseload he already had, but it would have helped to have a supervisor who treated him as one of the team rather than public enemy number one.

The call from Florence Turner arrived just as he unwrapped the jellied doughnut he'd brought for coffee break. He eyed it longingly as he picked up the receiver and identified himself. The woman on the other end sounded both reliable and sane, which he'd come to realize were rare qualities in the people he dealt with here.

He pulled an empty file folder out of a drawer, printed Annie's name on it, with Florence's underneath, and began to write, asking pertinent questions as he went along. It wasn't an urgent case by the sound of it, but it certainly had the potential to become one, what with a paroled criminal and a single male parent who worked long hours being the primary care-givers for a baby girl.

"You have my word that an investigation will be conducted in the very near future," he told Florence. "In the meantime, if you feel there's any immediate danger to the baby, if you notice any signs of abuse such as bruising, get in touch with me immediately."

He hung up the phone and picked up his doughnut, wondering what steps to take next in the investigation. He wished he didn't have problems with decision-making. It was his only weak area, he felt.

"Arbuckle." The stentorian voice rebounded off the walls of his tiny, windowless office, and he dropped the doughnut as he jerked to attention.

His supervisor glared at him from the doorway, her steely gaze making him feel hopelessly guilty, though for what he had no way of knowing. He swallowed hard and waited.

She let a small eternity pass before she said, "The order just came through for the children's apprehension in the Envelido case. It's a lucky thing I checked on that one. You made a serious error in not taking action sooner. I've found out that the father's psychotic and violent." She eyed the doughnut and his messy desk through narrowed eyes. "I trust this squalor isn't indicative of the way you always conduct your affairs, Arbuckle." As she stalked off down the hall, she called over her shoulder so the whole department could hear, "I hope this has been a learning experience for you, because we can't afford costly errors in judgment. Lives are at stake here."

Arbuckle was shaking. He tried to calm himself enough to think clearly. The thing was, he stood in danger of losing his job. He'd have to make certain he made no mistakes.

"BELLA, YOU WANT TO COME to the zoo with Annie and me this afternoon?"

The blistering late August heat had finally given way to a cool air mass blowing down from the mountains that had made life almost bearable for the past two days. Bella had gotten up early this Sunday morning, determined to test two new recipes for her next cookbook, which was going to feature texturized vegetable protein. Her editor was nudging her gently to get on with it.

"Ace said you're off today, and I figure it's time to introduce Annie to the animals. Besides, it's years since I went myself. But it wouldn't be the same without you. Whattya say, Bella?"

What she ought to say was a firm no. But Jake was holding Annie in his arms at her back door, and the baby, now almost five months old, gave Bella a wide, two-toothed grin and held out her dimpled arms, begging Bella to take her. She responded to all the adults in her small world with ecstatic smiles and outstretched arms, and not one of them could resist her.

Bella rinsed the onion off her hands under the tap and took Annie.

"Hiya, Toad. How you doing? You look pretty in those red rompers."

Bella had known she would; she'd spotted them in an exclusive children's shop and bought them for Annie.

"Her hair's getting so curly," she remarked to Jake, running her fingers through the white blond silk on the top of Annie's head.

"Yeah, she gets the curls from me, at least. She's blond like Carol, though. So what about it, you coming to the zoo with us? I'll feed Annie some lunch and then we'll go."

Annie patted Bella's cheek and tried to get a grip on her earring, blowing bubbles with her spit all the while. Ace had taught her that trick, and there were times all of them wished he hadn't. Now he was trying to get her to suck liquids up through a straw, which he felt would reverse the spit bubbles.

Bella made up her mind. The texturized vegetable protein would wait.

"Okay, I'll clean up here and get ready. I need a shower and then I'll make us some lunch. The stuff they sell at the zoo is hardly fit for human consumption."

Jake grinned at her, that crooked grin she had such trouble resisting. They'd made love for hours only two nights before, and yet it felt like forever since she'd been with him. She could tell by the sudden warmth in his brown eyes that he, too, was thinking of other things besides the zoo.

"If Annie didn't need tending to, I'd come over and wash your back for you." There was a suggestive, heavy timbre to his voice that made her shiver.

She gave Annie a kiss on her downy cheek and handed her to her father, but the baby wailed and tried to reach for Bella all over again.

"See, she's fallen for you, too," Jake said with a wink as he headed out the door.

Bella watched them cross the backyard. The tall, dark, muscular man posed such a contrast to the silvery blond, delicate baby. Jake was a study in contrasts, Bella mused as she wiped out her frying pan and wrapped the unused onion in plastic wrap and stored it in the fridge.

He was physically stronger than most men she knew, even the burly farmers she'd grown up among, and still he could be the gentlest of men, certainly with his daughter, but also as a lover. And he never pulled any domineering male stunts on her; he seemed too secure in himself to need to control anyone else.

He ran his construction crew with an iron hand, and yet he allowed Florence to nag at him about wearing his shoes in the house or dirtying the kitchen sink. And he never said a bad word about that ex-wife of his, even though it seemed he was talking about her more and more as the weeks went by. It was irritating, hearing about Carol all the time.

Bella swiped at the counters with a dishrag and headed for the shower, dropping clothes behind her as she went. He'd joked about Annie falling for Bella, too, hadn't he? Yet with all the incredible lovemaking they'd shared, Jake had never once mentioned how he really felt about her. He'd told her she was wonderful, beautiful, incredible, fantastic, irresistible—but he'd never once mentioned love.

She turned on the water full force and stood under it, feeling the needle-sharp prickles on her body. Oh, he'd said he loved her body; he'd admired every last inch of it in detail. He'd told her he loved their conversations. He'd said more than once that he loved her cooking. He'd even said he loved certain pieces of her clothing, notably some exotic underwear she'd bought with him in mind. He loved having her tell him stories about her childhood, and they laughed together more than any two people had the right to do.

So why didn't Jake ever say he loved *her?* Why didn't he ever create a scenario in which maybe, just maybe, they were together in some rosy future?

She shampooed her hair and rinsed it, putting on some banana conditioner she'd treated herself to the day before. She'd blown her clothing allowance for the month on Annie and had happily settled for conditioner instead. Mindful of California's chronic water shortage, she turned off the taps while she let the banana rinse do its work.

What was Jake's problem, anyway? she asked herself. Sure, she'd told him in the beginning she was never getting married, never having children. Hell, she'd also told him she wasn't interested in making love with him, and look what had happened there. He ought to realize a woman changed her mind now and then.

The stupid man seemed locked in a time warp, back where Bella had insisted she wanted nothing to do with little Moreno babies and a house in the country with a white picket fence. Maybe she still didn't, but she wasn't absolutely clear about it anymore.

She turned the water on full force and rinsed her hair.

The least he could do was ask her.

CHAPTER NINE

IT SEEMED all of San Diego had decided that this was the day for the Zoo. Family groups and lovers crowded through the gates and into the semitropical atmosphere of the hundred-acre wonderland.

Annie bounced happily along in the infant backpack Jake had strapped on. She bobbed along, alternately smiling and drooling happily.

"You know," Bella confessed as they strolled through the flamingo lagoon on their way to the monkey cages, "I've only ever been here once before."

"Carol and I used to come here a lot when I first met her," Jake remarked. "We used to take the aerial tram from one side to the other. She didn't like walking."

Bella immediately decided they'd avoid the aerial tram. Jake was doing it again, talking about his ex-wife at every opportunity, and it was getting under her skin. They stopped to admire a peacock strutting his stuff, tail fully fanned out.

"Do you miss Carol?" Bella was careful not to look at Jake as she asked the crucial question. He considered the query much longer than she felt should be necessary, and tension built in the pit of her stomach.

"I don't miss her in the sense of having a wife," Jake finally said. "We tended to fight quite a bit and I sure don't miss that. What I do miss is having a mother for Annie. I'm beginning to believe a kid does better if it has two parents. The way it is now, I make all the decisions and I'm not always sure they're the right ones. Think how much harder it's going to get as she gets older. Hell, I never even had a sister. I just don't know much about little girls."

For a moment, Bella's jealousy took second place to warm compassion. "But you're doing a great job with Annie, Jake. I don't think two people would necessarily do a better job than you can alone. There are lots of screwed-up kids around who have two parents, you know."

Jake smiled at her and put an arm across her shoulders, giving her a thank-you hug.

A white-haired woman standing beside them had been more interested in Annie than she had the monkeys.

"You have such a lovely baby," she said to Bella. "Even though she's fair, she looks just like you, especially the shape of her face."

"Thank you." Bella caught Jake's teasing grin and felt a little abashed. She was irrationally proud and pleased these days when people mistook her for Annie's mother, and she'd stopped explaining the situation a long time ago.

They had the lunch Bella had packed, and then they bought immense bags of popcorn and sat eating it near the children's zoo. Annie was still too young to appreciate the animals, but other children, dozens of them, crowded around the nursery area, watching the baby animals being bottle fed by the cheerful attendants.

Bella studied the children, wondering if Annie would look like this little girl or that one... or maybe that angelic little thing over there with the blond curls and overalls? Her musings were interrupted by Jake's wistful voice.

"I wonder sometimes if Carol ever even thinks about Annie. I see people out with their kids and I wonder how it would be to have a partner help raise her."

Jake was looking at the children, as well, and Bella realized that what he was seeing were families—man, woman, child, man, woman, child. His words reinforced her earlier conviction that he didn't see her in the role of wife or mother, and that stung as nothing else had.

"I'm sick of hearing about your insecurities and your ex-wife," Bella lashed out. "If you miss her that much, why don't you ask her to come back?" The words were out before she could stop them.

Jake was astonished. "That's not what I meant at all. I told you I don't want Carol back."

Bella was angry, and she didn't quite understand why.

"Well, you'd never know it to listen to you. It seems all I hear about these days is Carol this or Carol that." She got to her feet. "I've had enough of this zoo thing, I'm going home. I've got a ton of work to do. I feel as if I'm wasting time."

She knew she was being awful and she didn't care. Something deep inside was hurting too much to ignore, and she had to get away from Jake and from Annie.

Jake was standing up. "I'll just put this stuff in the garbage and then we'll go."

"Don't bother. You and Annie stay here, I'll catch a bus home." She started to walk away, but Jake grabbed her by the arm and swung her around to face him. Now he was angry, as well, and puzzled.

"What the hell's gotten into you, Bella? If I said the wrong thing, I'm sorry. All I was doing was thinking out loud. I thought you understood that, for crying out loud."

So his thoughts *were* on Carol most of the time. Did he think about her even when his arms were around Bella?

She wrenched out of his grasp and glared at him. "Let me go. You say you don't know much about little girls. Well, you don't know much about women, either, do you? I've had enough of hearing about your ex-wife. I've..." Tears were threatening, and she used her anger to fight them off. "I've had enough of talking about babies and families and..." She groped for words and they were the wrong ones, but she used them anyway. "And...and teething and diaper rash. I'd like an adult conversation once in a while."

That wasn't at all what she meant. It wasn't at all what she was angry about. She knew by the stricken look on his face that she'd hurt him, and something inside her seemed to crack and crumble. But she was still too angry and confused to back down.

"I really would rather take the bus, if you don't mind," she said in a cold voice, and she turned and walked away.

It was hard to see where she was going for the tears, and every moment she kept thinking Jake would come after her. But he didn't.

It was late that evening when he tapped at Bella's back door. He appeared uncertain and contrite and held a huge bouquet of brilliantly colored straw flowers, which he knew she loved. He held them out to her, and after a moment she took them.

"Bella, I'm sorry for being such a selfish, inconsiderate moron," he apologized. "I probably do talk way too much about Annie and my ex-wife. I've treated you badly. It dawned on me that I haven't even taken you out on a proper date. How does dinner and dancing sound next Friday night?"

It sounded fantastic, but she didn't want to seem desparate, in spite of the fact that she'd spent the entire afternoon weeping. She'd burned, dropped and overspiced every single dish she tried to make because all she could think about was Jake.

He was impossible, sure, but not half as impossible as any other man she'd ever known. Thanks to him she had a car that ran faithfully, a house in better repair than it had ever been, and a love life she'd never even had the imagination to fantasize about before he came along. So what was making her crazy here?

She figured it had a lot to do with the fact that she'd gone along all these years totally clear about what she wanted from life, and now she was no longer certain about anything, and as far as she could figure, it was all Jake Moreno's fault, damn his gorgeous hide.

"So what do you say, Bella? Is Friday night okay with you?" He shuffled his feet and leaned an arm on the doorjamb. He sounded anxious, and she realized she hadn't answered him yet.

"Friday's fine. It sounds terrific. I have to work in the afternoon, but I should be off by five at least. Woody and Ace can manage as long as the food's mostly prepared." She looked up at him, the deep-set brown eyes, the curly dark hair, the cleft in his chin, and she crumbled.

"You want to come in for a while?"

He let out a breath he must have been holding. "God, Bella, I figured you'd never get around to asking me."

His arms were around her before the door was even closed, and his kiss sent waves of desire shooting through her.

"Bella, I was so scared all afternoon. I figured I'd wrecked it between us, and it drove me nuts. Please, don't walk away like that on me again."

She tightened her hold on him and lifted her chin. After several minutes of frantic kissing, he swept her into his arms and headed for the bedroom. Things were back to normal.

More or less.

IT HADN'T TAKEN ACE LONG to realize that the Artichoke Heart wasn't exactly San Diego's most successful restaurant. The same small group of people frequented the place, with maybe a few strangers now and then who wandered in off the street or heard about the Artichoke from vegetarian friends. There were times when all the tables were filled, but those times were few and far between. The sameness of the routine and the familiar faces of all the customers soon got to Ace. The place needed a little excitement, in his opinion.

He thought about the problem for a couple of days. It was obvious some advertising was in order, but he was at a loss as to how to go about it. Then he remembered a man he knew, Dictionary Jones, who had made a small fortune through advertising.

Granted, Ace had met Dictionary behind bars. In fact, he was still in the big house as far as Ace knew, serving time for innumerable counts of false advertising. He'd put ads in hundreds of magazines promising some weird thing or other if people would send five dollars to a box number. Ace thought one of the ads had had something to do with a magic cure for cancer or arthritis, and one claimed to take off ten pounds overnight. Anyhow, Dictionary cleaned up for several years on those and other advertising scams until the feds got him.

"The general public is an untapped reservoir of gullibility, waiting for an enterprising individual like me to exercise my skills," Dictionary used to claim to anyone who'd listen. He talked like that, which was how he got the nickname Dictionary, of course.

There would be problems getting Dictionary's help. Everyone inside the joint suspected that all phone calls and letters were monitored, and one of the conditions of Ace's parole was that he have no contact with any of his former inmates.

He made some inquiries at a bar he'd heard of, and he got the number of a woman who, for an agreed-upon—and in Ace's opinion, exorbitant—fee, visited the prison for him and got to talk to Dictionary by claiming she was his sister. Through her, Ace offered Dictionary a piece of the action; after all, a talented dude like him wasn't about to write the ads for nothing.

Being Dictionary, he wanted special esoteric books he couldn't get his hands on inside the joint instead of money, so Ace promised to search them out for him in return for Dictionary's professional services. It wasn't a problem; Adams Avenue had more than its share of dusty, cavernous secondhand bookstores.

Within a couple of weeks, the wheels were set in motion, and Dictionary outdid himself, in Ace's opinion. Ads that didn't resemble ads appeared in most of San Diego's smaller newspapers proclaiming the Artichoke Heart as an eating place for healthy, happy folk despite the fact that it was vegetarian and served food low in fat and cholesterol. Or it was billed as the place to go for the crowd in the know who wanted food that tasted superb and was also good for body and soul. These declarations were phrased as if someone on the paper's staff had visited the Artichoke and loved it enough to write about it. Dictionary was a genius.

Just as Ace had planned, business increased dramatically. Woody and Bella were mystified and delighted by what they considered free advertising; Ace was managing the till, and it was child's play for him to skim off enough to pay for the ads.

It had been Dictionary's idea to mail one of the write-ups to the well-known food critic for the San Diego *Union*, Emmanuel Short. But even Dictionary couldn't have foreseen that Emmanuel had been sternly advised by his doctor that very week to cut out fats and cholesterol and lose twenty-five pounds, which meant eating more vegetables and cutting red meat entirely from his diet.

Emmanuel arrived at the Artichoke at six-fifteen one Wednesday evening and took a seat by the window, dusting off his wooden chair with his embossed handkerchief and eyeing the homey ambience with suspicion and not a little dread. He'd already noticed there was no wine list, and no bar, either, and he didn't hold out much hope for anything extraordinary, or even edible, for that matter. What could one expect from a vegan restaurant? It was too, too depressing.

Bella had made vegetable tofu potpie, Woody had baked yeasted soy milk dinner buns, and together they'd concocted a rich, deep apple tart with pear cream for dessert.

Ace didn't recognize Emmanuel Short—the picture that appeared daily in the critic's column was ten years old and twenty pounds light, and showed a lot more hair on his head than was evident at present. The only part of the critic that looked like his photo was his bushy eyebrows, and Ace didn't pay much attention to them.

"Well, young feller, haven't seen you here before. Guess it's your lucky day," Ace enthused, grinning in friendly fashion at the portly man who overflowed the wooden chair. "Don't bother reading that menu, just leave things up to me, whattya say?"

Emmanuel didn't say anything. Familiar with deferential serving people who catered to his every whim, he was speechless at such effrontery.

Ace didn't notice. He whipped the menu out of Emmanuel's pudgy fingers and went ahead and served him the Artichoke's special salad, mounded scoops of grated carrots, grated beets and alfalfa sprouts with mustard-honey dressing, along with a couple of Woody's buns, warm and yeasty, served with generous scoops of carrot-rich veggie butter.

Emmanuel took suspicious, minuscule tastes of each item. He rolled them around in his mouth and his bushy eyebrows went up to his nonexistent hairline.

Ace was waiting for his reaction, and he laughed. "Tastes better than it looks, huh? Stick around, son. It even improves as it goes along."

Emmanuel ended up eating all the buns and most of the salad.

Ace served the tofu potpie, succulent vegetables encased in flaky pastry. Without asking, he brought two more buns and more veggie spread, as well as the bottle of sparkling water Emmanuel had sulkily settled for when Ace confirmed the fact that the Artichoke didn't serve even so much as an unpretentious little chardonnay.

"You oughta switch to drinking juice instead of wine anyway," Ace advised. "What with all the chemicals in the wine these days, it's not safe. Besides, you're gettin' to an age where you oughta watch that old waistline. Juice is lots healthier for you."

The deep dish apple tart arrived smothered in pear cream, along with a pot of peppermint tea. Emmanuel ate his way through everything and made fastidious notes in his pocket notebook as he sipped his tea.

It was a customer who pointed out the review to Ace in Friday's edition of the *Union.*

"Farewell, vegetarian virginity," it blared, and went on to praise the Artichoke's food in glowing terms while abhorring what Emmanuel labeled "impudent and intrusive service." He praised the "quaint atmosphere and superior, albeit unfamiliar, cuisine."

Ace didn't take the crack about the service personally. He was too elated at the success of his advertising endeavors, which of course he couldn't even take credit for. He raced into the kitchen to show Bella and Woody the review, but there was barely time for them to read it before the crowds began arriving.

Friday afternoon was hectic, and that evening was the first time in the history of the Artichoke that there was actually a lineup to get in the door, much less sit down and eat. The telephone rang incessantly with requests for a table. Until now, no one had ever dreamed of making reservations. Ace was finally forced to unplug the phone—there wasn't time to answer it and look after customers, as well.

Bella and Woody cooked themselves into exhaustion, and Bella naturally stayed on past her five o'clock quitting time. It was like a movie on fast forward, with the three of them always a beat behind. They ran out of everything just after nine o'clock and had to close and lock the door with people still waiting hopefully to get in. It was almost ten before the last enthusiastic customer paid his bill and left. Ace locked the door behind him and pulled down the curtains.

The old-fashioned cash register was bursting with money. Ace whistled as he counted it. They'd brought in five times the usual amount, and he stacked the bills neatly into fives, tens, twenties and fifties all along the counter. Ace scrupulously added up every last cent of his tip money and divided it between the three of them.

"Look at that, would ya?" he crowed. "We oughta do a deposit. It's not safe, leaving all this here overnight."

Bella and Woody were slouched at an uncleared table, sipping tea and trying to find the strength to finish cleaning up the truly prodigious mess in the kitchen. They'd both been on automatic pilot for hours already, and they sat shell-shocked, like victims of a battle. Both had their shoes off, their aching feet resting on a chair.

Ace interspersed his whistling with plans for expansion, moving around the restaurant with vibrant energy as he talked nonstop. "This is only the tip of the iceberg, folks, you mark my words. I'd say this is gonna be one of our slower nights when we really get up to speed around here. We gotta find some more young able bodies to clear off the tables and reset them, and we need a busboy who'd run errands and help keep the kitchen in order while you guys cook. We can phone unemployment in the morning. They're bound to have somebody who'd be glad of the job. I'll break him in and keep an eye on him. And we need way more supplies. No point in having all the customers if we don't have anything to feed 'em, now, is there? We better phone all the suppliers in the morning and tell 'em the good news. What's that produce guy's name again, the one who grows the organic vegetables out in the valley?"

He glanced expectantly at Woody and Bella, but it was obvious Ace's mind was far ahead of either of theirs. They stared at him in dull amazement, too tired to assimilate anything he was saying.

"Now, I can manage the till and the deposits as well for you, if that'll help," he offered magnanimously. "Fact is, I'll make this one out right here and now. I've had a good bit of bookkeeping experience in my time, won't be any trouble at all. Just until you get your sea legs, so to speak." He laughed and started whistling again as he found the deposit books and filled them in, then zipped the money into the night deposit bag they'd hardly ever used.

An insistent knocking at the kitchen door brought Bella out of her stupor, and an awful realization hit her on the head like a hammer.

"Oh, my God, I'll bet that's Jake. We were supposed to go out tonight for dinner and dancing, and in this chaos I completely forgot."

Woody gave her an incredulous stare. "You're telling me you forgot a real date, where the guy asks you out and then takes you somewhere special? Where *Jake* takes you somewhere special?"

"Oh, be quiet, Woody. What the heck would you have done tonight if I'd folded my apron and walked out of here at five? Anyhow, it got so busy I totally forgot it was Friday." Bella was running frantic fingers through her hair, even though she knew it was beyond redemption. Steam had turned it into an unruly halo of tight curls.

"If you'd walked out, I'd probably have made Ace boot out all those famished bodies and close at six. Then I might have had a relaxing evening in front of the television instead of cooking my fingers to the bone and suffering through a ten on the stress scale."

Woody sounded downright grumpy for the first time Bella could remember.

"Bella *mia,* you've got your priorities all screwed up, if you don't mind my saying so."

She did mind. She glared at him and staggered to the door.

It was Jake all right, but a Jake she'd never encountered before. For a moment, all she could do was stare. He was wearing a black silk shirt with well-cut gray trousers and a narrow leather tie. A matching gray sports jacket was tossed over one shoulder. His shoes gleamed, his hair had been trimmed, and he smelled the way male models on television looked as if they smelled. The leathery scent drifted in along with a whiff of the dry evening air, and Bella realized how deeply the cooking smells had permeated the kitchen—and probably every pore of her body, as well. She was also aware of a sinking sensation deep in her stomach.

"Jake, I'm so sorry, we got crazy here, I've never seen so many people. We ran out of everything and had to make more and more. I couldn't even think there for a while, and I should have phoned you but..." She was babbling. "Ace unplugged the phone."

She stopped for a breath and added with a sick feeling in her stomach, "The truth is, somewhere in this chaos I forgot it was tonight we were going out." Another thought struck. "Where's Annie?"

"I knew Ace would be working so I got a sitter. I waited around awhile, tried to phone here and kept getting a busy signal. When you didn't make it home by nine, I figured maybe something had gone wrong over here, so I drove over." His voice was controlled and reasonable, but Bella could see the spark of anger in his eyes.

She didn't blame him; he had every right to be furious with her. She was furious with herself.

"Come out to the front, Ace and Woody are there. I'll just get my things and then we'll go. It won't take me long to get ready."

She led the way through the battleground that the kitchen had become, aware of the greasy stains on her shirt, the flour that had somehow become ingrained in the fabric of her cotton jeans. Even her feet were dirty, she realized when she looked down at them. She hadn't glanced in a mirror since before noon, and she knew it wasn't going to be encouraging when she finally did. And Jake was nothing short of resplendent. She noticed the kitchen clock and her heart sank. It was five minutes to ten.

"Hi, Jake. Nice threads," Woody commented, giving Bella a significant look. She frowned at him. "I guess Bella told you what happened around here tonight."

Ace had a copy of the *Union,* opened to Emmanuel Short's review. He held it out to Jake, triumph in every deeply etched line of his face. "Getta loada this. The Artichoke is on the map, but good."

Jake skimmed the article and gave his father a long, narrow-eyed look, but all he said was, "I hear this kind of thing is the best advertising you can get. I guess you and Bella are going to be famous now, Woody."

Woody looked dejected. "Being famous isn't exactly my idea of a good time. I'll take anonymity any old day." He brightened for a moment. "How's that remarkable child of yours, Jake? Ace showed me some pictures of her the other day. She's getting a lot bigger every time I see her."

"What pictures?" Jake turned to his father. "I didn't know you'd taken any pictures of Annie."

Ace looked disconcerted. "Saw your camera just sitting there doing nothing, so I snapped a few here and there," he mumbled.

"A few?" Woody's tone was teasing. "You must have close to a hundred by now. He's filled six of those pocket albums," he told Jake with a conspiratorial wink.

Bella was ready. She handed Ace the keys to her Volkswagen and asked him to drive it home for her.

Once they were in Jake's truck, she tried again to apologize for what had happened, but Jake just nodded.

"It won't take me long to shower and get dressed," she promised. "I'll be ready in half an hour."

He turned and looked straight at her at last, his eyes flat. "There isn't much point, is there, Bella? It's after ten, and our reservations were for seven-thirty. Nobody'll hold a table this long. And I can see you're exhausted. There's no way you'll feel like dancing tonight. We'll just forget it."

She *was* tired, bone tired. She was also miserable, mortified at herself for forgetting something so important.

They pulled into Jake's driveway and he got out and came around to open her door. He was impossibly handsome, and she felt hopelessly frumpy.

"Would you like to come over? I could fix something, you haven't eaten..." The very thought of food was enough to make her gag, but she felt she owed him that at least.

He shook his head. "Thanks, but I'd better let the sitter go home." He walked her formally to her door, but he made no move to kiss her or even touch her.

"Night, Bella." He was gone before she could formulate any words. She heard the front door of his house close softly behind him, and as she stared into the night, she noticed how clean and shiny his truck looked in the moonlight. The usual construction clutter was missing from the back, and the interior had been gleaming, as well, she remembered belatedly. He'd gone to all the trouble of washing and vacuuming his truck for her. And she hadn't even managed to remember their date.

She slunk into her house and took all her clothes off, shoving them neatly in the laundry bin instead of leaving them all over the floor. She had a scalding hot shower, and then sat by the phone for more than an hour, figuring out what to say when she finally got up the nerve to call Jake. When at last she did dial his number, it rang busy.

It rang busy the next fifteen times she dialed, and reluctantly she gave up and went to bed, sick in her soul and convinced that he'd probably taken the phone off the hook to avoid having to talk to her.

The worst part was, she didn't blame him.

CHAPTER TEN

"SOMEBODY'S BEEN PHONING you all evening," the young baby-sitter informed Jake the moment he walked in the door. "It's a woman, but she didn't leave her name or number. She called four times."

When the girl was gone, Jake checked on Annie and then slowly took off his fancy clothing and hung it carefully in his closet, pulling on an old pair of sweat-pants and a loose shirt. He found a beer in the fridge, snapped the top and slumped into his favorite chair.

He clicked the television on and almost immediately turned it off again. He felt restless, let down, disappointed and not a little angry with Bella for spoiling the special evening he'd planned with such painstaking effort. He understood that emergencies could come up, and he appreciated that they'd had a rough time at the Artichoke tonight, but having her forget all about their date made him feel that she didn't put much value on what they had together.

He took a long slug of his beer and thought about that. What, exactly, *did* they have?

The plain truth was, he was crazy about Bella, but he was pretty certain she didn't feel the same way about him. Sure, they had this fantastic sexual relationship, but apart from that, Bella didn't want the same things he wanted. No marriage, no babies.

She'd made it clear in the beginning that she wasn't interested in a forever clause, that she had no intention of ever being anyone's mother or wife. He wasn't sure himself he wanted to get into another relationship with a woman; his marriage had been no hell, that was certain. So he'd made up his mind to enjoy whatever part of Bella's life she felt she could share with him and not worry about the rest. He'd figured he could live with that.

But that was before he'd fallen in love with her. Now he wasn't sure how much longer he could go on pretending.

And there was Annie to consider, as well. The baby absolutely adored Bella; her little arms went shooting out whenever she laid eyes on her. It was unfair to let Annie become so attached. He was increasingly afraid that one of these days Bella would move on and leave both of them.

He took another gulp of his beer and admitted that that wasn't all that was bothering him, either. Seeing his father casually handling the day's take from the restaurant had set every warning bell jangling. Was it just coincidence that a few scant weeks after Ace started working there, the place suddenly got discovered by some artsy food critic?

Jake couldn't for the life of him figure out how Ace might have engineered it, but he was fairly certain his father had something to do with the increase in business. Ace was smart, you had to give him his due. And that was fine, as long as he was sticking to his vow to live the straight life. The trouble was, Jake was far from convinced a leopard his father's age could change his spots.

The old man had certainly changed as far as Annie was concerned, though. Jake had been amazed and touched tonight to hear that Ace actually carried around pictures of his granddaughter and showed them off. Hell, maybe the old reprobate *had* turned over a new leaf. Maybe Jake was being too suspicious.

Still, he wished there was some way of alerting Bella and Woody to the fact that it wasn't the smartest move in the world to let Ace manage any of the money at the Artichoke, some way besides coming straight out and telling them Ace was an ex-con. He had to figure out a way of warning them that would leave Ace his dignity.

And Jake wanted more than anything to give the old man the benefit of the doubt. He was beginning to understand how very much he wanted a father who managed to stay on the right side of the law. There were times now when the two of them were here alone that he actually enjoyed having the old man around, enjoyed sharing details of his work and having someone to gloat with him over Annie's newest accomplishment.

The phone rang.

He was sure it was Bella, and he felt a warm sense of relief at the thought that they would talk things over. He'd tell her straight out how disappointed he'd been about their date, and maybe he could even find a tactful way to let her know a little about Ace's background.

"Jake, honey, you finally got home, I've been calling all evening."

The soft, breathy voice was familiar, but it wasn't Bella. Jake felt every muscle in his body tighten, and he had to struggle to control his voice.

"How are you, Carol? *Where* are you?" There was nothing to indicate the call was a transatlantic, and his hand clenched the receiver.

"Here, you silly old thing. I'm back here in San Diego. I'm staying with Maria, you remember Maria? But the guy next door's moving out. I'm getting his apartment next week. It's not much, but it has a bit of a view of the bay."

Jake remembered Maria as a grabby little brunette who'd struck him as terminally dissatisfied, but that was the least of his worries at the moment.

"So what happened to acting school in London?"

She made a rude noise. "London's the absolute pits. I've never seen so much rain. And RADA really had nothing to teach me, I felt I was wasting my time over there. The London scene just isn't where it's at, so I came home."

Jake was silent.

"Anyway, Jake darling, I called to find out how our dear little baby is."

"Her name's Annie." Jake's voice was suddenly caustic.

"Did you actually think I'd forget her name, Jake?" There was a warning note in Carol's voice that he remembered well. It foreshadowed trouble. Well, trouble was inevitable where Carol was concerned. Funny how he'd almost forgotten that in the months she'd been away.

"I wasn't sure if you'd remember her name or not, Carol. You haven't seemed too concerned about her up till now."

"Don't be an idiot, Jake. After all, I *am* her *mother*. Nothing changes that. In fact, not a day goes by that I don't think of her and wonder how she is. It's just that I've been incredibly busy, crazy, really, what with England and then the move back here and trying to find a place to live." There was a pathetic tone in her voice. "It isn't easy when you haven't much money, you know."

A significant silence ensued. Jake could have asked her what she'd done with the substantial sum she'd gotten from their divorce, but didn't.

"By the way," her voice went on, a mock teasing in it. He realized she was using all her considerable acting skill on him. "I hear you're doing pretty well for yourself. Someone told me you landed a cushy contract building some big shot a house. It must be nice to be rich." Her tinkly laugh sounded, but there wasn't any real humor in it. "Anyway, now that I'm back, I'm longing to see my baby."

Jake gritted his teeth. *My* baby. It rankled him. He remembered that Carol hadn't even so much as asked to hold Annie after she was born. But legally there was probably little he could do to stop her if she decided she wanted to see Annie. Under the terms of the divorce agreement, Carol didn't have visiting rights, but he was certain any judge would change that if she pursued the matter. The last thing he wanted to do was get involved in a legal battle.

"I'll be home tomorrow afternoon if you want to stop by and see the baby then." Jake felt cornered, but he also wanted to face Carol as soon as possible. Face to face he might have a better chance at figuring out what it was she really wanted. He'd never been much good at second-guessing Carol.

"Tomorrow? Oh, that's sweet of you, Jake, but a friend and I are driving to L.A. tomorrow. We're touring the garment district, the new fall designs are on sale. We won't be back until Monday."

So much for longing to see her baby. Jake kept his tone as neutral as he could. "I work late during the week, so weekends are the only time it's convenient for me to have you come by."

"No problem. I'm rather busy myself during the week, what with auditions and appointments with my agent and everything." She sighed as if it was a bore, being beleaguered with offers. "I'll give you a call next week and we'll work out a time that's good for both of us, how's that? I think it's better to be civilized about these things, don't you?"

Jake agreed and they said goodbye and hung up. He realized that his hands were shaking and there was a bitter taste in his mouth. He almost ran into Annie's bedroom. She was asleep in her favorite position, pink terry-covered bottom stuck high in the air, head to one side, thumb in her mouth. Her cheeks were flushed delicate pink, her golden hair shone in the soft light, her eyelashes were long and curling. She looked like a sleeping angel, and fear gripped Jake's gut at the thought of Carol seeing her.

No one could be around Annie and not fall in love with her. Look at what had happened with Ace. At first he wouldn't come within an arm's length of Annie, and now he'd almost fight with Jake for the privilege of holding her. And Bella. She'd made it plain she wasn't fond of babies, and yet it was obvious she adored Annie.

Carol would fall in love with this child, too, and then what? Would she go for custody? His breath caught in his throat. He leaned over the crib and tucked the soft blanket around his daughter.

The thought of a court battle made Jake feel physically ill. And just say it came to that, who would win? The courts were partial to mothers, he knew that. His heart was hammering against his ribs, and he wished to God there was someone he could talk to. He'd never felt as lonely in his entire life as he felt at this moment.

He went to the window and drew the brightly patterned nursery blind aside, peering across at Bella's bedroom window, hoping there'd be a light on. If only she was awake, he'd phone her and...

And what? Hadn't she made it plain she was fed up with hearing about his ex-wife and his baby and his problems? Like a fool, he'd run off at the mouth too often. Who could blame Bella for getting annoyed? Her bedroom was dark, anyhow.

He'd never needed her more than he needed her this minute. *Bella, I think I love you.* As soon as the words formed in his brain, he recognized their irony. What the hell was the matter with him, always falling in love with the wrong women? First Carol, now Bella.

Even Ace wasn't home, and tonight Jake would have welcomed the chance to talk with him. Feeling bereft and almost desperate, he wandered to the living room, picked up his stale beer and turned on the television, trying to force himself to be rational. But the only thing he could think of was a movie he'd watched one time, about parents fighting bitterly over the custody of their son.

Jake was pretty sure the father lost.

"SO HOW'D YOUR DATE turn out?" Woody and Bella were mixing muffins and pancake batter early Saturday morning, doubling what they usually prepared just in case Friday's deluge of people somehow spilled over to Saturday brunch.

Both of them were weary.

"It didn't turn out. We didn't go anywhere. It was too late." Bella added soaked raisins to the bran muffin mixture and spooned it into muffin tins.

She'd watched for Jake before she left for work this morning, hoping she'd have a chance to talk to him, but his house had seemed to slumber in the early morning sunshine. She hadn't even heard Annie's usual morning summons, the whimpers and short, expectant cries with a waiting silence in between that the little girl had perfected to call her father or her grandpa to her cradle.

Bella found herself listening these mornings, even in her sleep, for those soft little cries in the morning. She could usually hear through the open windows the soft, deep murmur of Jake's reassuring voice when he came to pick Annie up, the delighted coos and babbling sounds the little girl made. But everyone next door must have slept in this morning. Bella had felt bereft.

"I hate to lecture you, Bella *mia,* but are you sure you're not making a fatal mistake with this guy?"

Bella looked over at Woody. "Mistake? What kind of mistake?"

"The mistake of a lifetime. The one where you're too stubborn to admit maybe you were wrong about what you wanted out of life."

She'd thought about exactly that half the night. She didn't need Woody nagging her about it, as well. Bella turned her back on him and slid the muffin tins into the oven.

"I had a letter from my mother the other day," she said. "She's stopped going to the exercise class she joined a while ago at the community center. She says Father doesn't approve, he feels she gets enough exercise working around the house. This, Woody dear, is a fifty-one-year-old woman we're talking about who doesn't even seem to realize it's her body, it's her right to do what the hell she wants to with the rest of her life."

"So? You're a bright lady, Bella, but you're mixed up here. You're confusing you with your mother. Not every marriage is like hers, y'know, or like the three my mother battled her way through, either. I've heard underground rumors that there's actually some happy unions out there, where two people are equals and share life instead of turning it into a war zone."

"You've been reading romance novels again, Woody."

Someone had left a romance behind on a table one day and Woody had devoured it, giving Bella a rundown on how fascinating it was, making her laugh with his earnest involvement in the plot. Several times since then, she'd caught him surreptitiously reading others, and he'd shamefacedly admitted he was hooked on them.

"You oughta try reading a few yourself, pretty lady. They specialize in happy endings and how to get there from here."

Ace arrived just then, and when the closed sign on the door was switched to open, two dozen people poured in like eager acolytes arriving at a brand-new ashram.

"Vegetarianism must be reaching epidemic proportions in southern California," Woody moaned, peeking out at them. "Maybe it's time for me to become a born-again carnivore, this is getting me down."

For the rest of the frantic day, there wasn't time to say more to each other than "We need more stir fry" or "Have you set the yeast bread yet?" The Artichoke Heart had been discovered by the in crowd, and Bella had no time to think about anything except cooking, cooking and more cooking.

Well, cooking...and Jake.

She couldn't seem to forget how handsome he'd looked the night before, how the dark silk shirt had emphasized his broad shoulders and wide chest. His image was superimposed on the tofu noodle soup she was trying to make, on the rice pudding, on the puffy biscuits, and she couldn't concentrate. Woody rescued several of her concoctions from disaster, pulling the biscuits out of the oven and turning the soup to simmer just before they burned.

"Fame doesn't agree with you, either," he commented at one point. "I've never known you to be so absentminded. Anything wrong that I can help fix, Bella *mia?* I'm an expert fixer."

She shook her head. She knew what was wrong. She needed to make things right with Jake so she could concentrate on what she was doing.

She decided she'd do just that as soon as she got home. She'd apologize, she'd prostrate herself at his feet, if that's what it took to get him to forgive her for forgetting about their date. And maybe she'd better give him some vague idea about how she felt about him, as well.

She wasn't quite ready to tell him she was in love with him—she needed time to think about that. But she could let him know she was heading that way. The thought scared her to death, but it also seemed like the right thing to do.

By nine that night they had locked the restaurant's door and served the last customer. Bella was exhausted and Woody offered to stay and make preparations for the next day.

"I liked the Artichoke better the old way, before it got famous," he grumbled. "Maybe I don't have the emotional stamina for all this success."

Ace was riding home with Bella. Her little car ran better now than it had when she'd first bought it secondhand, and each time she drove it she thought of Jake.

She stopped and waited impatiently while Ace shoved the deposit he'd made out into the bank's night deposit slot. But when they got home, Jake's house was dark, and her heart plummeted down into her sandals.

"Looks like Jake and Annie's gone out somewhere," Ace commented, and he sounded disappointed, too. "I was sort of hopin' Annie might be awake."

"When he gets home, would you tell him I want to talk to him?"

"Sure will." Ace waved and headed into the house.

Bella felt irrationally deflated and not a little angry with Jake. Here she'd been waiting all day for a chance to make things right with him, and he didn't even have the common decency to stay home so she could do it.

She took a fast shower and put on lacy underwear and a soft flowery rayon skirt that hugged her hips and flared around her legs. She chose a red silk top to go with it that bared her shoulders and arms, and she hooked a set of silver hoops through her ears. After adding deft touches of eyeshadow and lip gloss, blush and mascara, she surveyed the results with approval.

It wouldn't hurt to look her best when Jake finally did get back. Problems always seemed easier to solve when she was in Jake's arms. She put water on to boil for some calming herbal tea, looking out the window every couple of minutes to see if he'd gotten home yet. She was just pouring herself a cup when the front doorbell rang.

She ran to open the door. A taxi was pulling away, and her mother, surrounded by suitcases, boxes and several bulging shopping bags, stood on the doorstep.

"Mom?" Bella couldn't believe her eyes. Her mother had never gone anywhere on her own, and yet here she was, obviously alone. She was wearing the creamy silk blouse Bella had sent her for Christmas and a pair of black polyester pants. She looked flustered and rumpled.

"Bella, I know I should have let you know I was coming, but it happened so fast, I couldn't go to the other kids, they wouldn't understand. I hope you don't mind me landing on you like this. I had no idea your place would be so far from the bus depot, that taxi cost me twenty-four dollars. Heavens to Betsy, it's hot here in California, and at this hour of the night, too. Do you think I could come in?"

Marion Donovan's high, nervous voice quivered, and to Bella's amazement, her faded gray eyes behind the old-fashioned glasses filled with tears. She all but fell over the doorstep and into Bella's arms.

"Mom, for heaven's sake, what's wrong?" Bella felt as if she'd bungled into the wrong theater. "Come in, come in and sit, and don't cry, we'll talk about whatever it is." She helped her mother to a chair and dragged in all the luggage. Marion was sobbing in earnest now, so Bella got her a box of tissues and sat down beside her, hugging her shoulders.

"I had no place else to go," Marion gulped at last. "You see, dear, I've left your father."

IT TOOK BELLA almost an hour and numerous pots of calming bancha twig herbal tea to quiet her mother down enough so she could talk coherently. Still sniffling and making use of the economy-size box of tissues Bella had placed on the kitchen table, Marion tried to explain.

"I never told you, but I went to this meeting, about six months ago now. It was a group Leah joined after she came back from that trip she took with that awful young man, and she kept after me to go. Well, anyway, it was a women's group. I thought it would be something like the ladies' aid I always went to. Anyhow, Leah finally talked me into coming with her one night, but it wasn't like ladies' aid at all, Bella."

Bella would have smiled at the expression on her mother's face except that Marion was still fighting back tears. "Was it a woman's consciousness raising group or something, Mom?" She could just see her rebellious little sister gloating over tricking her mother into going.

Marion nodded. "Something like that, I suppose. You know, Bella, I was so shocked that night, hearing those women talk about things like..." Marion's face and neck flushed a deep crimson.

"Well, they talked about things I'd never heard women discuss openly before, and I was so mad at Leah for getting me into such an embarrassing situation. But you know, some of the things they said did make me think afterward. Anyway, I went back to the next meeting. There was another woman there, about my age, and I could tell she was as scared and embarrassed as I was, but she came back, too." Marion sipped her tea and made a face. "Do you have some sugar and milk to put in this, dear? It tastes awfully bitter to me."

"I don't use sugar or milk, Mom, I never keep them in the house. It's really bad for your system to put milk or sugar in tea. That's a macrobiotic mixture, it'll have a calming effect on your nervous system. So what happened after that?"

Marian sighed and resignedly took another gulp of the tea, shuddering a little. "Well, she and I got to be friends, and after Leah left we went to more of those meetings together. Dorothy, her name is. Dorothy Wallenbacher. Anyway, it was her idea we join the exercise classes. She's had six kids and both of us felt we were a little out of shape."

An expression came over her mother's face that Bella had never expected to see there, one of open defiance and outright rebellion.

"See, Bella, at those meetings they talked a lot about pride in yourself and taking care of your body, and things like having a sense of self-worth. I'd never even heard of such a thing. Anyway, Dorothy and I joined the community center, but after the fourth get-fit session, your father said I had to quit going. It was for men and women both, and he didn't like that."

"You wrote and told me he wanted you to quit, Mom." It was ironic her father had felt threatened by the exercise class and not the women's group. But then, he probably believed the meetings Marion went to involved sewing or something. The whole thing would be funny if it weren't also tragic.

"I really enjoyed that exercise class, I even lost an inch off my hips. So when Father put his foot down, I got to thinking about what those women said, how it was my body and my choice to do what I wanted to do, and for the first time in our married life, I stood up to him and said I'd go anyway. I've never defied your father before, you know, Bella. Oh, we've had our differences, but I always gave in to him."

Bella knew only too well. She was astounded at the courage it must have taken for Marion to defy Peter at this late date.

"It caused an awful lot of trouble." Marion shook her head and new tears began forming behind her glasses. "But I couldn't seem to give in to him on this, Bella. Oh, we had some awful fights, I can tell you. Finally Father said if I didn't do as he asked, then I could leave. That was the day before yesterday. Well, I sat up all night thinking about things, and I was so mad at him by morning, I packed my suitcases and got on the bus."

Bella reached over and took her mother's hand. "Well, I think you were right to leave. You know you can stay here as long as you like."

The ramifications of having her mother here for an extended period were beginning to dawn on her, however, and they weren't necessarily all good. Bella felt like an unworthy child even thinking such thoughts, but she couldn't help it.

"Did you tell him you were coming to me?"

Marion shook her head. "I didn't tell him anything. He was so mad he wouldn't have listened anyhow."

Bella thought for a moment. "Maybe you should call and say you're all right. Just so he doesn't phone the Marines." Bella meant that as a joke, but her mother appeared stricken.

"You know, dear, I didn't even tell the other kids I was leaving. And Penny's about to have her baby. She's counting on me being there for her. I'll give her a call and tell her where I am, and she'll pass the message on to Father."

Marion talked on the phone for some time, and when she hung up, Bella could see the guilt taking hold as she thought about her grown children in Washington State.

"The other kids are all adults, Mom. Stop worrying about them and think about yourself for a change. They'll manage fine. Penny can have a baby by herself. She's already had one so she knows how it goes. Now, I'll put your suitcases in the spare bedroom—" Bella thought about the chaotic state of the spare bedroom and shuddered. She used it as a sort of dumping ground for all the books and stuff she didn't know where else to put.

Maybe she'd better give her mother her room...but she was sure there were socks of Jake's on the chair by the bed, and he'd left a shirt there last week. There could also be a set or two of jockey shorts under the bed. She hadn't vacuumed there for a good two weeks.

It would have to be the spare room. She would clear it out tomorrow and put the junk somewhere else. In the meantime, it would have to do.

Her mother was already on her feet, washing out their cups at the sink and using scouring pads on the pots Bella had left there to soak.

"My goodness, dear, didn't you try boiling these with some baking soda? The food's really burned on. I hope you haven't ruined them."

Bella's heart sank. Her mother was of the old school, and housekeeping chores were high on her list of priorities. They were near the bottom as far as Bella was concerned, and part of the joy of living alone was ignoring them if she felt like it. She had the feeling the next few days were going to be a trying time all round.

A familiar single tap sounded on the back door and Jake walked in. Bella's heart sank at the sight of him. She'd wanted so badly to see him tonight, and now things had taken an unexpected curve. She couldn't very well start telling him how much she cared about him with her mother listening in.

"Hi, Jake. This is my mother, Marion Donovan. Mom, this is my next-door neighbor, Jake Moreno."

Marion dried her hands on a towel and extended her hand, and Jake took it and held it a moment.

"Nice to meet you, Mrs. Donovan."

"Marion. Everyone calls me Marion." She was giving Jake a thorough examination.

"Marion. How d'you do."

He was obviously at a loss, wondering where Bella's mother had suddenly dropped from. Well, Bella was at a loss herself.

"You want some tea, Jake?"

"No, thanks. I just came over to..." His glance went from Bella to Marion and back again to Bella.

He shrugged and finally improvised. "I just wondered if I left Annie's pacifier here the other day."

Bella knew he hadn't. She also knew it wasn't what he'd come for at all, but she pretended to do a quick search anyway, while Marion asked how old the baby was and how much she weighed and what solid foods she was eating. Jake chatted with Marion a few minutes and then turned to Bella.

"Ace said you were looking for me earlier. Sorry I wasn't home. Tho Van Chung invited Annie and me over to his restaurant for supper."

"It wasn't anything important," Bella lied. "How was your dinner?"

"Really good, but the best thing was having a chance to talk to Tho away from the work site. We've been having a few problems, and I think we got them ironed out tonight. And it sounds as if there might be another contract coming up soon. His cousin wants a house built."

"That's fantastic." They looked at each other, and Bella wondered if she only imagined the yearning in Jake's eyes.

"Well, I ought to get back home. Nice meeting you, Mrs.... Marian." He said a quick good-night and left.

"That's a nice young man." Bella could see the alarm in her mother's eyes. "You must be awfully good friends for him to just walk in here that way at this time of night, Bella. What's his wife like?"

She explained about Jake being a single father and then had to listen to her mother go on and on about how sad it was for all these poor little children having to grow up without a complete family. Bella could think of dozens of ways to puncture Marion's arguments like the hot air balloons they were, but she knew how fragile her mother was tonight, so she kept her mouth firmly shut.

At least this new subject kept her mother's mind off her own problems, problems that were going to affect Bella's life as well during the next...my God, how long? How long would her mother stay? And how could Bella carry on a decent love affair or anything else with Jake's father resident in his spare bedroom and her mother now moving into hers?

Wasn't it adult children who were supposed to be moving in with parents instead of the other way around? Something had gone seriously askew here.

She watched surreptitiously through the window, but by the time her mother finally stopped talking and went to bed, Jake's lights had been out for an hour. Bella felt sorry for her mother, but she also felt like tearing her hair out in utter frustration.

CHAPTER ELEVEN

FLORENCE WAS GIVING ANNIE her midmorning bottle of juice and watching a talk show when the doorbell rang on Monday morning. She tipped Annie up over her shoulder and grumbled under her breath as she went to answer it.

The young woman on the doorstep was both beautiful and very nervous, fiddling with her expensive handbag and shifting her weight from one high-heeled white sandal to the other. She gave Florence a winning smile and stammered, "I'm so sorry to bother you, but I had to come . . ." Her eyes widened, her attention riveted on the baby. "Oh, I can't believe how beautiful she is. She's five months old now, isn't she?"

Those startling blue eyes suddenly filled with tears and she reached a hesitant hand out to touch Annie. Florence drew back, a bit alarmed, and the young woman explained with a watery smile and an apologetic shake of her head, "I'm so sorry, of course you don't know who I am. My name's Carol Moreno. I'm Annie's mother."

"Annie's mother?" Florence was astonished. Young Mr. Moreno hadn't said a word about the baby's mother after that first interview when he'd mentioned, very gruffly, that he and his wife were divorced and he was raising the child alone. Alarm bells went off in Florence's head; she'd seen enough television dramas to know that there were people around who kidnapped babies.

"Do you have any identification?" Florence tightened her hold on Annie and frowned at the woman.

"Yes, yes, of course I have. How silly of me, I should have shown you that first." She fumbled in her purse and drew out a driver's license with photo. Florence scrutinized it carefully. It was the same woman all right, Carol Moreno; the license even had this address. The only difference was that she looked a lot more upset right now than she did in the picture.

Tears trickled down the young woman's cheeks, and her voice quavered. "I've...I'm afraid I had a, a sort of—of breakdown after Annie was born. I've only just...gotten back. Over it. It...it was awful." She began to sob in earnest, obviously unable to continue. "Oh, I...I've missed her so much. My own dear baby."

Florence's suspicions faded and her heart went out to the poor creature. Now that she really looked at her, Florence could see a definite resemblance to the child she held in her arms, the same soft blond hair and something about the shape of Annie's mouth, as well. And Mr. Moreno hadn't ever said a word about not letting the baby's mother in the house, had he? Thank goodness that awful old Ace was off at work; he'd cause trouble even when there was nothing to cause trouble about.

Florence made up her mind. "Come on in, Mrs. Moreno. Would you like some coffee?"

It didn't take long before Annie was perched on Carol's knee. The baby was at her very best, fresh from her bath and snapped into a white eyelet romper. She smiled and reached up to Carol's face with her chubby hands.

Carol was awkward with her at first, but she soon relaxed. "You don't know what a relief it is to me to know Annie's in the care of someone like you," she said. "Believe me, I'll sleep easier at nights. Men . . ." She didn't finish the sentence, but she exchanged a telling look with Florence, who of course knew exactly what she meant.

"Men don't always know what's best for little girls," Florence supplied, and Carol eagerly agreed.

She didn't overstay, and before she left, Florence assured her she could drop by and see Annie again. When Carol asked, Florence told her what hours she came to work and what time she left, and she told her also about Ace living there and her opinion of him. "Nothin' but a jailbird. It's a disgrace."

Carol was understandably shocked. "Jake never mentioned his father, I had no idea. I can't tell you how much this disturbs me." She cast a worried frown in Annie's direction.

"He works some mornings, but mostly afternoons. You come by any afternoon, dear, you just give me a call first." To make sure the coast was clear, but of course Florence didn't say that. She asked for Carol's phone number and address, and Carol gave it to her willingly.

Then, blushing and hesitant, Carol wondered if it would be necessary to tell Jake about the visits. Not that she wanted to hide anything, but he'd been very unfeeling about her condition, and . . . she was rather afraid of him, if the truth were told. She shuddered delicately.

Florence said of course she'd have to tell if Mr. Moreno asked her directly. He was her employer, and she had a responsibility. But, she added, she sure wasn't one to carry tales.

Florence thought about the visit the rest of the day. It went against the grain, keeping a young mother and her baby apart, she fumed as she changed Annie and put her down for her nap. Imagine him holding it against that poor young girl, just because she had a bad time with postpartum depression. And it sounded as if young Mr. Moreno might have a violent temper if he got riled. You never could tell. These Moreno men had a lot to answer for, in her opinion.

CAROL ALMOST SKIPPED down the sidewalk, she was so thrilled at the success of her scheme. She'd come on the spur of the moment and had done a great acting job, if she did say so herself. That old bat was so easy to fool; it was all she could do to keep from laughing out loud.

But who'd have believed the kid would be so cute? Carol felt a proprietary thrill thinking that she'd supplied the genes that made Annie beautiful. Granted, she'd drooled a little on her new linen dress, but Carol thought she could probably sponge it off. Kids were so damned messy.

Wouldn't it be fun to show Annie off to her friends? Just for an hour or so at most. She wouldn't want to be saddled with a baby any longer than that. She wasn't up to changing diapers or anything.

Maybe some of the studios in L.A. could use a baby that looked like Annie for ads. There were so many commercials with babies in them, and the kids weren't half as cute as Annie. What kind of money did baby models make, anyhow? She'd have to do some investigating. There were possibilities here she hadn't even dreamed of.

LIKE A PAIR OF TEENAGERS whose parents were always home, Jake and Bella found that the only way they could be alone together was to take a walk or a ride late at night. As if by mutual agreement, they didn't get into any serious discussions during those stolen hours; they were both too physically exhausted to expend energy on emotional issues, anyway.

By the second week in September, the house for Tho Van Chung was almost done, but it was still taking up long hours of Jake's time, and as the Artichoke became more and more popular, Bella found herself working six and sometimes seven days a week.

"Actually, except for not getting my cookbook finished on time, I don't mind all that much. At least it gets me out of the house," she told Jake late one evening as they sat in the cab of his truck. He'd driven Bella up to the construction site to show her the progress of Chung's house—and to escape from Ace in his house and Marion in hers.

They were sitting in the truck in Chung's newly paved driveway, the panoramic view of the city and harbor spread out below them under a moonlit sky.

Jake had an arm around Bella's shoulders, and every once in a while he touched her soft, springy hair, just for the pleasure of touching her. He wanted to kiss her, but she'd been talking nonstop for quite some time now, and he didn't want to act like a caveman and drag her into his arms.

He sure felt like it, though. He ached to touch Bella, to kiss her, to make love to her again. Their physical relationship seemed to be stalled, mostly because of parents and lack of opportunity.

Jake also knew there were issues the two of them were going to have to discuss before too much more time went by. On a superficial level, they seemed to be doing okay, but underneath he knew there were land mines they were both avoiding. They were going to have to talk sooner or later.

Not tonight, though. Tonight Bella's main topic of conversation was exactly what it had been for two weeks now—her mother. Marion had been with her exactly two weeks, and Bella freely admitted it seemed like two years.

"Honest to God, she's making me into a basket case. She's cleaned every room in my house so I can't find a damn thing, and now she's started cooking, using eggs and cream and meat and chicken." Bella shuddered. "Animal poisons, in *my* kitchen. I feel as if the whole place is polluted. I don't even know what she does with half the stuff. I won't eat it, but she keeps on making it."

"She's given most of it to Ace and me," Jake confessed. "Our freezer's getting pretty full." Jake didn't mention that he and Ace most often devoured Marion's offerings before they ever hit the freezer.

"Oh, Jake, I hope you're not eating all that awful stuff." Bella sounded horrified. "It's bad for your heart."

"We don't want to hurt her feelings."

"Never mind her feelings, think about your body. I know Ace wouldn't resort to meat anymore. He's converted since he's worked at the Artichoke. But I do worry about you, Jake."

Jake had worried a bit himself before Marion came along. She was as good an ordinary cook as her daughter was vegetarian, and for all Ace's lip service to the pure vegan food at the Artichoke, he scoffed down Marion's pork chop casseroles and hamburger stews like a man dying of thirst in the desert. Jake wasn't far behind; a man could get awfully tired of tofu, although neither of them would ever tell Bella that.

"I don't even know where she's getting the money for all the ingredients. I give her all I can spare, but the kind of cooking she's doing costs lots more than I'm able to give her."

Jake was diplomatically silent. He and Ace had made an agreement with Marion: they were joyfully footing her grocery bills and also paying her a generous extra in return for the finished products. She'd made them a chocolate frosted fudge cake yesterday that they'd eaten in one sitting, half for Ace, half for Jake. And she made strawberry shortcake with whipped cream the day before. Even the memory made his mouth water.

"I know cooking is probably therapeutic for her, but I can't stop thinking about all that fat and sugar and cholesterol."

Neither could Jake. He was getting hungry all over again. He decided they needed a change of subject before Bella found out what was going on.

"How's your father managing on his own, have you heard?"

Bella snorted. "All my many sisters and sisters-in-law are taking turns cooking, cleaning and doing laundry for him. In some twisted way they think they're helping Mom by doing it. I told one of them the other day they ought to just let the old chauvinist starve, and she hung up on me."

"Has he talked to your mother?"

"She's called him a couple of times. She doesn't tell me everything that goes on, but from what she does say it sounds as if he figures she just needs to come to her senses. At first she cried for hours after each call, but the last couple of days she's taken to hanging up on him. I never thought she had this much backbone."

Jake laughed at that. "She's your mother, I wouldn't have doubted it for a minute."

Jake could feel Bella's deep sigh. "I'm proud of her, but... Well, it's a terrible thing to say, but I wish they'd just settle it and she'd go home so I could have my life back."

She sounded forlorn, and Jake tightened his arm around her shoulders, giving her an understanding hug.

"I know what you mean. I feel like that, too, with Ace around all the time."

Bella's voice was low and contrite, and she fiddled with a button on his shirt. "I never could understand why you weren't happy about Ace being with you. I used to get annoyed at you for being impatient with him. Well, I sure understand now. Parents can be a real problem sometimes."

Jake held his breath. Here was the perfect opportunity to tell Bella all about his father, to explain there was far more to worry about with Ace than Bella realized. He was trying to figure out how best to begin when she turned and kissed him, full on the lips, wet and soft and sensual, making the hair on the back of his neck as well as other parts of his anatomy stand on end.

"I miss the nights we used to spend together, Jake," she whispered, nestling against him so he could feel the warmth of her breasts through the thin white blouse she wore.

"God, Bella, so do I." He was having trouble breathing.

He found her mouth and ran the tip of his tongue along the seam of her lips. Their tongues met, and he heard the harsh intake of breath that was part her, part him. His hand shifted down from her shoulder and found the familiar place it had been aching to hold, the soft, full mound of her breast. The nipple grew hard and throbbed for him. He could feel her heart thudding under his hand, and his own blood pounded painfully into his groin.

Needing to feel her against him, he gently turned her so she was facing him, pulling her legs up on the seat, stretching his legs toward the opposite door until she lay full on him, cradled between his knees.

It was awkward, but it was also heaven. Their bodies fit, her breasts against his chest, her soft weight pressing, agony and ecstasy, against his groin. Her fingers fumbled with the buttons on his shirt, and at last she slid her hands inside, touching his chest, caressing his nipples, running her fingers through his chest hair.

He kissed her, long, suckling kisses, until her lips were swollen and puffy beneath his. His hand stroked and rubbed across her breasts, and her hips began to move as the need within her grew overwhelming. She made tiny, hungry sounds in her throat that he knew well, and he slid his hand between them, reaching down to cup her warm, arching body, unable to stop himself from thrusting against her.

Her eyes were closed, face turned blindly up to his, when out of the corner of his eye he caught the beam from a flashlight coming toward them down the drive.

"Bella, there's someone coming, damn it. I forgot all about security..."

By the time the night watchman reached them, they were sitting side by side again, but it had taken a panicked scrambling and both were breathing hard.

Jake rolled down his window and cleared his throat. "Evening, Amos." His voice was still thick and husky, and he realized too late that the buttons on his shirt were all undone.

The elderly man ducked his head and peered in, nodding politely at Bella. "Evenin', ma'am. Thought that this was your truck, Jake. Figgered I'd better check it out, though, these days you never know." There was a knowing twinkle in his eyes, and he gave Jake a huge wink, which Jake thought it best to ignore.

"Right, you never know. Well, we'd better be on our way here, it's getting late. Night, Amos."

They were blocks away and Bella still hadn't said a word.

"Bella, I'm sorry about that."

He was probably going to be more than sorry after Amos finished telling the story to every last one of Jake's workmen tomorrow morning.

She turned and looked at him. Her hair was wild, and her eyes were huge and dazed looking. The freckles stood out like exclamation points across her nose, her clothes were crooked, and her voice trembled.

"I'm twenty-nine years old, Jake. The last time I was caught necking in a car I was about fifteen, and I felt totally humiliated. I felt exactly the same way tonight, for God's sake. You and I both have houses of our own, we're grown people—you're even a father. I can't believe our own parents have driven us to this."

He had to laugh, she looked so frustrated and fiery. She laughed, too, after a long minute. Suddenly he thought of a perfect solution to the whole mess, but he didn't suggest it. It involved marrying Bella and moving Ace next door to live with Marion.

He didn't say anything about it because he was afraid Bella might figure he was only joking.

BELLA CREPT QUIETLY in through the back door of her house, but Marion was waiting up for her, wrapped in Bella's old blue robe in front of the television. Bella's heart sank. She wanted more than anything to be alone.

Marion clicked off the late-night talk show she was watching and came hurrying out to the kitchen. "I wondered when you'd be coming home, I couldn't wait to tell you the news. Penny's husband, Stewart, phoned. Penny went into labor this afternoon and she had a baby boy at nine o'clock tonight, eight pounds fourteen ounces."

"That's great, Mom." Bella tried to inject the proper amount of enthusiasm in her tone, but after eleven nieces and nephews, it wasn't easy to get excited. "It's nice she got a boy this time. Are they both okay?"

Marian nodded. "Stewart said it was an easy delivery, but I'll believe that after I talk to Penny. I'm going to call her tomorrow morning, if that's all right with you."

"Sure, Mom, call her whenever you like." Bella was trying to edge toward the bathroom door. She wanted nothing more than to fill the tub to the brim with steaming water and soak away all the frustration and embarrassment of the evening.

"All these phone calls I've been making are expensive, and I want to pay you for them," Marion said. "Could you come and sit down for a few minutes, dear? There's several things I want to talk to you about and one of them is the telephone bill. I've made a lot of calls, and I've got some money of my own, but I'm afraid Father's refusing to send me any more." Marion's voice quavered.

Bella gave up on her bath and followed Marion into the living room, sitting down and curling her legs beneath her in one of the overstuffed chairs. "I don't think legally he can do that, Mom. Anyhow, didn't you have a joint account at the bank?"

Marion sniffled a bit and shook her head. "I always let Father take care of the finances."

Bella should have known that. "Well, half of everything belongs to you, anyway, I know that much. Let me talk to Woody tomorrow. His mother's been divorced so many times she must know every lawyer in San Diego. We'll go talk to one and see if—"

Marion was horrified. "Divorced? A lawyer? Oh, Bella, I wouldn't dream of getting a lawyer. How would Father feel?"

Bella was dumbfounded. "What the heck does it matter how he'd feel? For heaven's sake, Mom, if he won't send you any money you'll have to do something."

At her mother's stricken expression, Bella hastily added, "Not that the phone bill matters, I don't give a damn about that, but you have to have money of your own to do what you want with, so you can feel independent. Don't you see, he's just using the money as a way of controlling you, of making you dependent on him. He's always had you under his thumb and now he feels like he's losing control."

Marion nodded impatiently. "Oh, I know that, Bella, of course he's like that. But it's just because he's so afraid. Your father's always been afraid that if he lets go of what he loves even a little bit, he'll lose it. He thinks that loving means hanging on tight. He's always been that way, overly possessive. With you kids, he never wanted to let any of you grow up or go your own way. I guess he was afraid if he let go of you, he'd lose you forever."

Her father, afraid? Bella stared at her mother. Could they be talking about the same person here? Fear was the last emotion she'd suspect Peter Donovan of harboring.

Marion fiddled with the tie on the housecoat. "I've always known he didn't really understand about love. It bothered me, but I told myself a person can't have everything, and he was always a good provider, never drank or womanized. And over the years I just got used to the way things were, the way *he* was. But then I got on my high horse about that exercise class, and I realized that he's got to learn that he can let people have their own lives and they'll still love him. I mean, he can't go through his whole life trying to force others to care about him, can he?"

"He's giving it his best shot, as far as I can see." Bella was too tired to be diplomatic. "And it's worked up till now, too. With you, I mean."

"Being here on my own, I've had time to think about it, and I've been just as much at fault as he has, Bella, for allowing him to act that way."

Bella was surprised at her mother's quiet assertion, and she had to admit, albeit reluctantly, that Marion was right. She remembered being angry at her father for taking away her mother's selfhood. But he couldn't have taken it if Marion hadn't allowed him to, could he? Why hadn't Bella realized that before? she wondered.

Was it because she'd fallen into the habit of thinking of her mother as a victim and her father as a tyrant? Now those stereotypical images didn't seem to fit as well as they had done in the past. Marion had definitely grown and changed over the past few weeks. Bella felt proud of her, but it didn't solve the immediate problem.

"So what are you going to do about him, Mom?"

Marion seemed to dissolve. "That's just it, I don't know, dear. I love your father, I miss him terribly, but I won't go back to him until he admits he's wrong and promises to let me have more freedom."

Bella's heart sank. As far as she knew, her father had never admitted he was wrong about anything, and she couldn't imagine him starting at this late date.

"Have you told him that, Mom?"

Marion nodded. "That's when he said he wouldn't send me any more money."

Stalemate. Bella sighed. "Well, don't back down. You know I'm not that short of money, and we can manage fine."

She could, for a while. But what if this went on for months? Or years? It didn't bear thinking about.

It wasn't the money at all. It was her privacy that was at stake here. But a person couldn't put her mother out on the street because she needed her privacy.

Damn it all to hell, it was all her father's fault.

"Honestly, he's so damned stubborn he'd cut off his nose to spite his face," she burst out.

Marion gave her a strange look. "Of course he's stubborn, dear. But he has many good points, as well. You're stubborn, too, you know. In lots of ways you're just like him. Of all the kids, you're the most like your father."

Bella knew for certain her mother was losing her marbles. Peter Donovan was bullheaded, selfish, inconsiderate, narrow-minded and fanatical, as well as stubborn.

"Me? Like *him?*" Bella gave a hollow laugh. "Don't be ridiculous, Mom."

"I know you can't see it, dear, but don't you remember how you used to argue with him all the time? Heavens, if he said something was white, you'd insist it was black. Neither of you would ever back down. Both of you have those fiery tempers and strong convictions. And then there's this thing you have about marriage. Your father was the same way, you know. He never wanted to get married or have children. I forced him into it." Marion looked embarrassed all of a sudden, as if she'd said more than she'd planned.

Bella uncurled her legs and sat forward on her chair. This conversation was getting interesting.

"What do you mean, you forced him?"

Marion's face turned scarlet. "Well, I'm afraid I was pregnant with John before we were married."

"Heck, Mom, I knew that. We kids could add and subtract. We all knew John came along just a few months after you were married."

"Yes, it always bothered me that you kids knew. Well, it...it wasn't altogether your father's fault, you see." She glanced away. "I'm afraid I...I sort of tricked him."

The implications of her mother's confession took long moments to reach Bella's brain. Her mouth dropped open. "You don't mean...you mean you *seduced* him?" She gaped at her mother. It was hard enough to visualize any sort of a sex life between one's own mother and father, never mind imagining a scene like the one her mother was hinting at.

Bella's mind went uncomfortably back to the first time she'd made love with Jake. She'd sort of tricked him, too, if the truth were told. Except that she hadn't gotten pregnant. But then she hadn't planned to, either. Still, she'd acted just like her mother. Too bad it wasn't an example she could bring up right now to prove to Marion how wrong she was about Bella being like Peter Donovan. But Bella was reasonably certain that particular example of mother-daughter likeness wasn't something her mother wanted to hear.

Marion cleared her throat, shoved her glasses up her nose and stared at Bella. There was both appeal and defiance in her gaze.

"Yes, well, I loved him with all my heart, and I knew he'd change his mind about a family once he held his own dear little baby in his arms. And he did, too. We got married, of course, and then when John came, he did a complete turnaround about having children."

Marion sighed and pursed her mouth. "And I will say, once your father changes his mind, he sometimes goes too far in the opposite direction. I would have been quite content to stop after Andrew was born, I felt seven was ample, but by that time, Father decided ten was a reasonable number. Not that I don't adore Carl and Leah and Ben," she added hastily. "It's just that sometimes he can get a bit carried away. He was the same about the farm, and then about his ministry. He tends to be a bit overzealous at times."

Bella felt shell-shocked and slightly ill. "Boy, you can say that again." She sighed.

"Well, you're much the same in that regard, as well," Marion snapped. She saw the look on Bella's face and her voice gentled. "Not just about babies or marriage, although it's too bad you've stuck to your guns about that. I think you'll be sorry when you get older. But take this vegetarian thing, for instance. You've certainly gone overboard there, running a restaurant and writing cookbooks and all. I'm not criticizing, I'm just drawing a comparison," she added as Bella opened her mouth to level a tirade at her. "Dear, I'm terribly proud of all the things you've accomplished. I'm afraid the other kids get awfully jealous that I keep bragging about you all the time."

Bella's world was turning upside down. "You talk about me? I always thought you hardly noticed what I was doing."

Marion laughed and waved a hand at Bella as though that was too foolish to even consider. "Don't be silly. Your father and I are both really proud of you."

"But you never said so. You never ask me questions or seem the least bit interested in my life."

"Of course we're interested. We just don't want to pry, that's all. We bend over backward to let you have the life you want. You made it quite plain when you left home that you wanted to live your life your own way. Heavens to Betsy, I remember that last fight you had with your father. I think your exact expression was, 'Butt out of my life, and stay out.' Don't you remember that, Bella?"

"Yeah, I guess I do." It rankled, being forced to see things through her parent's eyes. "But that was the time Dad cornered that perfectly nice Rudy Pisetsky I was seeing and asked him his intentions. Rudy was so freaked he signed up for the Peace Corps."

All of a sudden, for the first time, Bella could see the funny side of that debacle. She caught her mother's eye and they both started to giggle. It eased the tension, and soon they both got ready for bed.

Bella was sitting up in bed rubbing moisturizer into her elbows when her mother tapped at her bedroom door.

"There's just one more thing I wanted to say, Bella."

"What's that, Mom?" Bella was starting to think this night would go on forever.

Marion took a deep breath. "I don't want to sound like Father, and I know you think you don't want to get married, but Jake Moreno is a very fine young man, and that baby needs a mother. And you've made him fall in love with you, and I hope you're aware of the responsibility of that."

Before Bella could say a word, Marion had scuttled down the hall and ducked into the spare bedroom, closing the door firmly behind her.

CHAPTER TWELVE

TWO WEEKS WENT BY. It was the end of September before Carol called Jake again to arrange for a visit with Annie.

Tho Van Chung's house was completed, and Jake was enjoying a perfect lazy Saturday morning at home alone with Annie. Ace had gone to work with Bella an hour before, and Annie was bouncing up and down in her jumper, suspended from the kitchen doorjamb, and carrying on what she considered a conversation with her father. Almost six months old now, she'd discovered that people talked back to her when she babbled, and she'd learned to pause politely for their response after each outburst.

Jake had two of Marion's frozen egg waffles toasting and a country station playing on the radio. He was telling Annie all about his favorite country singers, and he felt at peace with the world. The rich smell of coffee filled the room, and he'd just poured himself a mugful when the phone rang.

"Jake, sweetie, how are you?" The rich tones of Carol's voice caught him unprepared.

"Fine, how are you?" He reached over to turn down the volume on the radio.

"Apart from being broke, you mean?" Her laugh was brittle. "But then, we can't all be rich contractors, can we?"

He supposed her tone was meant to be teasing.

"Anyway, I thought I'd take you up on your invitation to come and see Annie today. You did say any Saturday or Sunday, didn't you, lover?"

Jake didn't remember saying precisely that. He noticed that Annie had upchucked a good portion of her breakfast all over her pajamas and the floor. He'd planned to give her a bath right after he ate.

"I'll be over in an hour, if that's all right with you."

He wasn't sure it was, but he figured he might as well get this over with. He hung up the phone and rubbed a hand through his hair, releasing his pent-up breath in a whoosh. All of a sudden the perfect morning had taken on ominous overtones.

"Let's get you cleaned up quick, Peanut. Your mother's coming to meet you." His hands were clumsy as he removed Annie from her jumper and took her into the bathroom. Why the hell should a visit from Carol make him this nervous?

She arrived forty minutes later by cab. She was wearing artistically faded, skin-tight blue jeans and a red filmy blouse that did nothing to hide her bare, firm breasts. Her spectacular body was definitely on display. Her blond mane was pulled to the top of her head in an ingenious loose knot, and her perfect features were subtly emphasized with makeup. She wore outrageously large silver hoops in her ears and an armful of jangling bracelets. She gave Jake a hug, and before he realized she was going to, she reached up and kissed him full on the lips.

"No point in being enemies, right, lover? Mmm, you always did taste good." She flicked her tongue provocatively over his lips.

He stepped quickly away and wondered at his total lack of response—not even the faintest tingle of sexual desire. A profound sense of relief came over him.

"Annie's in here." He led the way into the kitchen. Annie was sitting in her high chair, gumming a teething ring.

She looked up expectantly when Carol and Jake came in. He'd dressed her in a blue-and-white striped one-piece romper that Bella had bought for her. Her freshly washed blond hair curled absurdly around her head, and after a moment of observation, she grinned hugely and held her arms out to Carol.

"Oh, she's adorable. She looks just like me, don't you think? And she recognizes her mommy, too, don't you, angel?"

Annie cooed and clapped her hands, her newest trick. Jake's heart sank. It was juvenile of him, but he'd hoped Annie would scream blue murder at the sight of Carol. Instead, she was greeting her like an old friend.

Carol took the baby out of the high chair and jogged her on her knees, far more adept in the role of mother than Jake had expected her to be. It gave him an uneasy feeling, watching Carol hold Annie. She was paying more attention to the house than the baby, however.

"I see you've fixed the place up. It hardly seems like the same old dump anymore. God, I used to get so fed up with the mess. It actually looks quite good now. I like that wallpaper."

Bella had helped him choose it.

"Is there any coffee? I was going to ask you if you use the coffeemaker much. I could sure use one at my place, and I'm really low on funds at the moment."

Jake poured her a coffee, setting it on the table carefully out of Annie's reach. "I use it, yeah, but you can take it if you need it." He'd give her the whole damn place as long as she didn't decide she wanted Annie, as well.

"Thanks, Jake. So how've you been? How's your love life—anybody sharing that queen-size bed with you yet?" She winked at him. She was paying no attention whatsoever to the baby, holding Annie so casually Jake was afraid the active little girl would wriggle from her mother's lax grasp and fall to the floor.

"Better hang on to her, she's pretty strong," he warned.

Carol nonchalantly tightened her grasp and at the same time picked up the hot coffee, totally unaware that Annie was already reaching for the cup. Jake lunged just as Annie's fingers closed around the rim of the mug. His fingers gripped Annie's arms and he snatched the baby from Carol's lap.

"For God's sake, be careful," he roared at Carol.

Coffee flew everywhere, and Annie started to scream. Carol leaped up and swore, swiping at her stained jeans and soaked blouse.

"Damn! What did you have to do that for, you idiot? Look at me, I'm a mess, and that coffee was boiling hot, too." She glared at him and fled into the bathroom.

Jake was oblivious to Carol. He was talking softly to the baby and putting cold compresses on her hand and arm in case she'd been burned. He didn't think she had, but he wasn't sure. She was crying hard and struggling against the wet washcloth on her arm.

After a few minutes, she snuggled her head into Jake's shoulder and he rocked her back and forth. It was long past the time for her nap and she was exhausted from crying. In a few moments, her sobs quieted, her little body relaxed and she slept. Jake carried her into her room and settled her into the crib, taking a final, careful look at her tiny hand and arm.

Alarm filled him. Her skin was pretty red after all. He found some vitamin E ointment and tenderly smeared it on.

"You'll have to loan me a shirt, Jake, mine's soaked and all stained from that damn coffee. Lucky I didn't get burned. Do you still have that stripy thing I used to wear sometimes?" Carol's strident tones were loud and invasive. She was standing right behind him, and he whirled around and made a shushing sound. He hardly even noticed she was bare from the waist up. He did notice she hadn't asked if Annie was burned.

"You ought to teach her not to grab at things like that. I'm not sure if coffee stains come out or not. That top cost me a fortune. It's raw silk, and it has to be dry cleaned."

Rage began to build inside of him. How could he have forgotten that Carol's world consisted only of Carol, her comfort, her appearance, her interests? How could he have thought for an instant that she'd give more than a passing thought to a tiny piece of humanity like Annie, even though the little girl was her daughter?

He all but shoved her out of Annie's room and half closed the door. Stalking into his bedroom, he pulled open a drawer and tugged out the first T-shirt his hand fell on.

She was lounging behind him in the doorway, looking around the room. He hadn't yet finished the renovations in here, and she was quick to comment on it.

"Not much improvement in here, is there? What did you do with our wedding picture on top of the dresser?"

He tossed the shirt to her. "I threw it away, Carol," he snapped, wanting to hurt her. "Everything's over between us, there's no point in keeping old pictures around, right?"

Actually, it was in the top drawer of his dresser. He was keeping it in case Annie wanted to look at it someday—Bella had told him kids liked to look at family photographs.

She pouted. "You should have kept it, it was a good picture of me." She eyed the shirt he'd given her, obviously in no hurry to cover her naked breasts. "This isn't the one I liked."

He shrugged. "Take it or leave it." He brushed past her as she pulled the shirt on, stopping at Annie's door to check on her and then going to the kitchen. He used a rag to mop up the spilled coffee while Carol poured herself a fresh cup.

"Let's sit where it's comfortable, we've got a lot to talk about." She led the way into the living room and sinuously wound herself into Jake's favorite chair.

It took all Jake's willpower to keep from ordering her out of the house. Some small voice of reason reminded him that she had a purpose for being here and that it had nothing to do with wanting to see their daughter. It was important that he find out what she really wanted so he could protect Annie from her.

Stay cool, Moreno. Stay cool.

Carol fussed with her hair and tied a knot in the bottom of his shirt so once again her breasts were outlined. She sipped her coffee and snuggled back in the chair.

"Turn some music on, sweetie. You still have that Duran Duran tape I used to listen to?"

"You took it with you when you left, Carol."

"Oh, yeah, I guess I did. Well, turn the radio to a rock station then." She smiled at him, assuming he'd jump to do whatever she ordered him to do, just as he always had.

It was hard to believe there'd been a time when a smile from her had seemed a gift, when he'd worshiped that near-perfect face and body without realizing how shallow and empty the woman behind it really was.

"Jake?" There was that trace of petulance he remembered so well. He could almost imagine her snapping her fingers at him. "The radio? You were going to turn it on, remember?"

"Nope. I don't feel like music right now, Carol."

He'd fallen hard for this woman, but it seemed aeons ago now. He'd had no other women to compare her with, no sisters, no mother, and he'd been overwhelmed by the idea that someone as physically beautiful as Carol would see anything in a guy like him. He'd married her within weeks of their first meeting, believing himself the luckiest man in San Diego to have captured a beauty like her.

She pouted for long minutes, and he sat and stared at her, totally unmoved. After the wedding, he'd thought maybe her moods, her selfishness, her petulant rages were somehow his fault. She'd ranted about how little money they had, how few things he could give her, how uneducated he was about the theater and the arts, and he'd believed her when she implied that he was much less than she deserved.

Now he knew better. Now he had Bella to compare this selfish, self-centered child-woman to, and he saw Carol for exactly what she was. Despite her ideas about marriage and children, Bella was warm and loving and honest and endlessly generous with her affection and her laughter.

"I've been thinking about the baby, Jake." Her tone was frosty. "I should never have signed away my rights to her for as little as I did. I'm sure any lawyer in the state would agree."

He thought about the second mortgage he'd taken out to give her the cash she'd demanded. He thought about the ticket to England she'd insisted he pay for, the new wardrobe, the fur coat, and his blood pounded in his head.

"Is that so? What do you think would be fair, Carol?" A man could have a coronary, suppressing this much rage.

"Well, see, I wasn't thinking of just money. I was thinking that we really ought to look into getting Annie into TV advertising. There's an absolute bundle to be made on babies that look like she does. Diapers, soap, all that sort of thing. Of course, it takes someone who knows the ropes to get them in the door, but hey, I'm a pro, right?"

She winked at him, caught up in the money-making scenario she envisioned. "We could work out a deal on the money, but I'd be doing the legwork and everything, so of course I'd want at least a seventy-thirty split. She'd go on living here with you, naturally, and we'd have to have a nanny or something to take care of her on shoots—you must already have a nanny, right? So all that stuff is cool."

"Of course. All that stuff is cool." His voice seemed to be coming down a long tunnel. Slowly he got to his feet. He walked over to the door and opened it. "Get out, Carol. Now."

She gaped at him.

"Move. Fast." He was trembling. "I'm doing my best not to murder you, but it's tough. Don't tempt me."

Something lethal in his voice must have convinced her, because she grabbed her handbag and scuttled past him. Halfway across the lawn, she turned and shrieked, "You'll be hearing from my lawyer, I'll sue you for everything you've got, you..." A stream of foul words poured from her mouth.

Marion had been sweeping Bella's front walk, and she gave Carol one shocked look and then hurried inside.

Jake waited until Carol stalked off down the street before he closed the front door. He was shaking in earnest, his stomach knotted. As always, he hurried to Annie's door to reassure himself that she, at least, was unaffected.

She lay on her back, thumb stuck in her rosebud mouth, lashes fanned across the delicate pink of her cheeks. As he watched, her face puckered and she cried for a moment, still asleep. The trauma of the past hour had affected her just as it had him. He stood a moment, letting the consuming love he felt for her wash away the rage Carol had roused in him.

Back in the kitchen, he slumped into a chair. The first thing he had to do was contact his lawyer. He doubted Carol would ever sue for custody—it was obvious she wanted nothing to do with caring for the baby. The trouble was, he wasn't sure how far she'd go if she got it in her head that Annie could earn her big money.

It was Saturday, and he wouldn't be able to contact his lawyer till Monday. He picked up the phone and dialed the Artichoke. The only other person in the world he desperately needed to talk with right now was Bella. He wouldn't tell her what had happened; he'd just ask her to go for a drive after work or something. He needed to hear her low, melodious voice in his ear, he needed reassurance that he wasn't alone. He needed to be with the woman he loved.

But the restaurant number yielded a busy signal, all twenty-seven times he dialed it, and he finally slammed the phone down in frustration. Ace must have taken the phone off the hook again. Jake felt abandoned.

He was still slumped in the kitchen chair beside the phone when a tap came on the back door. It was Marion with a pan of freshly baked cinnamon rolls.

"I wondered if you'd like to have a cup of coffee and a warm bun with me?" She was shy and she had a sweet smile, reminiscent of Bella's. "It gets a bit lonely next door when Bella's working these long hours."

Jake smiled at her. "Come on in. If ever I needed a warm cinnamon bun, it's right now," he declared. He was pleased to see her, glad to have her in his kitchen, settling herself at the table. He made fresh coffee, and while it was perking, they chatted about the house Jake was going to start building for Tho Van Chung's cousin, the renovations he'd made here in his own house, the water shortage in California, Annie's teething problems.

Marion was tactful enough not to mention Carol and the tirade in the front yard until Jake brought it up himself. He apologized for the disturbance, explaining who Carol was and briefly what the argument had been about.

"She said she wanted to come by and see the baby—she hadn't seen her since she was born and she is Annie's mother," Jake explained with a sigh. "But then I found out she's only interested in exploiting Annie, trying to get her jobs as a baby model on television. Can you believe it?"

Marion was frowning at him. "You say this Carol hasn't seen Annie until today?"

Jake nodded. "She left the country right after Annie was born, and she hasn't come by to see her till today. She phoned a couple of weeks ago, but it wasn't convenient."

Marion looked puzzled. "But I'm absolutely certain she's been here at your house several times before, during the day."

Jake slowly set his cup down and stared at her.

"I'm not the type to spy on neighbours," she went on, "but I happened to see her here twice at least. I remember thinking what an attractive girl she was. Last week, when I was coming home from the grocery store, I saw her getting into a cab out front. And I saw her another time, at your front door. The mailman brought a parcel for Bella, some special books she'd ordered, and while I was signing for it, I saw your ex-wife arriving, again by cab. The baby-sitter came out on the step to greet her, they were talking together as if they knew one another quite well, and then they both went into the house."

Marion saw the thunderous expression on Jake's face.

"Oh, dear. I do hope I haven't caused you any more trouble. I just thought you should know. I mean it's your baby and your house, and that young woman today didn't sound to me like a person who ought to be around children, whether or not she's Annie's natural mother. Her language was dreadful."

It was all Jake could do to control himself. He felt like hunting Carol down there and then and throttling her. He wanted to take Florence's shoulders in his hands and shake her until her teeth rattled. The sanctimonious old witch had never mentioned a word to him about Carol being at his house.

And of course, Carol was an actress. It was easy for her to pretend she'd never seen Annie before today, although he'd been amazed this morning at how easily the baby accepted her. No wonder. Annie had probably seen Carol plenty of times already.

How dare they deceive him this way? He was livid with rage, and his stomach was churning.

Annie woke up just then, and when he saw the flaming red stain the scalding coffee had made on her arm, fear took the place of anger. The area hadn't blistered, but Annie flinched and cried out when her arm touched the changing table, scaring the heck out of Jake. Maybe he should have taken her straight to the doctor. All his insecurities about being a single father rose up to envelop him.

Jake bellowed for Marion. She hurried into Annie's room and examined the tiny arm.

"Calm down now, Jake. It's not a bad burn at all. Goodness, I remember once when Jacob, he was my fourth, put his poor little hand on the oven door just when I was taking bread out. His whole palm was one big blister. I used aloe vera on it. That's what we need here, a piece of Bella's aloe vera plant. I'll just nip next door and get some."

She was back in a moment with a long leaf, which she split to expose the gel. She spread this tenderly on

Annie's arm. The baby whimpered, but within moments the sting must have gone because she was smiling at them both and wriggling in an effort to get down to the floor, sore arm totally forgotten.

Annie was learning to crawl and pull herself up on furniture, with Ace's enthusiastic encouragement, and the floor was her favorite place. Ace had filled one of the bottom drawers in the kitchen with measuring cups, spoons, toys and a set of brightly colored plastic bowls, and Annie loved emptying the drawer all over the kitchen floor. Jake suspected Ace loved the complaints Florence made about the mess.

"She'll be fine now," Marion declared. "Just put more gel on her in an hour or so, and then later, spread some more of that vitamin E cream on."

Marion played with the baby for a while, tossing the toys back in the drawer each time Annie emptied it. After a while she glanced at the clock and announced she had to leave. "I'm making banana cream pie this afternoon. I'll bring it over when it's done."

The moment she was gone, Jake dialed Florence's number. He'd decided to fire her. If she was devious enough to have Carol come to the house without telling him, then as far as he was concerned she wasn't a suitable person to care for Annie. He'd give her a chance to explain why she'd done what she had, but he couldn't think of a single legitimate excuse for such gross dishonesty.

But it wasn't his day for telephoning. There was no answer at her number then or for the rest of the afternoon.

JAKE WAS GIVING Annie a bath when he heard Bella's car pull into the next-door driveway that evening. Fifteen minutes later, as he was putting fresh sleepers on the baby, Bella burst in the back door.

"Is she okay?" she demanded without preamble. "Mom said her arm got scalded today." She took the baby from Jake, concern evident on her expressive face, and began murmuring soothing nonsense phrases that delighted Annie.

She sat down on the couch and examined the burn, obviously relieved when she discovered it wasn't serious. Then she played peekaboo, and the baby exploded with delighted giggles each time the soft blanket Bella was using to hide behind revealed her face and eyes.

Jake looked at the dark, curly head bent over the small blond girl. The day's events had left him feeling sour, betrayed and very alone, yet Bella's presence seemed to ease all that.

"Mom said Carol was here today." Bella raised her head, her deep blue eyes questioning.

"She didn't tell you what happened?"

Bella shook her head.

"Come in the kitchen, we can talk while I give Annie her supper."

"Let me do it, okay? I enjoy feeding her."

While Bella spooned mashed vegetables into Annie's eager mouth, Jake sketched the day's events for her, then added that Carol had phoned him two weeks earlier.

Bella was shocked. "You didn't say anything to me about her phoning," she said, frowning at Jake as she wiped Annie's mouth. "We've seen each other almost every day, and yet you never said a word." She sounded hurt.

Jake groaned. The day was going from bad to worse. "I was going to, but I figured you didn't want to hear any more about her. You said so yourself that day in the park."

Annie was fussing to get down, so Bella put her on the floor, where she squirmed her way over to her drawer.

Bella's face was flushed and she didn't look at Jake. "I've always wanted to say how sorry I was about that day. I should have before now. I was such a bitch. I didn't mean to be. I love to talk about Annie, and of course I understand that sometimes you have to get stuff off your chest. That's what friendship's all about. What I said that day wasn't what I wanted to say at all. I wanted to..." She glanced up at him then looked down again, stopping and clearing her throat before she tried to continue.

"I've thought about this thing between you and me and I've wanted to tell you for a while now that I..."

Annie had unloaded the toys and was balancing precariously on her knees, one hand clutching the edge of the drawer. She tried to lean over and lunge for a red plastic bowl on the floor nearby. She slipped and toppled, her head smashing into the drawer's corner.

Her forehead landed hard against the sharp edge, splitting the skin open just between her eyes. She drew in a big breath and then screamed, first in surprise and then in pain. Blood began to trickle out of the wound on her head.

Jake and Bella both scrambled to reach her. Jake picked her up, appalled by the blood and horrified at the cut.

"Oh my God." Bella raced for a cold cloth, and Jake tried to comfort his daughter, but she was screaming in earnest now.

They held the cool washcloth against the baby's forehead and after a moment or two the bleeding stopped, but the gash was much deeper than either of them had suspected. Annie went on screaming, the long, urgent cries of a baby in pain. Her arms and legs flailed and she turned her head from one side to the other, unable to be comforted. Jake and Bella stared at each other, totally aghast.

"I think maybe she's going to need a stitch in that," Bella said faintly. "It's pretty deep." She was white, her freckles standing out vividly against her skin. "I'll get her diaper bag and a bottle."

Within moments, they were in Jake's truck and on their way to emergency.

CHAPTER THIRTEEN

THE YOUNG INTERN finally managed to put two stitches in Annie's head, but the baby fought her every inch of the way. It was hard to believe a girl Annie's size could create such havoc, but she did. Jake felt proud of his feisty daughter, even though she made the procedure difficult. At last, a small adhesive bandage was in place.

"She also scalded her arm on some hot coffee this morning. Maybe you'd better take a look at that, too." Jake figured he might as well play it safe, even though the arm didn't seem to bother Annie one bit.

His voice was husky and he kept clearing his throat. It had made him queasy, watching stitches being put in Annie's tender skin. Annie wanted nothing more to do with the doctor. She screamed all over again and struggled as her arm was being examined, and by the time the whole ordeal was over, Jake had broken out in a cold sweat.

Bella felt as though she was going to be sick. Annie, totally exhausted, slumped in Bella's arms and sucked on her bottle, emitting a heartrending sob every now and then, while Jake filled in innumerable forms and went to the accounting desk to pay the bill.

The intern appeared at Bella's side. "The burn isn't severe, it looks as if you're doing the right thing with it, but here's a tube of ointment you can use on it tonight. Exactly how did it happen?"

"She grabbed at a cup of hot coffee." Bella was diplomatic, but she really wanted to add a few pithy words about a mother stupid enough to let her baby burn herself that way.

The doctor put a gentle hand on Annie's curls and stroked them. "You've had a rough day, little girl." She glanced from Annie to Bella and gave her a long, assessing look. "Babies need to be watched every minute at this age," she remarked. "Accidents can happen in the blink of an eye."

Bella wholeheartedly agreed, and it wasn't until they were in the truck heading home that she realized perhaps the doctor had been issuing a subtle warning. Could she have thought that Annie was being mistreated? It was preposterous, but she recalled the expression on the woman's face and wondered.

She thought of asking Jake about the incident, but when she glanced over at him, she realized he didn't need anything more today to upset him. His rugged, suntanned features were drawn and tense, and his knuckles showed white on the steering wheel. Muscles bunched in his arms and shoulders, and his mouth was drawn into a tight, hard line. Under his tan, his skin looked pasty. Bella reached across the car seat where Annie was sleeping and touched his shoulder.

"Don't blame yourself, Jake. This is all part of raising kids. You should hear some of the hair-raising things that my mother went through with my brothers and sisters."

He nodded. "She told me a couple of them. It doesn't help much." He stopped at a light and turned and looked at her. His brown eyes were troubled. "Damn it all, Bella, I just feel as though I should be able to protect her better than I'm doing."

Bella sighed. "I think this is all part of the package, part of what you take on when you have a family. You do your very best, but accidents happen anyway." She was quiet for several moments.

"I remember once when I was about eleven," she said after a while. "I was supposed to be watching Carl out in the yard, he was two. I was reading this Nancy Drew mystery, not paying enough attention to him, and he crawled under the front steps. He stood up under there and a nail from the step above him went right down into the top of his head, impaling him. He started to scream, and Mom came running out. She took a look at Carl and figured out what happened, and just in time she kept me from grabbing him and trying to pull him out. I'd probably have ripped his whole head open in the process." Bella shuddered and felt icy cold just at the memory. "Mom stayed calm and together we eased him down off the nail and then took him to the hospital."

The memory was vivid and disturbing. "I was physically sick for days afterward, and I've never felt so guilty in my life. I worried over that kid until he was a teenager, always thinking he'd start having seizures or showing signs of brain damage or something because of me."

She was silent for a long time, oblivious to the traffic and the lights outside the truck window. "He's a fireman now in Oregon, a big, healthy guy with a good sense of humor. You'd like him."

She smiled at the thought of her younger brother, but then grew serious again. "You know, Jake, I think it was right then that I decided not to ever have kids," she said slowly.

She'd never really connected that incident before with the way she'd chosen to live her life, but it came back vividly now and she saw the link clearly. It surprised her. "I felt that I never wanted to be that responsible for another human being again. I felt so inadequate, so guilty and angry with myself, so...so damn stupid and careless. When I thought about what could have resulted..."

She looked down at Annie, sleeping soundly, thumb in her mouth, still giving those small, touching sighs every now and then. The flesh-toned bandage the doctor had applied was already distended by an egg-size lump forming on her forehead. Come morning, Bella figured Annie was liable to have two black eyes and an impressive goose egg.

"You're so brave, Jake, taking on the responsibility for another human life. It takes a lot of courage to do that." Her voice was quiet and sincere.

"I wish I could believe that, but thanks anyway, Bella." They were just pulling into the driveway behind his house, and Ace and Marion came hurrying out to meet them, both of them concerned about the baby. In the confusion of anxious questions and answers and reassurances that greeted their arrival, Jake didn't have a chance to say any more to Bella.

Marian announced that she'd made a vegetable stew for everyone, and she brought it over to Jake's house. She brought the banana cream pie as well, and Bella was too distracted to even notice.

After Annie was snug in her crib, the four of them sat down to eat, although neither Jake nor Bella had much appetite. Ace and Marion chatted a bit, but the atmosphere was subdued. Both older people seemed to have as much on their minds as Bella and Jake did. Each of them tiptoed at least twice into the bedroom to check the baby.

Marion served the pie and poured tea for everyone, then sat down and toyed with her spoon for several minutes. Finally, she caught Bella's eye and blurted, "Well, I guess this is sort of a farewell dinner for me, I'm flying home tomorrow. I'm going to miss all of you. This month here has been . . ." She paused, at a loss for words. "This has been a real experience for me," she finally stammered.

Bella put her spoon down and stared at her mother. "Flying home? Tomorrow? But you never said anything about it this morning."

She'd longed for this very thing for the past four weeks, yet now that the moment had arrived she found she had mixed feelings about Marion leaving. She'd grown close to her mother in a way she never had been before. In a strange way, she'd been her mother's only child for this little time, and for all the problems it had created, it had also been comforting.

"Yes, well, things have changed since this morning, Bella. I'll explain it all to you later, dear."

The men insisted on doing the dishes, so the women left soon afterward. Ace said an affectionate goodbye to Marion and planted a kiss on each of her cheeks, making her turn fiery red. Jake offered to drive her to the airport the next afternoon, because Bella and Ace were both working, and Marion accepted graciously.

They were barely inside Bella's front door when Bella turned to her mother. "Okay, what's this all about, Mom? How come you're suddenly going home?"

Marion plunked down in an armchair and smiled at Bella.

"Peter phoned this morning after you left for work, dear."

It actually took Bella a moment to figure out who Peter was—her mother had never called him anything but Father for as long as she could remember.

"And? He's been phoning you almost every day, so what was different this time?"

"This time we had a long talk. A *real* talk, about the things I want and whether or not he can adjust to them. Also, it seems Peter's arthritis is worse, and the old doctor we've always gone to, you remember Dr. Wilkins, well, he's turned his practice over to a younger man. This new doctor, his name is Anderson, he's put Peter on a new medicine, but he also told him he has to start exercising." A spark of something very like mischief lighted in Marion's eyes. "So Peter suggested this morning that maybe he should come with me to that exercise class at the community center.''

Bella whistled. ''I don't believe it. I just don't believe it. He actually changed his mind about something? I don't suppose he got around to saying he was sorry?''

Marion shook her head. ''He didn't actually apologize, but he did say he'd try to be more understanding, which is all I ask, really.'' Her eyes were shining behind her glasses. ''I don't expect miracles, after all, we're both only human. And, oh, Bella, there's also a bit more to it than that, dear. Leah phoned Peter. She's quit her job as a nanny and she's coming home next week with some young Russian man she met in France. It seems she's talking about marrying him.''

Marion didn't seem at all perturbed at this new turn of events in her youngest daughter's life. ''Of course, Peter's having a fit,'' she added complacently. ''He's worried that this man, Sergio I think his name is, wants to marry Leah just so he can get citizenship. I told Peter not to make judgments until he knows for sure, but you know your father.''

Bella did, but in this case she was inclined to think maybe her father was right. Judging from past performances, Leah wasn't exactly a great judge of human nature.

''And so Dad wants you to come home and do something about that?'' Bella shook her head. ''You'd think he'd have realized by now that Leah's going to do exactly what she wants, no matter what either of you say.''

"Don't you think we both know that?" Marion sounded impatient. "Neither of us has ever had much success talking sense to either you or Leah. No, all that Peter wants is moral support. He doesn't want to have to meet this Sergio without me there with him." Marion got up and came over to sit beside Bella. She put an arm around her daughter's shoulders and hugged her close. "He loves me, Bella, and he wants me with him. So he gives a little and I give a little, that's really what marriage is all about. I felt before as if I was doing all the giving. It feels good to have your father compromise a bit."

"It's about damn time," Bella growled. She felt very close to her mother at the moment, and some part of her was loathe to let her go.

"I've enjoyed being here so much, but it's time to go home." Marion was quiet for a moment. "Past time, actually. It's done me the world of good, though." She lowered her voice to a confidential whisper. "You know, dear, I'd never tell your father this, but Ace asked me to go out with him. Not only once, either. Quite a number of times."

"So why didn't you go?" Bella winked at her mother, teasing her a little, certain that Marion would never even consider going out with anyone but her father. "Ace is kind of cute."

"He is, isn't he?" Marion's color was high and her eyes sparkled. "I did go with him once, to an afternoon movie. He's asked me out several times since then, but I decided against it. He's very persistent, though."

Bella was taken aback, although she tried not to show it. This wasn't her idea of a joke anymore. She'd had no idea Ace Moreno was hitting on her mother like this, or that they'd actually been out together on...on a date, for God's sake. She wasn't at all sure she liked the idea. For some weird reason, she suddenly felt lonely for her father.

"It gave me back something I needed, having him treat me like a desirable woman," Marion was explaining. "I've gone on too long being just a mother and a wife. It's nice to be reminded I'm a woman as well, an individual, and that somebody still finds me attractive after all those pregnancies." She giggled a little, and Bella gaped at her.

"He brought me flowers twice, too. Having Ace around gave me the backbone to stand up to Peter, and I'm not going to back down to him from now on when I truly believe in something." There was a note of resolve in her voice, and her chin was set in a stubborn, determined fashion that surprised Bella all over again. It was so unlike her mother's usual benign, sweet expression.

"It's not good for him and it's not good for me, letting him get away with being so domineering. Besides, I know now that I could manage on my own if I ever had to, and I wouldn't necessarily have to be alone, either."

Bella was flabbergasted. She wondered if her father had any inkling just how much Marion had changed in the past month. The Donovan household was in for some interesting times when Marion got back. Bella was almost sorry she wouldn't be around to listen and watch. She felt seriously put out with Ace Moreno, though, and she couldn't help but wonder just exactly what her mother meant by describing him as "very persistent."

The old goat.

THE NEXT MORNING as the Artichoke geared itself up for Sunday brunch, Bella told Woody about Annie's accident and her mother going home. She left out the part about Ace taking Marion out; it still gave her a funny feeling to think about her mother dating Ace.

"I went over to see how Annie was this morning, and she's got two real shiners," Bella prattled on. She was mixing batter for corn fritters. "Jake was up all night. The doctor told him to watch Annie in case she had concussion, and so he just stayed up. She doesn't, though—have any concussion. She was back to her own sweet self this morning, smiling and playing patty cake with me, so I guess she's feeling okay."

Woody impaled her with a narrow-eyed look. "Bella *mia,* you're as much in love with that baby as you are with Jake. When are you going to get around to doing something about it? These things can slip away on you before you know it, and then you're sorry the rest of your life."

Bella poured far too much liquid into her batter and had to add more cornmeal than she'd intended, which annoyed her. Damn Woody anyway, he knew just how to get under her skin.

"You're a great one to talk, Woody," she snapped. "I don't notice you making any major changes in your love life."

"That's because you haven't been looking, then," he said complacently. He was frying up neat slices of tofu into something he called believable bacon.

During the last month, they'd both taken to coming in earlier and staying later, because so far the Artichoke showed no signs of slowing down. A lineup that stretched out the door at the dinner hour had become standard, and it seemed there were always people waiting to get in before they opened in the morning.

They had another forty minutes to go this morning. Before opening and after closing had become the only time Bella and Woody had to talk about anything but cooking and business. Sometimes Bella missed the old easy companionship they'd had before, but she also appreciated the extra revenue.

"What do you mean, I haven't been looking? Have you gone and gotten a lady friend behind my back, Wood?"

He laughed and shook his head. "No lady on the horizon, but I've enrolled in some night school courses that'll eventually turn me into a day-care supervisor. Remember telling me I ought to take some courses before I got pregnant?"

Bella lost all track of what she was doing. She abandoned the fritters and stared at him. "Day care? As in taking care of kids while their parents work?"

Woody laughed. "Yeah, like that exactly. I figure the odds of me finding an agreeable lady and having a family aren't that hot, so if I want to be around the younger specimens of the race, which I do, I'd better make it happen some other way." He busied himself over the griddle, dabbing the tofu with soy sauce and liquid smoke and not looking at Bella. "I'm not exactly at my best dealing with adults, as you've probably guessed by now. I figure I might do a whole lot better with babies. I want to give it a shot, anyhow. If I like it, I'll eventually open a day-care center or two of my own. I've done some research, and good day care is hard to find."

Bella was astounded. "But...but what about the Artichoke? What about our partnership? What about...?" she was at a loss for words. She felt as if he'd smacked her hard on the head from behind.

He sighed and took the tofu off the griddle, then poured two mugs of tea from the pot on the back of the stove.

"This isn't an overnight thing, Bella *mia*. It's going to take a few months at least, during which I'll still be here right beside you, cooking up meals for discerning vegans. It gives us plenty of time to find you another partner, although you're so darned cantankerous, it's going to be tough going." He smiled at her, a tentative smile that begged for understanding.

Bella didn't smile back. She felt more like bawling. She felt as if her world was falling apart. She counted on Woody to be here with her, always reliable, always willing to talk things over, always...always in control, even when she wasn't. He was her friend, her partner, her...her mentor, in a strange way.

"I just don't understand," she wailed. "I thought you were happy doing this, I...I thought this was forever."

He reached over and took her hand, holding it between both of his huge ones. "I was happy, love, until this place got discovered by the yuppies." He frowned and shook his head, his dark eyes sad. "See, I loved the Artichoke the way it was before, sort of laid back, same old crowd most of the time, comfortable, predictable, lazy." He waved one hand toward the front, where they'd crammed in five extra tables. "Now I feel as though I'm working on an assembly line. There's never time anymore to fool around with different recipes the way we used to, or make our own tofu, or make gluten from scratch, or dream up some new dessert on the spur of the moment." His eyes begged her to understand and go on loving him.

"I know I'm being selfish as hell about this," he admitted. "I know even though I don't need the extra money the place is making, you sure as heck do. But I can't just ignore the way I feel about it, either."

She looked at him, and regret almost overwhelmed her. "No, I know you can't. I do understand, I just wish..." What did she wish? She wasn't sure. She only knew she didn't want to lose Woody's friendship.

Ace came through the back door just then, whistling. He clapped his hands and grinned at them.

"C'mon, you two, let's get this show on the road. It's quarter to ten, there's already a crowd out front. Our public awaits." He donned one of the orange aprons with the huge artichoke on the front that he'd talked them into buying for the staff and headed out front to make certain everything was ready.

Woody's eyes followed him thoughtfully. "Too bad Ace can't cook, he'd be the perfect partner for you,

Bella. He's got more ambition in his little finger than I've got in my whole overweight body."

Bella was still more than a little annoyed with Ace for making such a play for her mother, and at times like this she resented his eternal exuberance, the endless flow of ideas he proposed.

"No thanks, Woody, not Ace. I'll choose my own partner when the time comes."

BY MONDAY MORNING, Annie looked both dramatic and pathetic. The adhesive on her forehead only partially hid the purplish goose egg, and both eyes were ringed with bruises turning purple and blue. She was obviously feeling fine, though, devouring the breakfast Jake was spooning into her anxious, open mouth, grabbing the spoon and rubbing her cereal into hands, face and hair with cheerful abandon.

Florence arrived exactly on time, unaware that Jake had been trying to phone her at regular intervals since Saturday. She'd gone to Reno on the bus for the weekend, and she'd been lucky, so she was in an unusually expansive mood.

Jake had decided that because of Annie's accident, this wasn't the time to change baby-sitters and upset his daughter more than she already had been. He wasn't going to fire Florence on the spot as he'd planned, but he intended to lay down the law to her about Carol, and dishonesty to one's employer.

She bustled in the back door, casting a critical eye around the kitchen and giving a disapproving "humph" before her gaze finally settled on the baby in the high chair. She put a hand over her mouth in horror.

"Good heavens, what on earth's happened to my dear little girl?"

Jake explained in short, precise sentences, adding, "I tried to contact you this weekend, there's a very serious issue I want to discuss with you." He wiped Annie off and lifted her out of the chair, giving Florence a long, cold look even as she began holding forth about the dangers of open drawers.

"I understand you've been entertaining my ex-wife, Carol Proctor, here in my house and behind my back," he interrupted her. "I called you several times this weekend, but you weren't around, so we'll have to deal with this now, and I don't have much time before I have to leave for work. Exactly what did you think you were doing?"

Florence's chin came up and she pursed her lips. Her skin grew mottled red and she folded her arms defensively across her flat chest, but she didn't answer Jake's question. Her nostrils flared and she tried to stare him down, but her eyes dropped after one look at him.

He waited a few ominous minutes. Then, in icy, exact tones, he spelled out for her how angry he was and what he expected of her as Annie's baby-sitter and his employee. He made it clear that her job was in jeopardy because he wasn't certain he could trust her.

"From now on," he grated out, "I want to know exactly who comes to the door, who you let in this house and why, and I don't want you taking Annie out anywhere without telling me where you're going and how long you'll be gone. Understood?''

After a moment, Florence jerked her head up and down.

''Under these conditions, do you feel you want to stay on?''

Florence still hadn't said a word, but she nodded again. ''Yes, I do.'' Her voice was reedy and her thin mouth was sewn into a tight knot. Jake could see leashed fury in her eyes.

''I love this child as if she were my own, and I want her to have the very best of care.'' Florence's words were jerky and erratic, but Jake felt she meant what she said.

Jake hesitated, but at last he gave Annie a kiss and placed her in Florence's arms. He had to meet his new client this morning, and if the man was anything like Tho Van Chung, it could take most of the day to get even a few things sorted out. He stated exactly when he'd be home and asked, as he always did, that she call him on his mobile number if there was the slightest problem.

''My father's still asleep in his room. If there's anything you need him for, wake him up.''

Jake's truck was hardly out of the driveway before Florence, smarting from Jake's tirade but determined now to do the right thing, dialed the number of the Children's Home Society and in a trembling voice demanded that she be put through to Manuel Arbuckle. She tried to keep her tone low, just in case that awful old man should wake up and listen in.

"Mr. Arbuckle's in a meeting with his supervisor at the moment and can't be disturbed, but I'll leave him a message to call you back if you give me your number," syrupy tones informed Florence. Florence thought fast. It could take all morning for Arbuckle to return her call, and the phone would awaken the man sleeping in the room down the hall. She looked at Annie's poor little bruised face and made up her mind.

"Will he be in the office for the next couple of hours?" she whispered. "This is an urgent matter."

When she was assured that he would be available, Florence hung up and hurriedly set about getting Annie ready to leave. She packed with great efficiency a number of bottles of formula and jars of baby food and enough clothing for at least a week.

She bathed the baby and dressed her, then called a taxi, afraid the entire time that Ace Moreno would wake up and demand to know what she was doing. But there wasn't a sound from his room, and when the taxi drew up, Florence was ready and waiting on the front steps, Annie safely in her arms. She shoved various bags at the driver and scuttled into the cab.

As they pulled away, triumph rose in her breast, sweet and satisfying. She'd outwitted those awful men and probably saved this dear little baby's life. It was perhaps the most valiant thing she'd ever done. And whatever happened, she already had another job offer. It had been all she could do not to throw that up to Mr. Moreno this morning when he was being so high-handed. But she'd kept her counsel because of this dear baby.

The trip to Reno had been worthwhile even though she hadn't won much money; going down, she'd sat beside a woman about her own age, expensively dressed and well groomed, and they'd started talking. The woman, Mrs. Margaret Peabody, had confided that she had a disabled husband and had recently been forced to fire the young practical nurse who'd been caring for him; apparently Margaret had caught the woman stark naked one afternoon with the man who cleaned the pool. Both women agreed that they didn't know what the world was coming to.

One confidence led to another, and when Florence told her newfound friend about the shocking situation in the Moreno household and her own credentials as a practical nurse, Margaret had asked Florence to consider working for her. Florence hadn't wanted to seem too eager, but she'd certainly left all the doors open. At this moment she had Margaret Peabody's card in the side pocket of her purse, and the address was in a very nice area indeed. Besides, what a blessing it would be not to have to put up with that awful, mouthy Ace Moreno any more.

ACE WALKED OUT of the waterfront hotel, closing his bloodshot eyes for a second when the morning sunlight sent arrows of white-hot pain shooting through his head. He'd had too much whiskey and too many cigars, but he felt like dancing in the street, shouting with joy, grabbing the nearest female and giving her a hug and kiss she'd never forget.

He'd been playing poker for the past twelve hours—all Sunday night, in fact—and he'd won. He'd won big, by God! The wad of bills wouldn't even fit in his wallet, so he'd shoved them deep into his hip pocket, where he could feel their reassuring bulk with every step he took.

Granted, some of the money in his pocket wasn't his. Some of it—the sizable amount he'd used as a stake when he got into the game last night—belonged to the Artichoke, but of course it was only a loan. It wasn't as if he'd stolen it; he'd even left his personal check in the cash drawer as an act of good faith. Not that the check was much good. He didn't have that kind of money in any bank, of course, but to him it seemed a nice gesture, a good-faith gesture.

He'd earned that money in a way, after all. He'd done the advertising that put the old Artichoke on the map, and then he'd watched the daily totals double and triple and finally quadruple, but it wasn't until Sunday afternoon that he'd yielded to temptation.

Bella and Woody had fallen into the habit of relying on him to make the bank deposits for the restaurant. Saturday had been frantic, and he'd made out the slip but failed to put the money into the night deposit bag, so when Sunday evening came, there was an unusually large amount of cash around. One hell of a wad, in fact. The Artichoke didn't take credit cards, which Ace felt was a smart move.

He'd conscientiously made out the deposit slip again, but somehow he hadn't made it to the bank that night, either. One of his contacts had tipped him off about a game downtown where a sharp player could really clean up.

And it wasn't as if he'd stolen the money from the restaurant. He'd just had the use of it for twelve hours or so, and by the time the Artichoke opened for business today, he'd have the money safely in the deposit book. He squinted up at a clock on a tower. Plenty of time. It was his lucky day, nothing could go wrong.

He happened to pass a used car lot, and there, up on a podium, was the sweetest little red convertible sports car he'd seen since he got out of the joint. He stared at it for a long time, and lust stirred in him.

The price on the card in the window was only two thirds of the amount he had in his pocket. And he'd kept his driver's license valid, just in case. He wandered over to look at the car a little closer, and a salesman materialized beside him.

"She's sweet, and going for a song. Guy that owned her was old, wanted air-conditioning. Want to take her out for a spin?"

Within an hour, the car was his. Ace felt giddy with the pride of ownership.

The next stop was a men's clothing store, and then a shoe shop, and finally a barbershop. The whole procedure took quite a long time, but it was worth it. You could always tell a gentleman by the shine on his shoes and the trim on his hair.

When he checked the roll of bills, which fit easily now into his wallet, there wasn't enough to cover the Artichoke's deposit slips anymore, and for a moment or two, a nasty, sick feeling gnawed at his gut. The new watch on his wrist also confirmed that it was long past opening hour, and he'd have to do some sweet talking about the missing money.

He drove around and thought about it, and finally he made a phone call. Sure enough, there was another game that afternoon, but it was in L.A. Well, lucky thing he had the car.

He thought about calling the Artichoke, but he would have to do a lot of explaining. Better to win the money back first and explain later. Maybe he'd just mail it to them, head for another city; he'd only been to Miami once, and he'd liked it.

A rolling stone gathers no moss.

He drove to Jake's house, thinking maybe he'd pick up his suitcase, just in case, but then he remembered that old prune face Turner would be there today, and he didn't even stop, just headed straight back to the freeway.

He had his little white pills in his pocket, there was nothing else he needed all that bad. Jake could forward his things once he settled somewhere. He blotted all thoughts of Annie out of his mind. With no trouble at all he found the turnoff for the San Diego Freeway and followed the signs marked Los Angeles.

CHAPTER FOURTEEN

IT WAS WELL PAST lunch hour when Florence was at last ushered into the tiny cubicle that was Manuel Arbuckle's office. She was fed up with waiting and greatly out of sorts by that time. Her arms were aching from trying to keep Annie amused—the baby kept wanting to get down on the floor, and the rug was filthy.

"It's indecent, keeping people waiting this long when all they're trying to do is protect an innocent child," Florence huffed, but after a few minutes Arbuckle had her feeling much better.

He clucked over Annie's injuries then found a small playpen somewhere. They settled Annie in it with some toys and her bottle of juice, then he brought Florence a cup of coffee and offered her a sweet bun from a box in his desk.

He had a file with Annie's name on it, which Florence found reassuring, and she filled him in on what had occurred since the last time she'd called him, telling him all about Annie's natural mother and how attached she was to the baby and how she, Florence, felt that Carol would be a far better person for Annie to be with than the young and old Mr. Morenos.

"Remember you told me to get in touch with you right away if there was any sign of her being mistreated," she reminded Arbuckle. "Well, just look at the poor little mite, bruised and burned and heaven alone knows what else."

Florence had to admit that once you got in to see him, Manuel Arbuckle got things done. Within the next couple of hours he had Annie examined by a staff doctor, who pronounced her a wonderfully healthy, well cared for baby. Of course, the doctor added, he had no idea how she had gotten the gash on her forehead or the minor burn on her arm. He'd checked the hospital computer system and there was no record of repeated admissions with injury.

Arbuckle verified from other hospital records that Carol Proctor Moreno was indeed Annie's natural mother, and while Florence was occupied filling in endless forms, he called the number Florence had given him, told Carol who he was and asked her to come to his office immediately, explaining that it concerned her baby, Annie Moreno.

"Ms. Turner is here with the child, and she feels the baby might be in jeopardy in her present situation. We'd like you to come down and give us your story. Ms. Turner has told us how concerned you've been about your child."

Carol was in the middle of a manicure when the official-sounding call came.

She had a date that night with a guy who was a cousin to one of the studio heads in Hollywood, and she wanted to look her very best. He was a stockbroker, and he drove a Porsche.

As she hung up, she cursed Florence Turner. She'd never dreamed the old bat would go this far; all she had wanted to do was squeeze Jake for a decent amount of money. Now, by the sounds of it, stupid old Florence had gotten them all in a mess.

As soon as she walked into his office, Carol could tell that Arbuckle was impressed with her. He fussed over her like an old hen, getting her a chair and offering her a cold drink. She was glad she'd taken the time to put on the demure blue sailor dress and do her makeup.

Of course she had to lie to him, reinforcing all the crap she'd fed Florence about desperately wanting Annie, and how she was pretty sure Jake smoked dope, and how irresponsible and unfeeling he'd been when they were married, and how she'd had a breakdown when the baby was born, and how worried she'd been about Annie being in the house with an ex-convict. It was either keep up the fiction or admit she'd been lying all along, and she sure as hell wasn't going to do that.

Maybe she embellished her story a bit because she was still good and mad at Jake over the scene on the weekend. He hadn't even given her the damned coffeemaker. She managed to squeeze out a few tears as she explained how she'd been treated during her pregnancy, and she added that he'd literally kicked her out of the house last weekend when she tried to visit her baby.

Arbuckle asked for the name of the hospital she'd been in after her breakdown, and she had to think fast and tell him she'd stayed with an aunt in London and attended a clinic there. He wasn't about to call England to check up on her, she'd bet on that.

When he asked for her aunt's adress, she gave him the address of the bed-sitter she'd been renting. He wrote everything down, then asked them to wait and left the office. He was gone what seemed a long time. The clock on the wall read five-fifteen, and Carol was beginning to wonder if she couldn't just leave, when Arbuckle finally came back.

"I've checked this out with my supervisor, and I'm releasing the baby in your care tonight, Ms. Proctor."

It took a minute for what he was saying to sink in. When it did, Carol was both speechless and horrified.

"I need some time to investigate the charges you and Ms. Turner have made about the Moreno household. I've tried to contact Mr. Jake Moreno, but there's no answer at his home, and I feel the situation is serious enough to warrant apprehension of the baby, at least until I have a chance to investigate further."

Florence gave Carol a self-satisfied smirk and plopped Annie into her arms. She turned over Annie's diaper bag and a small suitcase of clothing to her and rattled off instructions about the baby's dinner before she hurried out, murmuring something about being late for a bingo game.

Arbuckle called a cab, helped Carol down with the luggage and gave the driver her address. The driver solicitously helped her in. Annie was a limp, warm little bundle in Carol's arms, and she decided maybe it wouldn't be that bad after all, having her baby for a sleep over. The cabdriver smiled at her admiringly through the rearview mirror, and she knew she made an attractive picture with her curly-haired baby girl in her arms. She could probably get a baby-sitter for tonight—there were agencies in the phone book—and she sat back and started to scheme ways to turn this into a paying thing as far as Jake was concerned.

They hadn't gone six blocks before Annie woke up, took a long look at Carol and started screaming. She stopped only long enough to get a concentrated look on her face and turn quite red. A few minutes later, the driver muttered under his breath and wound his window down. A decided odor was wafting up from the baby's diapers.

The driver wasn't at all helpful at the other end. Somehow Carol managed to wrestle bags and baby into her tiny apartment. Dumping the screaming child on the floor, she raced to the telephone and started calling baby-sitting agencies. Three were closed for the day and the fourth had no one available at such short notice. And no, the bored woman drawled, she didn't do baby-sitting herself. Fed up, Carol dialed Jake's number, but it rang twelve times with no answer.

Her date would be along in less than an hour, and the kid was still screaming. The apartment was beginning to smell worse than the cab had, and Carol had never changed a baby in her life.

She found a diaper in Annie's bag and, kneeling on the pale blue rug, gingerly unsnapped the baby's rompers. Annie stopped crying and turned over just as Carol figured out how to undo the tabs on the disposable diaper. Annie thought it was a game and took off across the carpet, leaving the soiled diaper behind. Her bottom wasn't at all clean, and somehow her knees had gotten into the diaper's contents.

The mess was indescribable. It got on the rug, on Carol's dress and all over the baby's clothing. The entire apartment stank.

Eventually Carol attached a diaper to the baby and cleaned up most of the mess, but she was still gagging as she desperately dialed Jake's number again. There was still no answer.

The doorbell rang.

Her date had arrived. She felt like screaming, but Annie already was.

BELLA FOUND Ace's sizable check in the empty cash drawer that morning when she opened it to make change for a customer. She had to use money out of her own wallet for a float and she wondered what the heck Ace was up to, but she didn't worry too much about it for the first hour. After all, Ace was Jake's father. He was totally reliable, and she knew he'd be coming in soon to explain what this was all about.

It was Woody's morning off, and the Artichoke was busy. She kept expecting Ace to turn up for work any minute, and her annoyance grew as the hours passed and the workload increased. Mrs. Montgomery, their part-time cooking assistant, was helping her in the kitchen, but the woman was slow, so Bella had to serve out front and cook, as well.

Between customers, she tried to call Ace at home in case he was sick, but Jake's number rang and rang with no answer. She wondered where Florence was, then decided she must have taken Annie out to a park or something. It wasn't until after two that she became seriously worried about Ace and called the mobile number Jake had given her if she needed to contact him at work. Ace must have had a serious accident, she decided, and her fingers shook as she dialed.

Jake answered right away, and Bella blurted out how concerned she was about Ace not turning up for work or calling. At first there was silence at the other end of the line, and then Jake said the strangest thing.

"Is there any money missing?"

Bella frowned at the receiver and felt a whisper of apprehension run down her spine as she told him about the check in the cash drawer. Jake swore, a string of words that raised Bella's eyebrows.

"I'll be right over, it'll take me half an hour."

He hung up, leaving Bella more confused than ever.

IT WAS THE DAMNED AD for disposable diapers on a freeway billboard that got to Ace. The baby didn't even look like Annie, yet his granddaughter's sweet little face started popping into his mind no matter how hard he tried to think of other things.

He turned on the radio, a golden oldies station from L.A., but that only reminded him of singing to her when nobody else was around to hear him. She was fond of old Hank Williams tunes, and Ace figured he was pretty good at belting them out.

He thought about how she smiled at him and wriggled and held up her arms when he went in to get her early some mornings. He thought about how she sucked her thumb and snuggled against him when she was tired, how she grinned and banged her spoon on her high chair when he came in the kitchen, how she clung to his fingers when he taught her to take clumsy steps, how she loved to ride on his foot.

How she trusted him. How she seemed to love him.

He'd never thought having a grandchild would get to him the way it had. Hell, she didn't weigh thirty pounds yet and she had more influence on him than any full-grown woman he'd ever known. Except maybe her grandmother.

Ace had fallen hard for Annie's grandmother, but she'd dumped him. And now he was doing the same thing to their granddaughter.

What memories would Annie have of her grandpa? He didn't think babies her age remembered much. Hell, she probably wouldn't even remember how he'd taught her to crawl. Would Jake tell her the truth about him, that he was an old jailbird who took off with a friend's money?

All of a sudden he didn't feel as young as he had an hour ago. He hated to admit it to himself, but he'd lost more poker games than he'd ever won. If he lost the last of the money in his wallet, what was going to become of him? He could never go back to Jake's if that happened.

He'd seen men not much older than he was, rooting through garbage cans, broke and sick and alone, and he always gave them whatever he had in his pocket because they scared the hell out of him.

He thought uneasily about the vial of pills he carried in his pocket, the pills the prison doctor had prescribed after his old ticker had acted up. He wasn't at death's door or anything, but he wasn't as young as he'd been, either.

He was on the outskirts of L.A. when he made up his mind. At the next exit ramp, he turned off the freeway, watching for the signs that would head him back to San Diego.

He'd have to think up one hell of a whopper to explain what had happened to the money from the Artichoke, but he had a whole hour in which to do it. He'd offer to work off the difference, or maybe he could sell the car back to the guy he'd bought it from. That would help some.

If Bella and Woody had already called the cops on him, he'd just have to face the music. Either way, he was heading back.

Inexplicably, his spirits rose. He was going home, and even though he was scared witless, it felt better than anything he'd done in a very long time.

WOODY ARRIVED FOR WORK at three, and Bella just had time to tell him about Ace and the missing money and the check in the cash drawer when Jake strode through the back door.

He was in his work clothes, huge and bronzed and sweaty, and he looked like an advertisement for beer. Bella took one half second to admire him, then saw that he appeared angry, sad and resigned all at the same time. Suddenly she felt frightened. She held out the check, but Jake barely glanced at it before wadding in his fist.

"It's worthless but I'll cover it, so don't worry about the money. Can you get away from here for a while, Bella? I have to talk to you, and I also want to see if Ace is still at home." His jaw was clenched and a muscle jumped in his cheek.

"Go." Woody tied on his apron. "I'll cook and Mrs. Montgomery can serve out front, can't you, Mrs. Montgomery?"

Bella could hear the older woman strongly objecting to the idea as she and Jake walked out the door. The moment they were in the truck, Jake let his breath out with a whoosh and began to talk.

"There's things I should have told you about my father a long time ago, Bella." He started the engine and pulled out into the afternoon traffic. "He's taken off with your money. Maybe there's a chance we can still catch him, if he stopped at the house, but I doubt it, I think he's long gone. See, my father is a petty crook, has been all his life."

His voice was even but remote as he detailed his father's long history of passing bad checks. He described the way he and Jake often had to leave town in the middle of the night, just ahead of the law, and the times Ace hadn't managed to get away and had stood trial and been convicted.

"Just before he came to live with me this time, Ace had served almost a year in the pen. When he turned up at my door, he was down on his luck, and I know I was nuts to ever let him stay. I told him he could only live with Annie and me if he stayed clean. He promised he would." Jake snorted. "What a fool I was, thinking he'd keep a promise like that."

"Why didn't you tell me all this before? You never said a word about any of it." Bella felt stunned. She could hardly believe what she was hearing. The character Jake described was so different from the Ace she knew at the restaurant, the conscientious, clever man who showed off pictures of his granddaughter to the customers, the charming waiter who knew all about bookkeeping.

She swallowed hard. The persistent man who'd tried to date her mother.

Anger began to take the place of confusion, and she felt a sense of utter betrayal. It wasn't just Ace's dishonesty here that bothered her. Ace might be a thief, but it was Jake who had lied to her right and left. She'd never dreamed that he could have been dishonest with her about something this important.

"You...you never warned me, even when he began to work at the Artichoke. Didn't you think we had the right to know what kind of person we were hiring?"

Jake's forehead knotted in a frown and he sighed. "Bella, I knew I should have told you about him, but damn it all, things got more and more complicated."

He smashed a fist down on the dash and Bella jumped. "Don't you see, I wanted to give the old geezer a chance. I wanted so much to let him make a life for himself for once without having everyone know his background and judge him by it. Then he fell for Annie, and I thought maybe having a grandchild he loved would help keep him straight." He shook his head. "And most of all, I guess I didn't want you to think less of me because of him. The very first time I ever really talked with you, you told me about your father being a preacher." He grimaced. "A preacher. God, I couldn't turn to you right then and say, Bella, my father's a jailbird, don't you see that? I figured you'd never talk to me again."

But Bella didn't see. The one thing she'd valued above all else was honesty. It was devastating to realize that the first man in her life she'd come to love and trust and even consider marrying could have lied to her this way.

As if he'd read her mind, Jake said, "Bella, I know how you must feel about me now, and I don't blame you. I know only too well how you've always felt about marriage and kids and everything, but I'm in love with you anyway."

He blew out a lengthy breath, as if the words had been bottled up and it was a relief to finally let them out. "I think I've been in love with you a long time, but I was pretty screwed up over Carol and I had to get it through my head that she wasn't going to ever change or come back to me and Annie. It took me a long time to understand that I didn't even want her back." He wasn't looking at her but he stared resolutely out the front window of the truck.

"See, my pride was hurt pretty bad. It's a hell of a thing to realize that a woman you figured you loved enough to marry sure didn't feel the same way about you. And then you told me right at the beginning you never wanted a husband or a family, and I started to wonder if I just had a bad habit of falling for women who don't want what I want out of life. What I want more than anything is a wife. And more kids." He nodded his head as if he was figuring it out as he went along. "Not just any wife. You, Bella. I'm in love with you. And the damnedest thing is, so is Annie. She adores you, and she needs a family bad. Which is another part of the reason I didn't tell you about Ace. I guess I was hoping maybe he'd stick around and be a grandpa for Annie, be there for her while she grew up."

They were pulling into Jake's driveway, and Bella opened her mouth to tell him he was jumping to conclusions, that she'd changed her mind about a lot of things, but then decided against it. She had a lot of thinking to do before she committed herself to this man. If he'd lied to her about his father, maybe he was lying about his feelings for her, as well. How the hell was she to know?

Jake was out of the truck and taking the front steps two at a time. Bella followed and found the house strangely quiet.

"It doesn't look as if Ace is here," she said as she walked into the living room.

Jake strode down the hallway and threw Ace's bedroom door open. "He hasn't taken any of his things, but that's no guarantee."

He walked into the living room where Bella was waiting, and it dawned on both of them at the same time that not only Ace was absent.

"Where are Florence and Annie?" Bella remembered phoning hours ago and assuming they'd gone shopping or to the park, but it was now almost six o'clock. Surely they ought to be home. She told Jake about the phone calls. "Florence always makes a big thing about leaving on the dot of five, doesn't she, Jake?"

Jake didn't answer. He hurried into Annie's bedroom, his eyes taking in the empty crib, the missing diaper bag from the top of the bureau. He yanked open several drawers.

"Is... is anything missing? Are... are her clothes gone?"

Jake met Bella's frightened gaze and gave a jerky nod, his eyes slowly filling with the same terror that was making Bella's stomach cramp. Her throat felt as if she were being strangled. It was one thing to have Ace take off with money. It was quite another to think of anything happening to Annie.

She began to shiver. "Could...could Ace have taken her with... him?" It sounded unlikely, but she was grasping at straws.

Jake's face was pale beneath his tan. "I doubt it. If he'd tried anything like that, I'm pretty sure Florence would have called both me and the cops. She despises him."

"Florence, then?"

Jake nodded. "I all but fired her this morning. I wish I had. I figure it has to be her or...or Carol." He picked up the phone and called both Florence and his ex-wife, but there was no answer at either number. "I'm calling the police."

Bella had to sit down. Her legs felt as if they wouldn't hold her, and her entire body was trembling. Her baby...

Jake was in the midst of explaining to someone at the emergency number he'd dialed that his baby daughter was missing when the back door opened and Ace slunk in.

The moment he saw Bella, he straightened his shoulders and came over to her, a sickly smile pasted on his face. "Just the very person I wanted to see," he began in a forced tone. "I'm sure you're wondering..."

Jake slammed down the phone and took two steps toward his father. Ace backed up when he saw the expression on his son's face.

"Just shut up, Ace." Jake's tone was ruthless. "Whatever lies you've dreamed up won't work, and right now they're not even important. Do you have any idea where Annie is? We came home a few minutes ago and she's gone."

"Gone? Whattya mean, gone?" Ace looked around as if he expected Annie to come crawling out from behind the sofa.

"Some of her clothes, her diaper bag, bottles of her formula from the fridge. Someone's taken her."

Ace seemed to wilt. He staggered back and lowered himself into a chair, his face a strange greenish white. His breath came in short gasps and he put a hand to his chest and leaned over, his head almost touching his knees, his body trembling visibly. Bella and Jake both started to go to him, afraid that he was having a heart attack.

"Never... never mind me. I've... I've had these... before, they're... they're nothing. It's... it's that woman, that Florence, that took Annie. She's twisted, I knew it all along. Should never have... have trusted that bloody woman."

Bella brought him a glass of water and Ace swallowed a tiny pill from a vial in his pocket. In a few moments he straightened. His colour was still sickly but he seemed stronger. He got to his feet and motioned to Jake with a take-command gesture that would have been amusing under different circumstances.

"Let's go, son. You can drive, I know where that old bat lives, I made it my business to know. Let's go pay her a visit before she has a chance to take off with my granddaughter. My car's out back."

Jake hesitated, but Bella could see that any kind of action was better than waiting around.

"I'll stay here," she offered, and he gave her a grateful look.

"Will you explain to the police where we've gone? Carol's number and address are in the book beside the phone. Tell them she's the other person who might have..." He swallowed painfully. "Have taken Annie. They're sending a car over here right away, but Ace is right. If there's the slightest chance that Florence has her..."

Ace and Jake had just driven away when the police arrived. They'd parked in the alley and came to the kitchen door. Bella led them into the living room and was doing her best to explain the situation when a white sports car screeched into Jake's front driveway.

"That's Jake's ex-wife and...and she's got..." Bella made a dive for the door as Carol staggered out of the low car with Annie, gripped like a sack of flour under one arm. She had Annie's diaper bag and small suitcase clutched in the other, and Annie was crying.

Bella was out the door and down the walk before Carol had taken three steps. She snatched the weeping baby from Carol and cuddled her against her shoulder, relief and utter fury washing through her.

"Annie...God, honey, it's so good to see you," she crooned, kissing the baby's cheek and at the same time giving Carol the nastiest look she'd ever leveled on anyone in her life. If her arms hadn't been full of baby, she knew she'd have physically attacked the other woman.

"What exactly did you think you were doing, taking..." Bella's voice quivered with rage.

Without a word, Carol dropped the bags she was carrying and hurriedly started toward the white car, but the two officers had emerged from the house by that time. They blocked Carol's way, suggesting she might like to come in and answer a few questions.

The man in the Porsche still had his engine running, and he swiftly backed up and drove away, screeching his tires as he rounded the corner. An officer calmly wrote down his license number and went inside the house and over to the phone.

After the first few moments, when she identified Carol and assured the officers that Jake's wife absolutely didn't have custody and hadn't let Jake know she was taking the baby, Bella didn't hear much of what they asked Carol. She really didn't care. All that mattered was the little girl in her arms.

She took a tired, dirty Annie into the bathroom, closed the door, ran warm water in the tub and swiftly bathed and dressed her. Then she heated a bottle and, cradling the sleepy little girl in her arms, fed her and sang to her until she went to sleep.

Bella had just settled her in her crib when she heard Ace and Jake return—an obviously reluctant Florence in tow.

"Dragging a person out of their bingo game for no reason at all..."

She must have noticed the policemen, because her strident, outraged tones faded away, and shortly afterward Bella could hear what sounded like a fiery exchange between the two women.

A moment later, Jake hurried into Annie's room, and the utter relief on his face when he saw his daughter touched a chord deep in Bella's heart. His shoulders slumped and tears trickled down his cheeks. He rubbed them away with his fist and Bella pretended not to notice. Ace came, as well, to look at the baby, and while the men hovered over the little girl, Bella quietly went out the back door and home.

Her house was very quiet and very clean. Her mother had arranged a huge bouquet of straw flowers in a vase on the kitchen table and scrubbed the entire place from stem to stern before she left.

Bella locked the kitchen door behind her and put on the chain Jake had installed. She turned on quiet, classical music and began taking her clothes off, leaving them in a trail from the living room to the bathroom, where she filled the tub with scalding water and sank into it.

The phone rang after a while but she ignored it, even though it continued persistently for quite some time. As the bath cooled she added more hot water and concentrated on not thinking. A numbing kind of calm crept over her finally, and she was grateful. It took quite a long time before she was relaxed enough to start to cry.

And then she couldn't stop.

JAKE HAD PIECED TOGETHER what had gone on long before Manuel Arbuckle phoned late that evening to explain it all.

The social worker identified himself in a smooth, professional voice, apologized for not calling earlier and explained that he'd been out to dinner. Then he began telling Jake why he'd seen fit to take Annie into custody that afternoon.

"I've released her in the care of her natural mother until an investigation is complete. The child's nanny was concerned about her safety."

Jake shut his eyes and tried to contain the rage that made him want to murder Manuel Arbuckle. When he finally had control of his voice, he gave the man a summary of what had occurred in the past few hours.

"The police have been trying to contact you," he said. "I'm sure they'll be there soon." He could sense the growing apprehension in the silence of the other man and it gave him satisfaction to think Arbuckle was squirming just a little. He'd squirm a lot more before Jake was through with him.

He told the social worker that he'd fired Florence, and he explained with icy clarity that he was considering laying charges of kidnapping against her and Carol. She and Carol were currently down at headquarters, being questioned in detail about what had happened. Arbuckle would likely be called in, as well.

He laid out exactly what had occurred in his marriage to Carol, the papers she'd willingly signed giving him full custody of Annie, the sum of money he'd paid her after the divorce. He described her visit the weekend before, detailing how Annie's arm had come to be scalded.

"Why didn't you ever come here and ask me what was going on in my home? Surely I had the right to know."

Arbuckle stammered excuses about being overworked and understaffed and needing to protect innocent children, and after all, the baby's nanny had sounded so reliable....

Jake told Arbuckle that as far as he was concerned, there were grounds for legal action here, and he was going to see his lawyer first thing in the morning. The social worker began stammering out an apology, and Jake took great delight in hanging up in the middle of it.

He was breathing hard and his heart was pounding. He should have felt victorious, but somehow he didn't at all. He felt dejected and a little sick.

It took a good half hour before it dawned on him that he and Arbuckle had both made an error in judgment—Jake had withheld information, and Arbuckle had jumped to conclusions. Arbuckle might have caused a lot of chaos and some outright terror today when Annie was missing, but Jake had caused Bella, and Woody, as well, an untold amount of trouble by not leveling with them about his father. In fact, Bella and Woody had good grounds for legal action against Ace.

His father had admitted to Jake that he'd spent a lot of their money on the car and the new suit of clothes he was wearing. The car could go back, but the clothes were another matter.

Even worse, until tonight Jake had never been the slightest bit honest with Bella about how he really felt. He'd never once admitted his love for her or given her a chance to say whether or not she loved him back. The fact was, he'd jumped to conclusions at every turn.

Ace had been having a shower, and now he came into the living room and sank down on the couch, wrapped in a tattered old terry robe of Jake's. He looked pale, but the sparkle was back in his eyes.

"Hell of a day, eh, son? Well, tomorrow's a new one, always get a second chance, that's life. Time I went off to bed." Ace sounded quite chipper, and he started to get to his feet. "Man needs his sleep when he gets to be my age."

He yawned and stretched, and the robe came up over his bony knees. He hadn't said one word about the missing money; he'd never even said he was sorry.

Jake couldn't believe the force of the anger that suddenly filled him, anger for this child-man who was his father and who had betrayed that role not only today but so many times before.

"You stay right here, Ace," he grated out. "You sit down and don't move. We're going to get a few things straight for once, you and I."

The last thing Jake wanted to do tonight was have it out with his father, but he was determined that Ace was going to answer questions and face the full consequences of what he'd done, not just today but all the times he'd let Jake down in the past. If it was time for honesty, and Jake knew it was, then it had to start with Ace.

CHAPTER FIFTEEN

"YOU WERE ALL SET to just drive away today and leave me here holding the bag, weren't you?"

The resentment and anger in Jake's voice captured Ace's attention, at least. The older man sat down with a thump on the sofa and leaned forward, hands clasped between his knees, staring at the rug.

Jake was trembling. "You did the same thing the whole time I was growing up, you know, Ace. Do you have the slightest idea what it was like for me as a little kid that time you got yourself that jail term in Phoenix? You fobbed me off with those alcoholic friends of yours, the Taylors, who hadn't the foggiest clue what a kid needed. I was never sure you were even coming back for me." Each word was laden with a bitterness accumulated over the years.

Ace glanced up, surprise on his face. "Course I was coming back. You were my kid, weren't ya?" He attempted a grin, but it came off more as a grimace. "I'm like a bad penny. Hell, I always turn up again, you know that."

Jake's expression made Ace blink and look down again.

"I know that now, but back then I was an eight-year-old boy. I spent nine months spit scared that you were gone for good." Jake made a monumental effort to control the viciousness in his voice. Even after all these years, remembering made him want to smash something, lash out and hurt the way he'd been hurt.

"I couldn't eat half the time, I was so afraid—not that there was that much to eat anyway. Most of their money went on booze. I thought of running away, but an eight-year-old can't take care of himself and I knew it. It's a wonder it never dawned on you, but then you never did think of much except yourself, right, Ace?"

Ace seemed to shrivel a little. "Didn't know what the hell else to do with ya," he mumbled. "I was scared, too, y'know, scared they'd send you off to some orphanage someplace where I'd never get you back. Lester and Carrie offered to take you, and I didn't have a hell of a lot of choice. It wasn't like we had relatives to turn to."

Both men were silent for a while, remembering.

"Damn it, boy, I never was much good as a father, I know that," Ace finally said. He shrugged, and Jake noticed how thin his shoulders were under the worn robe.

"Might have been different if your mother had stayed, but I wasn't much of a husband, either. Always figured it was my fault, her leaving and taking to drink the way she did." He clasped and unclasped his hands. "Bothered me, you growing up with me as a model. Then you started getting in trouble, lifting cigarettes from corner groceries, you remember?"

Jake did remember. He'd gone through a wild stage for a while in his early teens.

"That's why I got you that there apprenticeship with the Liposkis," Ace continued with a sigh. "Nathan and Sam were friends of mine from way back. They liked the odd poker game but they were nothing like me, they weren't drifters. They were good solid men with a trade, and I knew you'd learn with them. I figured the best thing I could do for you right then was butt out of your life."

"So you climbed in that blue Cadillac you had and just drove away and left me all over again." Jake felt a flash of new pain as he thought about that afternoon. It had seemed like the end of the world to him.

Ace grinned suddenly. "Wasn't that one honey of a car, though? God, I used to feel like a winner in that Caddie."

Jake felt totally defeated. The old man obviously had more affection for some damned old car he'd owned years before than he'd had for his son. Ace was incapable of understanding the load of resentment Jake had carried all these years, there weren't any words to make him understand. And even if he did, what the hell could he do about it now? Ace had always said you couldn't get blood out of a stone.

"Y'know, son, that old car paid for your clothes and shoes and food for a good year or two. Drove her straight down to a used car dealer that afternoon, got one hell of a good price, and sent the money to the Liposkis straight off before it burned a hole in my pocket. I was pretty broke right then, so that old car came in handy. Mailed the money and hopped a freight, took me all the way down to Mexico. Made me feel good, knowing you were taken care of." Ace nodded as if the memory still pleased him. "And just look what you've made of yourself now, this Ace Construction and all, I feel damn good, knowing you named it after me. And now you got little Annie, too. Makes a man feel like he's accomplished something in life to have a son like you. Makes me glad I did the best I could."

The words seemed to take hold of Jake's heart and squeeze until he could hardly breathe. The one thing he'd never thought of before was that Ace was simply doing the best he could all those years—the same as Jake was trying to do for Annie.

Ace had made plenty of mistakes, but hell, so would Jake. He might not ever make the same ones his father had—at least he hoped like hell he wouldn't—but he had already made some bad ones. He thought of Florence and Carol and shuddered.

"If you want me to, Jake, I'll clear right outta here in the morning." Ace sounded sad but resigned. "I know I broke our bargain about staying out of trouble. I want to try and sell that car back tomorrow morning, and then I'll figure out some way of paying the rest of what I owe Bella and Woody. But I don't expect you to let me go on living here."

His voice trembled, and somehow Jake knew the old man's emotion was genuine. "Sure gonna miss that little baby, though." He looked up at Jake from under his eyebrows. "Maybe..." His voice was humble, all bluster and bravado missing for once. "Maybe you'd let me come by and see her every now and again? See, I got no plans for traveling anymore. No, sirree, a man's gotta settle sooner or later, and I'm stayin' here, in San Diego. Good a place as any, better than most."

Jake digested his words and wondered how often he was going to regret what he said next.

"Then maybe you better stick around and pull your weight here for the next while, Ace. I'm in a tight spot. I've got another house to build for Tho Van Chung's cousin, and I've got no one to leave Annie with." Jake frowned at the impossible old man who was his father and tried for a suitably gruff tone. "You figure there's any chance you could take proper care of her and keep the place halfway clean until I find another woman to come in? I'll pay you the same I paid Florence, but I'm warning you, I'll make sure most of it goes to the Artichoke till you get your debt paid. Sort of like having your wages garnisheed."

Ace's mouth opened and closed again without any sound. When at last he spoke, his voice was thick and quavery.

"Could I take care of Annie? Hell's bells, son, you just watch me. I swear on a stack of bibles I'll take the best care of her anybody ever took of a baby. You'll see, you won't need to hire any bitchy woman ever again, Annie and I'll make out just great."

"No teaching her to swear or spit or play cards, you understand that." Jake did his best to look stern.

Ace held up his hand. "You got my word of honor on it."

Jake remembered something. "What pills were those you took this afternoon, Ace? You got something wrong with you maybe I should know about?"

Ace looked frightened all of a sudden. "Nothing wrong with me that'll keep me from taking care of Annie, that's for sure. Doc gave me these little pills to slip under my tongue. The only time I need them is when I'm under lots of stress, old heart starts acting up a bit. Haven't had to use them at all since I came here, not till today. Then I got so damned scared over that baby being gone... But you got to believe me, son, I'm not about to have a heart attack or anything like that. Doc said I was good for another twenty, thirty years at least." He shoved his sleeve up and flexed a rather scrawny arm. "Just look at that, fit as a fiddle and ready to whip a den full o' wildcats, that's Ace Moreno."

Jake made a mental note to take Ace to a doctor within the next couple of days. But he figured the old geezer was probably telling the truth. He hadn't seen any sign of heart problems before today.

"Well, if you're going to stick around and you're in such good shape, how about baby-sitting right now while I go next door and try and talk Bella into taking the whole works of us on? And don't go waking Annie up to keep you company, either."

Ace's grin stretched from ear to ear. "Now you're talkin'," he crooned. "Now you're talkin'. Never thought any son of mine would be as slow as you've been about that girl. You could take some pointers about romance from the older generation, young feller. You take your time over there. I'll just catch up on some of this here professional bowling."

He reached for the remote control and clicked on the television.

IT WAS AFTER MIDNIGHT and Bella should have been in bed, sound asleep, but she'd tried that when she'd finally managed to stop crying and it hadn't worked. The day's events played and replayed on a stage in her brain, and she grew more and more upset as the hours passed.

She thought about an old man like Ace being a career criminal, and about Jake making love to her and never saying a word about his father just getting out of jail, and about little Annie growing up without a mother and only those two ignorant, meat-eating men to rely on for advice. Finally it made her so riled up she got out of bed, pulled on a pair of jeans and an old shirt and headed for the kitchen. Cooking always calmed her, and she needed calming badly right now.

In a frenzy, she started four different dishes, all of them complicated. She put marinated tofu in the oven to brown, she mixed mung beans and rice and put them on to boil, and she started frying onions in one pan and gingerroot and garlic in another. Just for good measure she started a batch of whole wheat bread. She was stirring and kneading and braising all at the same time when Jake's special tap came at the back door.

"Bella, let me in, please. I have to talk to you."

Her heart rate accelerated at the sound of his deep voice, but she was determined to ignore it and him.

"Go away. I'm busy, and it's the middle of the night, and we've got nothing to say to one another anyhow."

"Okay." There was a rustling sound, then silence. She didn't hear his footsteps going away. At last, she brushed some dough off her hands and cautiously opened the door a crack.

Jake was sitting on her back steps. He turned and smiled at her, that same sweet, patient, lopsided grin that had captured her in the very beginning. His hair was mussed and his white T-shirt and his teeth both shone bright in the moonlight.

"Hi, Bella." He made it sound as if he sat on her back porch every night of his life, for goodness' sakes.

"What exactly do you think you're doing?" She sounded mad, and that was good. Anger was the answer here, she told herself.

"I figured I'd just sit here until morning, when you're not busy anymore. Then maybe you could make us some carrot juice and we could talk. Remember that night you made us carrot juice, Bella?"

She used a single, pithy, rude expression and he grinned even wider. "I sure hate to think of Annie learning that word, but I suppose it's going to happen, especially growing up with two men in the house, right?"

He got to his feet and loomed over her in the doorway. She could feel his energy surrounding her, she could smell the special man scent that was uniquely Jake, she could feel herself being drawn by the sensuality that seemed to ooze out of his pores.

"I think something's burning on the stove," he remarked in a conversational tone, and she whirled around in time to see smoke curling out of her good iron frying pan.

She hurried over to the stove and grabbed the handle, forgetting how hot it was. With a holler she dropped the pan, and the dark, oily mess spilled down the front of the stove and all over the floor that Marion had stripped and scrubbed and waxed.

Jake grabbed her hand and held it under the cold water tap.

"It's not burned, it just scared me," she insisted, but he kept her hand in the icy water until she was certain it was frozen stiff. Finally he examined it, his dark, curly head bent over her in concentration, his muscular arms bare and brown and inviting.

"It looks okay. You're sure you don't want something on it?"

She shook her head.

He bent over and pressed a moist kiss into her palm, and the feel of his warm mouth sent shivers up and down her backbone.

"All better," he murmured. "Y'know, I wasn't much good at things like this before I had Annie."

Somehow that reminded her of why she was so angry with him. She took several steps back, away from him, so she could think straight.

"About Annie," she began, crossing her arms over her breasts and tipping her chin up defiantly. "I'm so mad at all of you over what happened to Annie, I've got half a mind to apply for custody myself. At the very least, I'm hiring the next baby-sitter, and that's all there is to it."

"That's probably a good idea." Jake looked at her and nodded in agreement. "A really good idea. I don't seem to be a very good judge of females. Not counting you, Bella. With you, I did damn good."

She did her best to forget what he'd said to her in the truck that afternoon, but it was there between them all the same, in his eyes, in the way his body seemed to lean toward her. She turned away, because if she gave in now, there would always be unfinished business between them.

"I've also had it up to the neck with you not telling me the truth about things, Jake Moreno. If there's one other single thing you aren't telling me, such as the fact that you have an ax murderer for an uncle or something, you'd better spit it out right now."

"I don't have any uncles, Ace was an only child—at least that's what he said when I asked him. You can't exactly trust Ace to always tell the truth, though. And I've got no idea about the people on my mother's side. You'd just have to take your chances."

"I'm also really fed up with you telling me how I feel about things instead of asking me." She swallowed hard. This was getting close to the root of everything, and she felt nervous again. He was watching her with unnerving intensity, so she turned her back to him and pretended to do things to the bread dough.

"How do you feel about things, Bella?"

Here it was, the moment she'd spent a lot of time and energy avoiding. She stopped pretending and began punching the warm dough in earnest, her fists going deep, her rhythm smooth and strong.

"Woody's leaving the Artichoke, and I'm pretty sure it's all Ace's fault. I don't know how he did it, but I'd bet he was the one who got us written up in all those papers, and as a result the Artichoke got popular and Woody isn't happy there anymore. Now I have to find a new partner, and I hate the thought of it. I'm good and mad at Ace, and I'm going to tell him so."

"He needs to be told. I already had a few words with him myself. You'll be the best thing that ever happened to Ace."

She doubted Ace would think so when she got through with him. There was also the matter of Ace putting the make on her mother. She rolled the dough over, folded it in half and went on punching. "I won't cook meat, or chicken or fish or eggs or..." she ran out of *or*'s and added firmly, "I run a vegetarian kitchen, and that's that."

"No problem. I figure I can live without meat and all the rest of that stuff. I just can't live without you, Bella."

This was hard. It was worse than she'd expected. She added a bit more flour and began working it into the dough in a frenzy.

"There's no way in the world I'm ever going to have ten children. Two, maybe. Three in a pinch."

"Three's more than enough." She noticed he chose the largest possibility, but she decided to let it pass.

This was frightening. It was all the things she'd told herself for many years she'd never do. It was commitment. It was taking responsibility for other people's lives. She was punching like a madwoman, and he waited patiently.

Gradually her movements slowed and finally stopped. The dough was a warm, shiny ball, and its yeasty smell filled the kitchen. Jake reached out and took her shoulders in his hands, turning her to face him. She stared up into his gentle brown eyes and the fear inside her began to fade away. Soon it was entirely gone, and desire took its place.

He had that funny, crooked smile, and she'd always been partial to a man with a cleft in his chin.

He had Annie, which was an enormous advantage.

He had Ace, which was rather a detriment, but then she had her whole complicated family with all their problems. It wouldn't surprise her if Leah decided to come and visit, bringing her Russian with her.

Jake would deal with all of it. Jake was strong.

"I love you, Jake Moreno. I think I'd like to marry you."

The moment the words were out, she realized he hadn't even asked her yet. It didn't seem to matter, though. He'd probably get around to it after he kissed her.

It was the smoke coming from the oven that eventually alerted them to the fact that the tofu was burning.

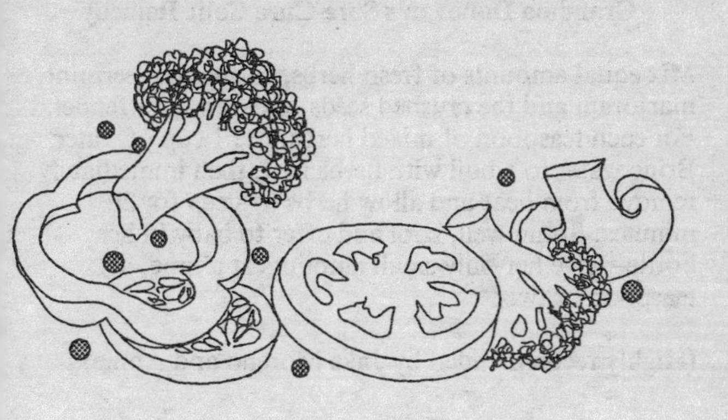

RECIPES FROM BELLA, WOODY AND THE ARTICHOKE HEART CAFÉ

I've always believed that making good healthy food for people is a way of loving them.

Woody Finch

Grandma Donovan's Sure-Cure Colic Remedy

Mix equal amounts of fresh herbs, catnip, peppermint, marjoram and the crushed seeds of caraway or fennel. For each teaspoon of mixed herbs, use 1 cup of water. Bring water to a boil with herbs in it, then immediately remove from heat and allow herbs to steep for 20 minutes. Strain well, cool and offer to baby in her bottle—give her only small amounts at a time, a teaspoon or two.

(Highly recommended by Jake Moreno and Annie)

Woody's Lentil-Dal Stew

10 cups water
3 cups lentils
⅛ cup safflower oil
2 onions, chopped
4-6 cloves garlic, chopped
2 tbsp grated fresh ginger
3 tbsp curry powder
2 carrots, sliced thin
½ green cabbage, chopped
½ cauliflower, chopped
1 potato, cut small
2 small zucchini, sliced thin
minced parsley

Put water on to boil in large pot. Heat oil in frying pan, add onions, garlic and ginger and sauté until starting to brown. Add curry powder and cook mixture until well done. Add to boiling water with lentils, cook 30 minutes, add all the other vegetables and bring to boil again. Lower heat and simmer for one hour, adding water as needed. Season to taste.

Bella's Pear Cream

In a blender, put 1 cup of raw cashews and 1 cup of hot water. Mix until liquefied. Add 1 tsp vanilla, 2 tbsp honey and 1 can pears (sugar-free, packed in pear juice) including liquid. Blend until mixture is thick and creamy. Refrigerate. Will thicken in fridge. Use in place of whipped cream or on cereal.

Bella's Quick and Easy Boffo Bread
(Requires food processor)

4 cups whole wheat flour
1 tbsp brown sugar or honey
1 tbsp lemon juice
1 tbsp oil
1 tsp salt
1 tbsp yeast

Put all ingredients in processor bowl, blend about 10 seconds. With machine running, add about 1½ cups warm water in slow, steady stream until dough forms ball. Stop processor, turn out dough and shape into ball. Place in greased bowl, let rise until double, punch down and let rise another 15 minutes. Shape into loaf, let rise until just about height of pan, bake in preheated 375 degree oven for 40 minutes.

Woody's Special Bran Muffins

2 cups unbleached flour
1 cup bran or wheat germ
2 cups soy milk
1½ tsp baking soda
⅓ cup honey
½ tsp salt
¼ cup oil
½ cup raisins

Stir dry ingredients together, mix liquids in another bowl and add to dry. Add raisins, stir just enough to moisten, spoon into 12 oiled muffin tins. Bake for 20 minutes at 425 degrees.

Artichoke's Eggless Whole Wheat Pancakes

1 cup whole wheat flour
1 cup whole wheat pastry flour
1 tsp baking soda
2 tbsp soy powder (dissolve in 6 tbsp water)
2 tbsp honey
¼ cup sunflower oil
2 cups soy milk

Combine dry ingredients in one bowl, liquid in another. Add dry to wet and stir to form thick, lumpy batter. Cook on preheated, oiled griddle. Serve with maple syrup or sugar-free jam and pear cream.

Bella's Sugar-Free Jam

Soak overnight 2 cups strawberries, 4 rings dried pineapple and 3 papaya spears in enough orange juice to cover. In morning, drain juice off, put fruit in blender and blend, adding juice in small amounts as needed to obtain good spreading consistency. Store in fridge.

The Tofu Potpie That Made the Artichoke Famous

Drain 1 pound of firm tofu, roll in paper towel and let stand for about an hour. Then cut in one-half-inch cubes and toss with 2-3 tbsp soy sauce. Spread on oiled baking sheet and brown in 425 degree oven until brown and crispy, about 15 minutes. Set aside.

Heat skillet and in 2 tbsp oil sauté 1 cup chopped onion and ½ cup celery until soft. Add slivered carrots, frozen corn, frozen peas. Set aside and make gravy.

Gravy: In heavy saucepan whisk together 1 tbsp corn oil, ¼ cup tahini, ½ cup nutritional yeast (engevita), 4 tbsp soy sauce and ¼ cup flour to form smooth paste. Add 2 tsp basil, 1 tsp rosemary and 2 tsp sage and simmer 5 minutes. Then whisk 3 cups water or vegetable stock into gravy and boil about 10 minutes to thicken. Pour over vegetables and tofu, stirring gently. Put in 9 x 12 baking dish and top with pastry.

Pastry

1 cup whole wheat pastry flour
1 cup unbleached white flour
⅓ cup light oil
1 tsp salt
½ cup ice water

Mix dry ingredients, add oil and water and mix lightly until dough holds together. Wrap in plastic wrap and refrigerate for 30 minutes, then knead a little and roll out on floured board to cover baking dish.

Bake tofu potpie at 350 degrees for 30 minutes until crust is golden. Serve to tofu-shy guests and bask in applause.

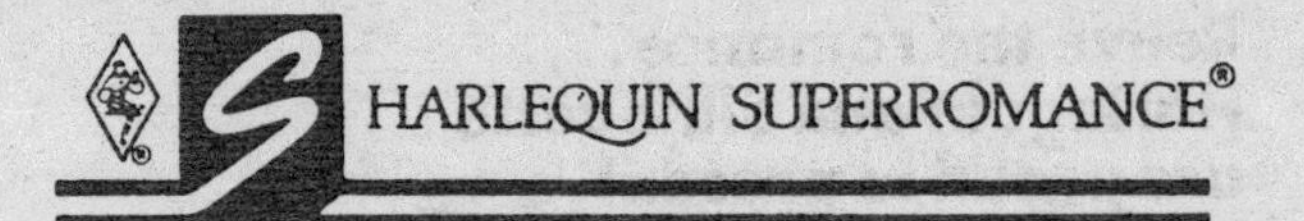

COMING NEXT MONTH

#558 ANOTHER WOMAN • Margot Dalton
Women Who Dare, Book 8

Leah Temple was living a nightmare. Somewhere in her past—a past she could not recall—was a secret she was terrified of uncovering. Paul Temple was fighting demons of his own. His estranged wife was back! Or was she? Gone was the scheming shrew who'd made his life hell. In her place, a strong, loving woman he didn't know... and didn't trust.

#559 FLASHFIRE • Judith Arnold

What happened when an old army buddy—a man you considered family—ripped you off? Matt Calloway figured he had another battle on his hands. But first he had to get past the thief's sister, his gorgeous single sister. Linda Villard was enough to make any man rethink his campaign.

#560 DREAMS OF GLASS • Brenna Todd

Haley Riverton was an actress with a dream, but it was shattered when she was stalked and shot by a demented fan. Rising star Keith Garrison tried to teach her how to dream again, but then her stalker escaped from prison, and the real nightmare began....

#561 HOME AGAIN • Janice Kay Johnson

Rebecca Halstead, divorced mother of a teenage son, had fallen for his boss—hard. Trouble was, Sam Ballard was the last man her matchmaking son wanted in the family. Which was just as well, since Sam had no interest in family. None at all.

AVAILABLE NOW:

#554 THE MARRIAGE TICKET
Sharon Brondos

#555 VALENTINE'S SUMMER
Terri Lynn

#556 MAN, WOMAN AND CHILD
Bobby Hutchinson

#557 BACHELOR FROM BANNACK
Sally Garrett